LOST
GIRLS
OF KATO

QUINN
AVERY

PRAISE FOR LOST GIRLS OF KATO

PRAISE FOR THE DEAD GIRL'S STILETTOS

"Fans of Janet Evanovich's Stephanie Plum and Willow Rose's Emma Frost will devour award-winning author Quinn Avery's Bexley Squires series. "Bexley is a great leading lady who, with a little sass, just enough self-doubt to make her relatable, and plenty of intelligence, will have readers coming back for more." -InD'tale Magazine

"Love, love, love these characters. Very awesomely told story that is attention-grabbing, action-packed, and impossible to put down. Twisting enough to keep me guessing until the end, this reader is hoping for more stories like these from this author."
-Booksprout Review

"The Dead Girl's Stilettos is such a fun murder mystery! I devoured this book. It is reminiscent of Janet Evanovich's Stephanie Plum series and I am here for it!! Amazing characters, a no nonsense plot, and fun world building."
-Instagram

BOOKS BY QUINN AVERY
www.QuinnAvery.com

BEXLEY SQUIRES MYSTERIES

The Dead Girl's Stilettos

The Million Dollar Collar

The Guard's Last Watch

The Skeleton Key's Secrets

The Notebook's Hidden Truths

STANDALONES

What They Never Said

In Her Father's Shadow

Woman Over the Edge

Deadly Paradise

Lost Girls of Kato

TIKI TROUBLE COZY MYSTERIES

Moscow Mules & Murder

BOOKS BY QUINN AVERY
WRITING AS JENNIFER ANN
www.authorJenniferAnn.com

KENDALL FAMILY SERIES
Brooklyn Rockstar
Midwest Fighter
Manhattan Millionaire
Oceanside Marine
Kendall Christmas
Miami Bodyguard
American Farmer

ROCK BOTTOM SERIES
Outrageous
Notorious
Courageous
Ferocious

STANDALONES
Broken Little Melodies
The Secrets Between Us

FALLEN HEROES DUET
Saving Phoebe
Saving Alexa

NYC LOVE SERIES
Adam's List
Kelly's Quest
Chloe's Dream

Lost Girls of Kato

Dedicated to my mom and dad for giving me nothing but the best of memories of my childhood in the beautiful (and not at all nefarious like I make it sound) city of Mankato

PROLOGUE

S weat lined the girl's brow as she waited in the tall grass for the comforting sign of headlights. The heat from the summer day was finally beginning to fade with a slight cool breeze that nipped at her bare legs. Fireflies danced in the sky around her to the call of nocturnal animals stirring to life. Her nerves were beginning to fray with the sight of the waning sunlight slipping beneath the long, expansive prairie. They'd agreed to meet at the edge of the park half an hour earlier. Where was he?

He was supposed to be the mature one in their relationship. He'd promised he would take care of her. What if she couldn't trust him? Agreeing to run away with him was a big deal. She could get into all sorts of trouble, maybe even wind up in juvie.

If she had to be honest, she was more afraid what

would happen if she stayed behind. In a couple of years she'd be done with high school, and she didn't have the money to go to college. She worried she'd be one of those local girls who never got away and settled for a boring husband and a mediocre job.

Still, with every minute that passed, she worried she had made a mistake. She had only saved up $100, and she didn't bring anything to wear beyond the summer months. How would they afford to eat? Where would they sleep?

Her fears were erased with twinned lights sweeping through the darkness.

Finally.

She huffed out an irritated breath.

She'd make him pay for scaring her like that. She swore she wouldn't let him kiss her for an entire week, even though she knew once she looked into his warm eyes the color of honey, she'd give in. She always did.

The car rolled closer. When the driver's side window cranked down, she was greeted with a face that was all too familiar.

It wasn't who she'd been expecting.

Not in a hundred years.

Little did she know, the familiar face would be the last face she'd ever see.

PART ONE

1
JACKIE - 1986

S tanding on the pedals of my pink Schwinn bike, I pant in the scent of freshly cut grass, pumping my legs like my life depends on it—or rather, *like the devil is chasing me,* as my grandma Anna would've said. My life really does depend on how quickly I can go since I'm not supposed to be riding this far from home on my own. If my mom finds out I went as far as Minneopa State Park by myself, she might ground me from going to Becky Myers's sleepover next week, which I guess wouldn't be all bad. I've been looking for an excuse not to go without hurting Becky's feelings.

It's not my fault that my older sister by four and a half years ditched me to hang out at the arcade with Karrie Schaumberg, her best friend from the trailer park. They told me I couldn't come along, which was fine by me. I don't have any money, and Kato Arcade only has a bunch of old games like Q*bert and Dig Dug.

As I push my bike even harder across the bumpy field, my waist-length braid begins to stick to the back of my damp neck. Spiderwebs catch on the tips of my jelly shoes as a cardinal tells his story in one of the trees overhead. When my dry tongue drags across the roof of my mouth, I'm all at once mad I didn't grab my sister's last can of Jolt from the fridge.

I've always hated the hot and sticky weather of mid-August in Minnesota. Mosquitoes swarm my head, biting a little harder than usual, and my legs itch from the long grass. Then there's the never-ending, annoying chirp of stupid crickets and the trill of cicadas. I imagine my tires squishing the life from every last one, finally shutting them up for good.

Worst of all, it's the time of year when most kids' parents take them on shopping sprees at the malls in The Cities for new clothes and school supplies.

It's not fair. I'll never be like them. My clothes fit funny and the patterns are faded because they're old and once belonged to other girls. Our pencils, paper, and folders come from a donation box at the Lutheran church. If I'm lucky, maybe someone will donate a Trapper Keeper with puppies or hearts like every other girl at Roosevelt Elementary had last year.

My mom is always reminding my sister and me how lucky we are to have a roof over our heads since our daddies both split long ago. It's hard to believe that we're any kind of lucky when the older boys have always teased me for being "trailer trash" and "having a whore mom." When I was younger, I asked my sister what they meant about our mom, and it only made her mad at me for an entire afternoon. By the time I understood the cruel intentions behind their words, it made me want to punch every one of those boys in their dumb faces.

The golden glow from the sun slipping beneath the evergreens lining the park causes my heart to rise into my throat. If I'm not home for my mom's break between her shifts at the paper factory in North Mankato and Happy Dan's convenience store down the road, I'll surely be grounded for life. The trailer park is still at least half an hour away, and my calves already burn.

With a tight band across my chest, I glance over to my left where the Minnesota River runs along the edge of the park. My mom told Diane and me we weren't allowed to cross through that area as it's rumored to be the spot where Shannon Bentzen was last seen a month ago. But all the local kids say the 10th grader ran away from her grandma's place with a carny rat she met at the county fair, so I don't understand why my mom makes a big deal out of it.

Swerving in that direction, I soon hear water rushing over tree roots and rocks. A cool breeze skims over my bare shoulders, rustling the loose strands of hair framing my face and blowing the mosquitos away. At least I would finally cool down if I took a dip in the river.

I slide off my bike's long seat and begin to walk, stopping dead in my tracks once I realize I'm not alone. At the edge of the river bank sits a lanky brunette boy in a white t-shirt and ripped jean shorts, his back curved like a question mark. Facing the rushing water, he wears a set of headphones plugged into a Walkman clipped to his shorts pocket. At first I think he must be fishing until I see a stream of smoke drift over his head. Worried he's one of the older boys always teasing me, I begin to steer my bike back in the other direction. Being late for taking the long way is better than being bullied.

"Hey!" he calls out, his voice a confusing combination of rough and high like he's stuck between being a boy and man. "Where're you goin'?"

I peer back at him over my shoulder. He's twisted around to look at me, headphones slung around his neck. His hairstyle reminds me of Johnny in the *Outsiders*. Thick, sandy brown locks curl around his neck and above his ears, feathering across his forehead. His nose and bottom lip are both a little bigger than the rest of his features, and his cheeks are as round as balloons. Dark eyes beneath thick eyebrows catch the golden hue of the setting sun, making my heart drum a little faster.

Although he's definitely a grade or two older, I'm pretty certain he's not one of last year's sixth graders who loves teasing me. I'm not sure I've ever seen him around.

"Pretty sure that's none of your business," I finally answer.

He holds up a funny-looking little cigarette and flashes a dimpled grin. "Want a drag?"

Butterfly wings flutter through my stomach. With that grin, he's the most beautiful boy to ever come into my life. Before I think it through too hard, I'm already guiding my bike back in his direction. It's as if he's holding a giant magnet, drawing me in.

"I'm...trying to quit," I say smartly, lifting my chin a little higher.

He laughs, his voice crackling with the gruff sound. "It's not that good anyway. I think the guy sold me ditch weed."

I lean my bike against a tree and shuffle over to him. "Aren't you a little young to be smoking *weed*?"

Taking another drag of the strange cigarette, he shrugs. "I'm almost fourteen." His brown eyes are warm and friendly when they meet mine. "How old are you?"

"Twelve and a half," I lie, standing a little taller. Although I just turned 12 a few weeks ago, my chest is flat as a board and I have a chubby baby face, so most people assume I'm a year or two younger.

"Nice bike," he tells me.

I can't decide if he's being mean or not. My mom gave it to me on my eighth birthday. It was already old and worn, its pink and white plastic basket cracked, the tassels on the handlebars torn. I removed them, thinking the pink flowers on the white seat made it pretty enough. Looking at it now, I realize it looks like something only an 8-year-old would ride.

The boy pats the greenish blue soil at his side.

"Come sit with me. If you aren't going to take a toke, you can at least keep me company."

My gaze travels from his narrow fingers splayed on the earth up to his tanned arm and neck, slipping past his thick bottom lip the color of pale raspberries before settling on his eyes the same warm hue as the bark of the hickory tree behind him. My stomach tightens with an unfamiliar sensation. I can't seem to make myself walk away from this beautiful boy even though my mom will be super mad that I'm late.

Pressing my lips together, I lower down at his side and cross my legs, willing my throat not to tighten any more. I already feel as if I'll choke to death. Beyond the faint odor of sweat and something that reminds me of one of those scratch-and-sniff skunk stickers, his skin has a spicy scent. When I sniff him again, my stomach does a funny little dance.

"What's your name?" he asks.

"Jackie. What's yours?"

"Everyone calls me J.R.—it's short for Junior."

"What are you doing here by yourself?" I ask, pulling my legs against my chest and glancing at him over my knees. "Don't you have any friends?"

"Don't *you*?" J.R. fires back, one sandy brown eyebrow raised.

Eyeing the chipped orange polish on my toes, I think of Becky Myers. She was the oldest one in her grade before she was held back a year, so she's two years older than most sixth graders. We sometimes played together at recess in 5th grade. Even though she only lives four trailers down from ours, I haven't seen her around all summer. I was surprised when the pretty little invite to her sleepover appeared in our mailbox a couple of weeks after the start of summer break. The yellowed paper was folded in half with my name written among hand-drawn stars and rainbows. I have a feeling I might be the only person she invited since none of the other kids at school ever want anything to do with her. She's really pretty, but she wears dirty clothes and talks a little funny, like she isn't very smart. She also has a mean dad who drinks a lot and throws crushed beer cans at anyone who steps on his lawn. He's the only reason I really don't want to go to her party.

From behind my knees, I shrug as a blush spreads across my cheeks. I'm not about to admit I'm a loner.

"I'm just yanking your chain," J.R. says, finally letting me off the hook. "I don't have any friends here. I just moved to town with my old man." With another dazzling grin, he reaches out to gently tug my braid over my shoulder. "I guess I could become friends with a twelve-year-old *girl*."

"I'm not a *girly* girl," I declare, all at once wishing I hadn't let my sister braid my hair before we left home, and that I hadn't worn a pink and white striped tank top, or rode my pink bike. I nudge my braid back behind my shoulder. "I like riding bike… and listening to music."

"Oh yeah? What kind of music?"

Panic zaps down my spine. I only listen to whatever's playing on the K-Dog radio station while my mom's at work, and I really don't know the different "kinds." Some are fast paced with a lot of drums and a lot of yelling. Some are slow and dreamy with a gentle voice and softer music in the background. "Whatever," I say. "I like all kinds."

"My old man has a ton of electropop vinyls. I kind of dig it."

What the heck is electropop? I wonder. "I like electropop too," I say anyway.

"Cool." Head tilted to one side, J.R. studies my face, as if waiting to catch me in the lie. "What's your favorite song?"

Sweat pricks beneath my hairline. I don't know the name of a single song *or* band. I only remember our elementary music teacher, Mrs. Lewinsky, introducing us to certain melodies she enjoyed.

I say, "I really like that song that goes, *'you may be right, I may be crazy, but it just may be a lunatic you're looking for.'*"

He looks as if he's on the verge of laughter when his eyebrows squiggle up and down. "Never heard of it."

"I think it's new." I point to his Walkman. "What are you listening to?"

"Gary Numan. Some of the songs on this tape are crap, but I really dig 'Cars.' Have you heard it?"

"I love that one," I lie once again.

"I guess it wouldn't be so bad having a girl as a friend," he decides. With a chuckle, he reaches over to tug my braid a little harder. "Why are you out here by yourself, anyway? Don't you know it isn't safe for girls like you? My old man said there's a curfew coming soon."

Irritated that he's so focused on my braid, I nudge his fingers away. "How would he know that?"

"He's a police detective. We only came back here because of the girls that have gone missing in the area." He looks annoyed when he adds, "He's good at solving murder cases and shit."

A trickling cold spreads over my face, sending

painful chills down my back. More than one girl from Mankato is missing? Was my mom right about Shannon? Has she been murdered?

"What girls?" I whisper.

"My old man isn't supposed to talk about details of his cases with me, but I overheard him mention some names in a conversation with someone on the phone—Shannon Bentzen and Rebecca something or other. He's out now with the cops, leading a search party." He glances up at the sky, tapping his chin. "Wait...I know the other last name because it was the same as one of those slasher movie guys that kills everyone." He takes another drag of the strange cigarette. "Not Krueger...not Voorhees..." He glances back at me, his eyes wide as smoke curls out from his nostrils. "I know! It was *Myers*! You know, like Michael!"

A massive sob lodges in my throat. "Becky Myers?"

"Yep, that's it." He notices the tears in my eyes and frowns. "Oh shit. You know her?"

When my stomach folds over itself the same way it does when I get the flu, I scramble to my feet. My legs don't feel strong enough to hold me up when I stand. "I have to go," I tell him, turning away right as fat tears freely flow down my face.

Who would want to hurt someone as innocent as Becky? I've never heard her say a mean thing to anyone, even to defend herself. Could she really be dead? Everyone knows her dad is mean, but would he kill his own daughter?

J.R.'s sandaled feet crunch on the sticks behind me as I wrestle my bike away from the tree. "Hold on, Jackie." He touches the back of my arm, waiting for me to turn back to him. "Are you okay?"

Swiping my arm over my wet face, I close my eyes and slowly shake my head. "Becky's my friend."

His warm fingers encircle my wrist. "I shouldn't have said that thing about my old man and murder cases. Just because they can't find her doesn't mean she's dead. Sometimes missing kids like her are found and brought back home. Maybe she just ran away."

My stomach hurts too much to say anything in reply.

"Why don't I go with you?" he offers, his voice gentle. "I'll stand on the pedals and you can ride behind me on the seat. I give my little cousin a ride that way all the time. I promise it's safe—you just have to hold onto me, and tell me where to turn."

I allow the new boy with eyes the color of warm hickory to guide me onto the seat of my bike and wrap my arms around his waist when he climbs on in front of me.

As I direct him to my house, the little knots in my stomach keep churning over and over. What if he's wrong, and Becky *is* dead?

2
STERLING - 2018

Sweat pricks across my hairline as I sit upright, sucking in a sharp breath and taking in my surroundings. Where the hell am I? A second ago I was alongside the blonde little girl in a meadow, inhaling the scent of freshly cut grass. Now I'm in a nondescript bedroom, surrounded by moving boxes and the strong odor of disinfectant. Tiny little chunks of raw cauliflower stick to my thigh when I scoot to the end of the bed and glance out the little window across from me. A freaking real-life *deer* stares back at me from the thick of a meadow, chomping on a mouthful of grass with a bored look, like I'm interrupting its meal.

Everything clicks into place—it's my first morning in my new home in southern Minnesota.

I'd stayed up late into the night, snacking on a veggie tray from a nearby gas station while researching everything I may possibly need to know about the picturesque community. An empty container of ranch dip by my feet serves as more evidence of my nocturnal activities.

It still sometimes baffles me that I actually moved over a thousand miles to the idyllic city with a river running through its downtown. But after seven years of counseling at a juvenile shelter in Los Angeles and enduring a handful of years with a man who could never be taken for his word, I was desperate for a drastic change. Then one day, my phone dinged with an open position in a county child services department within the southern Minnesota city. I realized I had failed to specify in my search that I was seeking openings in social work in California, but it ended up being a happy accident. A chance for a new start. For the first time in my life, I've made a substantial decision akin to free-falling from an airplane, and it feels amazing.

A mere day after I'd landed the job, I'd purchased the Craftsman-style house sight unseen with the trust fund my parents had started when I was a newborn. When I first set foot inside my new home yesterday afternoon, I was a little taken aback to discover it was a serious fixer-upper. Yet I quickly felt a thrill with the idea of flipping it on my own. The one-bedroom with a gabled roof, rustic wood framing, open floor plan, and a tiny front porch is a stark contrast to the massively cold mansions I'd known as a kid and the bland apartment I'd shared with Stefan. The house's bones have the potential to become a Pinterest-worthy masterpiece.

I nearly jump out of my skin when my cell phone chirps with the generic ringtone I haven't bothered to change since I brought it home from the wireless store in the midst of leaving California. My mother's youthful face—one that has netted hundreds of millions for various production studios over the years—beams back at me from the screen in a selfie she'd sent me last Christmas. Inheriting her genes, even though it means I'm still sometimes carded at 32, was akin to winning the lottery. We share the same lightly tinted skin, raven hair, and bright green eyes the shade of ripe watermelons. I also tend to embrace her untamed spirit and occasional anxiety —both of which she displays most when she's preparing to shoot a new movie, like the action-comedy that started production last week.

My above-average height, broad shoulders, and narrow nose came from my father—a former college basketball player who garnered the attention of every girl on campus before my mother stole his heart. Their superior genes mashed together created an extraordinarily average daughter who enjoys observing movies and sports from afar.

Stretching one arm to the ceiling, I answer in a sleepy voice. "Hey, Mom."

"Sterling? Are you alright?" From the crispness of her words, I sense she's one heartbeat away from hopping on the next flight here from Los Angeles. "Why can't I FaceTime you?"

"They're coming to install the internet today. And I'm fine. I just didn't sleep the best last night," I admit as I stumble into the kitchen. "You know, change of timezone and everything."

There's no chance in hell I'm disclosing the details of my latest dream. Although the same little girl has visited me in my sleep ever since I was 3-years-old, something about this dream felt more...*tangible*. When I was little, my father wrote the girl off as an imaginary friend created by an over-active mind. My mother—a fan of new-age nuances—was certain there was something more sinister involved. If she were to learn I've had hundreds of dreams about the same girl in the past several decades, I'm certain she'd force me to move back home and mentor under my aunt Constantine, her best friend who's a renowned psychic to the stars.

My mother releases an overly dramatic sigh. "I'm so sorry this new film's schedule didn't allow for me to help you settle into your new place."

"I already told you it was no big deal." I'm secretly grateful she wasn't able to make the trip. Had she been here, she would've come unglued with the house's subpar condition. When I was 9, she completely remodeled our newly constructed home after a mere six months because my aunt Constantine thought it was omitting bad vibes when Mom was turned down for a coveted role. "It's not like I owned any furniture after my breakup with Stefan, and that company you hired was great. They had everything put away before dinner."

Okay, so that last part was a fabrication. I had let the movers load everything inside the house and set the newly purchased mattress in the bedroom, then told them I wanted to unpack the boxes on my own. It was weird enough letting a bunch of strangers pack all of my belongings in the first place. I couldn't stand around and watch a bunch of sweaty men rifle through my things a second time. I dig inside a few open boxes marked "KITCHEN," searching for the coffee maker.

The brisk click of my mother's tongue amplifies through my phone. "If you hadn't left L.A. to move halfway across the country, I could've stopped by with a calming cup of tea and my decorator. I'm sure your new pad could use some serious feng shui."

Once I locate everything needed to make coffee, I plug in the maker to the only outlet in sight. "You'd be too busy to stop by even if I still lived there," I say while nestling a filter in place.

"That's not fair."

"It's the truth," I say, attempting to keep my tone light, "and you know it."

It was the same reason my father had divorced her when I was in junior high, right after she'd filmed her fifth blockbuster. I've never held any ill-will against her for not being around, mostly because I never knew any better, but my father claimed it was too lonely of a life. I suppose I would've felt the same way if it hadn't been for my live-in nanny, or the close friendships I forged with other actors' kids in private school. I know she loves me, even if she loves her career more, and that has always been enough.

I flip on the faucet to fill the carafe, wincing

when the pipes moan and groan before spewing out brown-tinted water. *Maybe the remodel of this place can't wait very long,* I think to myself.

A shrill ring followed by the shouting of voices amplifies through the phone.

My mom sighs loudly. "Babe, I have to go. The director's calling for me."

"I'll FaceTime you when I'm more settled," I promise. "Love you."

"Love you more, Sterling-bug! Feel free to use the black AmEx card for anything you need!"

When the call ends, I shake my head and laugh. If she had her way, she'd replace everything in the house right down to the studs. Now that I'm over fifteen hundred miles from the glitz and glamour of Hollywood, I've finally attained a calming sense of normalcy. Even though I opted out of premiere parties and any other events that involved celebrities when I was a kid, the life of a famous actress tended to follow my mother everywhere we went. I'm lucky my father convinced her to guard me from the spotlight throughout my entire life, allowing me to live an otherwise normal lifestyle. Let's just say I'm no stranger to wigs and oversized sunglasses.

A brisk knock falls on my front door, followed by

the piercing voice of my realtor. "Yoo-hoo, Sterling! Are you up?"

"Like anyone could sleep through that," I mutter, shuffling toward the door. When my heel scrapes across a loose board, I wince. When I swept the house the day before, I'd already noted the worn state of the heavy oak panels. Along with new pipes and more electrical outlets in the kitchen, I add flooring to my mental list of required improvements.

Swinging open the heavy front door, I smile wearily at my new acquaintance. In a pale blue pants suit, matte heels, golden blond hair expertly coifed around her face, and tasteful gold jewelry hanging from her earlobes and neck, Carol Bratsch embodies the modern business woman with perfection. She's petite enough to fit in my pocket, but has the energy of a linebacker. During our first video call several months back, she promptly informed me that she only sleeps four hours every night due to a high-demand job, a workaholic husband, and two active children. I'm beginning to wonder if she makes up for it by snorting cocaine.

"Hi, Carol. What brings you by so early?"

"I just wanted to see for myself that you got settled in and aren't having any problems." Her sky-blue eyes behind dramatically dark lashes widen on the retro MTV t-shirt I'd altered to hang off one shoulder. "If that's what you wear to bed at night, it's no wonder you're still single...even if you *are* nearly as pretty as your mom."

As she barges in past me, I roll my eyes and let out a silent groan. She's the only one in the city who knows my mother is the world-famous April Marie, only because my mom had to sign off on the financing. Although I've asked Carol repeatedly to keep the fact to herself, her flippant reference makes me doubt she'll honor my secret.

She spins around in the center of my living room, frowning at the piles of boxes. "Looks like you still have a ton of unpacking to do, girlfriend. I don't understand why you sent those movers home when your momma hired them to do everything."

"I'm not going to settle in all the way until I have a few things fixed," I decide, dusting my toe against the loose board I'd tripped over. "Do you know any good contractors?"

"I most certainly do," she replies, wiggling her eyebrows. "There just happens to be a handsome bachelor a few blocks down from here who specializes in repairing old houses like this one. I heard he's looking for work, too. I can give Theo a call...ask him to swing by." She leans in closer, bathing me in her strong floral perfume. "If I weren't married, I'd ask him to swing by *my* place."

Even though I'm not totally convinced she still wouldn't consider the idea despite her commitment, I laugh because I think that's the reaction she was going for. "I don't care what he looks like as long as he does good work."

Her cherry red lips quirk with a grin. "You say that now, but wait until you meet him."

I ONLY HAVE to wait a handful of hours before deciding Carol wasn't being facetious when she'd described Theo Davies as handsome. Exceptionally tall and impressively muscular, his presence becomes commanding the moment he steps inside my small home wearing a faded gray t-shirt advertising a craft beer, worn blue jeans, and scuffed leather work boots. He somehow pulls off shaggy hair and a scraggly beard without looking homeless. His features are strong and nearly perfectly symmetrical except for a slight dip in the bridge of his nose and a jagged scar nestled inside one of his thick eyebrows. With the exception of his thick fingers covered in calluses, he would look at home on a stage with a rock band.

As his dark eyes jump around the room, scrutinizing every square inch, they never fully land in my direction. I'm kind of glad, because my body is reacting to him in ways I haven't felt since I was a hormonal teenager with a crush on the son of a famous rockstar who went to my school.

As he tucks his chin-length, mocha hair behind one ear, I realize he's the type my mother would fall for in a heartbeat. He's much closer to her 52 years, too. I can literally picture them acting out a scene together, his arms wound around her as they engage in a dramatic kiss. It's a good thing he still isn't looking my way when I shiver from the visual.

"This place is one step away from being bull-dozed," he informs me in a gruff tenor. "Looked at buying it myself...figured it needed too much work to bother."

Carol failed to mention Mr. Handsome's personality leaves a lot to be desired. Crossing my arms under my chest, I let out an irritated sigh. "If you aren't interested—"

"I'm interested," he says, finally meeting my gaze. "It has a lot of potential." His eyes are notably sad... haunted. I can't help wondering what made him that way. A surge of guilt zips through my gut for judging him so quickly. Years ago, I promised myself that I would treat everyone with equal compassion because every single person in the universe is battling something bigger than them. It became my mantra after working with countless homeless teenagers.

Something monumental passes between us, reflected in the shift of his dark eyes. With the thud of my pulse against my throat, I almost wonder if my aunt Constantine may be onto something when she talks about soul connections. My chest buzzes with relief when he tears his gaze away once again. "But you need to understand upfront it's gonna cost you a pretty penny, Miss..."

"It's Sterling," I say, injecting as much kindness into my tone as possible.

"What kind of name is that?" he says with a snort.

"The kind picked out by an incredibly eccentric mother." I throw him a genuine smile. "Write me up a quote. Then we'll talk."

He nods once. "I can do that." His eyes travel down to my left hand still resting beneath my breasts. "You single?"

Despite my initial reservations about him, some-thing flutters deep inside my belly when I hold his dark stare. I haven't dated since my last disaster of a relationship, and I can't say I wouldn't be interested in starting something with someone a little older. But only if I found a way to break through his stony exterior.

"You looking to hook up?" I spar with a slight grin.

A dark blush spreads over his cheeks as he shifts his weight and inspects his right thumb like he just developed a hangnail. "Just wondering how someone as young as you could afford a project this big."

"I sell *a lot* of drugs," I reply in a matter-of-fact tone.

His eyes snap back onto mine. "You serious?"

Letting out a lighthearted laugh, I shake my head. "Not at all. I'm a social worker. I start with Blue Earth County Human Services in a couple of days. I know it's not a glamorous job, but—" I clamp down on my tongue, stopping myself from saying any more. He doesn't need to know my mother's filthy rich and gets off on sharing her wealth with her only child. "Is someone as *old* as you able to keep up with a project this big, or do we need to schedule around afternoon naps and shuffleboard tournaments?"

Now he's looking at me like I'm unhinged. "I'd need a hefty deposit, and weekly payments."

"Include those numbers in your quote. If you know anything about plumbing, you can add that cost in too. The kitchen sink could use a little... something. Possibly an exorcism."

I'm admittedly disappointed when my attempt at humor doesn't even crack his serious expression. His arms swing idly at his sides as he steps past me and starts for the kitchen. "I'll get started on that quote after you show me everything you wanna fix."

Trailing behind him, I decide the thing I want to fix the most is the six-foot-something, insanely attractive man lumbering through my new home.

3

JACKIE - 1986

S ince finding J.R. on the river bank, we've met up dozens of times. Sometimes it's planned, and sometimes we run into each other in the very same spot where we met. He doesn't know I go there every single day, hoping to see him. I can't get enough of the warm, tingling feeling that stirs in my belly whenever he's near. And with Becky gone, there's no one else I can hang with anyway. I swear I hold my breath the entire time I'm with J.R., waiting for him to declare he doesn't want to spend time with me anymore because he's found a group of friends his age.

The day after I met J.R., his dad appeared on channel 12 KEYC's evening news, asking for the public's help in finding both Becky and Shannon. The first thing I noticed about his dad was that he shared the same brown hair and beautiful eyes as his son. He was so tall and utterly handsome, wearing a black suit jacket over a stark white shirt and red tie, voice deep and commanding. By the time the Mayor took his place behind the podium to announce a 7 o'clock curfew was in effect for anyone under the age of 18 until further notice, my cheeks had warmed with the idea of J.R. growing up to be even more attractive, like his dad.

Exactly a week from the day we met, J.R. spends the entire afternoon rambling on about something he keeps calling an "Atari." He even declares he's going to teach me all about "Asteroids." I'm a little unnerved by the idea after he told me it's more addictive than crack cocaine. At school, we sometimes watch videos on a TV brought into the room on a rolling cart. In one of those videos, the First Lady told us about the dangers of drugs—including crack cocaine—and said we should "just say no" to *any* kind of drugs, so I'm confused by J.R.'s intentions. But when he gives me directions to his house and tells me to sneak over after my mom leaves for her night shift, I convince myself that my new friend wouldn't pressure me into doing anything I don't want to do. When I asked what would happen if I was caught after curfew, J.R. said as long as I stick to the shadows and stay off the main roads, the police cruiser going up and down the streets won't be a problem.

My mom is in one of her foul moods when she stops home between jobs for dinner. She stomps around the kitchen in her high heels, slamming doors and swearing under her breath. Before going out to talk to her, I change into my Garfield night-gown to make her think I'm getting ready for bed. My sister's nowhere to be seen, so I assume she's at the arcade.

Even though my mom always looks as if she hasn't slept in a long time, she's still super pretty. We have the same strawberry blond hair and blue eyes the same shade as my favorite crayon out of the box of 64 Crayolas I got from Santa last Christmas. I almost never see her narrow lips without her favorite fire-engine red lipstick, or her eyelids without her usual robin blue eyeshadow.

Whenever she's on her way to dance at the club like tonight, she wears her bangs feathered with a stubby little ponytail and hoop earrings that touch her shoulders. She once told me she has a hard time finding clothes that fit right because her body has more curves than most other moms. The satiny pink dress she wears is so tight that I'm able to see every line of her large breasts, and the material dips down low enough that I can see the deep line running between them. When she bends to grab a plate from the cupboard, a little bit of her black panties covered in lace stick out from underneath her dress.

I once asked if I could watch her dance, but she told me only grown ups can enter Mettler's. A few times she's been in an extra good mood when she's home and will dance to really old songs on the radio with me and Diane. She sure likes to shake her hips a lot.

"Is there anything I can help you with, Mom?" I ask, half hidden behind the refrigerator wall. She has never hit me or my sister, but she has made me cry more times than I could count. I don't want my eyes to get all red and puffy before I meet with J.R.

"I don't have time to make you girls supper," she huffs while opening a bag of Wonder bread. "I have to be at work early tonight."

I don't tell her that Diane and I already ate at Pizza Hut. She might think we weren't being thoughtful by bringing her something back. The personal pan I ordered was free, thanks to the

BOOK IT! reading program I signed up for at the library. Diane had to use babysitting money for hers, because she thinks she's too cool to read books now that she's in high school.

"That's okay," I tell her. "We can make our own supper."

I move into the kitchen to hand her a butter knife and a nearly empty jar of Skippy. She bends to kiss the top of my head. "You're my angel."

In a matter of minutes, she's scarfed the sandwich down and she's heading for the door, fumbling with her purse and keys. She pauses to look back at me, her eyes heavy with concern. "Don't talk to any strangers, especially men, and steer clear of Becky's dad. There's a rumor going around that he bought a gun after Becky disappeared and he's been threatening to shoot people." Her eyes darken. "I don't know what I'd do if something happened to you or your sister."

"We'll be careful," I promise, trying to hide my surprise. Would she even notice if me or Diane went missing like Becky and Shannon?

Once I can no longer see the taillights of the old station wagon, I strip out of my pajamas and throw on a sweatshirt with jeans. After slipping into the $5 pair of white Adidas my mom bought at the secondhand store that are two sizes too big and marked with countless scuffs, I head out the door.

As I'm walking my bike through the trailer park, a crushed Hamm's beer can rockets over my head and clunks into something metal at my side. I stop dead in my tracks as a gruff voice demands, "Who's that? Who's there?"

Cold fear sends my stomach into a deep dive. *Becky's dad.* My pulse quickens as I remember what my mom said about him having a gun. I decide to step into view of the yard light to avoid getting shot. "It's me, Mr. Myers. Jackie Tanner."

"Who?" He waddles down from his broken porch to get a closer look. A stained white tank top barely covers his grossly round belly, and his light-colored pants are black with filth. My eyes quickly jump from the beer can in his fat hand to the butt of a gun tucked into his waistband. The dark shadows under his eyes shift when he frowns. "What're you doin' out this late, little girl?" His words are slow and slurry enough that I'm certain he's been drinking all day.

"I have to run an errand for my mom," I lie, praying he doesn't run into my mom anytime soon.

"Yer not s'posed to be out after dark," he reminds me.

"I'm just going to the gas station to get milk. I'll only be gone for a couple of minutes."

"Ain't you scared of them demons?"

A cold ripple grips my spine, and the hairs on the back of my neck rise. "What demons?"

"The ones that came for my Becky."

My teeth begin to chatter. I know there's no such thing as the boogeyman, and I always thought that covered monsters and demons too. "I—I have to go," I tell him, hooking a leg over my bike.

"Watch out for them demons!" Becky's dad yells after me.

WHEN I PULL up to the *Brady Bunch* style split-level house with green shutters and a picket fence, sitting on one of Mankato's many hills, I know something's wrong. Two people-shaped shadows appear behind a thin curtain—one's really tall, the other shorter and skinny like J.R. From their muted shouting, I'm guessing he's in the middle of a serious scolding from his dad. Goose bumps break out across my skin. J.R. recently admitted his mom left years ago because his dad has a mean side.

I jump off my bike, my feet becoming fixed like

tree roots with the sounds of their argument. If I were to ring the doorbell, it would probably only make things worse, especially as I'd get into serious trouble for breaking curfew. But I feel as if I need to do something to stop J.R.'s dad...to save my friend.

There's a roar of, *"God dammit!"* before the bigger shadow hits the smaller one, sending it sailing down out of sight. I slap my hands over my mouth, quieting a surprised cry. The dad-sized shadow spins away to leave the room as J.R.'s shadow rises from the floor. I stash my bike inside a set of bushes and sneak around to the backside of the house, crouching outside of the window in the corner like J.R. said. My heartbeats shake my entire body as I wait for him to come find me.

The sound of a door slamming drifts through the crack in his bedroom window. My chest hurts with every tight breath as I wait for him to come to me. For several minutes, everything becomes still. Then I hear faint crying. Even though it sounds as if he's holding a pillow over his mouth, his sobs are raw and deep.

My heart hurts, heavy with pain for my new friend as I try to decide what to do. Why was his dad so angry? Would J.R. hate me if I let him know I'm worried? He once told me the thing he likes best about hanging out with me is the fact that I don't act like a "girly" kind of girl. Do I pretend I didn't see what just happened? What if he's seriously hurt and needs to be seen by a doctor?

Eventually, I decide to tiptoe away from the window and head back home. If J.R. finds out I heard him crying, he might not want to be my friend anymore.

THE NEXT MORNING, a Saturday, J.R. shows up on the steps outside our trailer house. "Can we hang out in your room?" he asks.

I hesitate. If I left him in, he'll realize we're dirt poor and I'm far more girly than I let on. He'll maybe even decide I'm too much of a baby to hang with any longer. But when I notice the bright red mark under his left eye, my heart won't allow me to turn him away. At least my sister is babysitting the neighbors' kids all day and my mom won't be home until after 3 o'clock.

I nod and open the door. My heart thumps extra hard as we pass the brown and tan couch with ugly flowers and a wood frame that my mom brought home after my grandma Anna died. When you sit in it, you can still smell a trace of my grandma's menthol cigarettes. I can only pray that J.R. doesn't pay it any attention as we pass it and head into the narrow hallway leading to my bedroom.

"Why didn't you come over last night?" he asks.

Glancing back into his pretty brown eyes, I wonder what answer will make him happy. "What happened to your eye?" I counter.

He looks past me into the hallway. "I ran into a cabinet in the living room. Guess I'm still not used to the new house."

Even if I hadn't seen his dad hit him, I'd know it was a lie. "My mom once got punched by some jerk while she was dancing."

A snort rips through his nose. "Where was she dancing?"

"At Mettler's. She works there."

"My old man told me about that place." His dark eyes grow wider. "Your mom's *a stripper*?"

Sickness stirs in my gut as the warmth drains from my face. I have a small idea of what a "stripper" does, but my mom has never mentioned taking off her clothes in front of strangers. Could that be the reason the older boys call her a whore?

"It doesn't matter," I snap, gritting my teeth. "I'm

just saying…her eye looked exactly like yours after the man hit her."

His lips tighten. "So what?"

I pause in the doorway to my room. "You can tell me the truth, J.R. We're friends, aren't we? I won't tell anyone. I promise."

He drags a hand through his hair, making it stick up like he just rolled out of bed. "Sometimes my old man gets pissed off about stuff. It's not a big deal."

"But he works for the police," I protest, mirroring his scowl.

"And that's exactly why you can't tell anyone else, Jackie. He could lose his job…go to jail. And then they'd throw me in a foster home." He nudges past me, studying every nook and cranny of my small bedroom. I enter behind him and hold my breath, waiting for him to comment on it being a baby's room with its faded Rainbow Brite bedspread and second-hand collection of My Little Pony dolls. Instead, he pages through my small sticker book before pointing to a watercolor painting of the neighbor's dog pinned to my wall. "Did you do that?"

"It's just something I scribbled in Art class."

"It's gnarly." He points to another painting of the spot where we often meet by the river. I painted it one night when I couldn't sleep because he was on my mind. "That too. Looks just like our hangout."

A hot blush fills my cheeks. At least I didn't try to paint his face like I wanted. "Do you paint?"

"Only when forced. I'm not any good." He throws himself down on my bed and stares at the translucent stars stuck to my ceiling. "Those glow in the dark?"

"Not anymore. My dad won them at the fair when I was really little."

"Do you see him often?"

I step over to my window and glance outside. "He left my mom when I was two and a half. He hasn't come back since."

"Do you remember him?"

"Do *you* remember stuff from when you were a toddler?"

"You're lucky," J.R. grumbles. He motions to the creased poster of Jason Bateman, the teenage actor, taped next to my paintings. It was something I had stolen a few months earlier from an old *Teen Beat* magazine in the dentist's waiting room. I didn't know who he was at the time, but I thought he was super cute. I know stealing is bad, but sometimes I get jealous that I never get anything fun. "You watch *Silver Spoons*?" he asks.

"Once or twice," I lie. We don't have cable, so all I ever get to watch are lame shows that come in on UHF, like *Mash* and *Little House on the Prairie.* I like Laura Ingalls, and Almanzo is handsome, but I don't like how the show pretends they live nearby in Southern Minnesota when nothing looks like it does in real life, even though it was supposed to have happened forever ago. When my grandma Anna was still alive, I often stayed at her house on Friday nights, and we'd watch *Dukes of Hazzard.* Long before I met J.R., I would fantasize about marrying Bo Duke.

J.R. stares back at the ceiling. "Do you ever dream about running away?"

"Like running away and never coming back?"

"Yeah."

"I wouldn't have anywhere to go," I say. "And I don't have any money."

"Doesn't matter. You could totally find somewhere to work."

"Who's gonna hire a kid?"

"Lots of people," he tells me. "But if money wasn't a problem, would you leave?"

I consider his question for a minute. There are so many places I've seen on TV and in magazines that

I'd like to visit. "Only if my mom and sister came with."

J.R. forces out a sigh. "That defeats the point of running away."

"Would you leave your dad to live on your own?"

His eyes darken and he makes an expression that makes me think he's in pain. "Yeah," he grunts through clenched teeth. "I would."

4

STERLING - 2018

After Theo hand-delivers a relatively reasonable quote two days later, I write him a check on the spot for the deposit he requested. Early the next morning, as I'm preparing a pot of coffee before my first day with Human Services, he returns with a fairly new pickup truck full of tools. I wait in the open doorway as he's climbing out from the driver's seat, eager to have any connection with another human before reporting to my new employer.

Another dream involving the little girl being fearful of something tore me from a deep sleep. After once binging a ghost hunting show with Stefan, there was a period of time in which I considered I could have some kind of a psychic ability.

Then I came to my senses and realized my aunt Constantine's new age beliefs were the only reason I'd entertained the idea in the first place. I've wondered if I should speak with a psychologist to discuss the dreams, but it seems unnecessary considering I studied more than my share of psychology in college. I'm well aware my brain is likely compensating due to the stress of moving and starting a job in which I'll once again be working with abused children. I'm eager to focus my thoughts on something else for a little while, even if the only way available involves pestering a prickly carpenter.

"Good morning," I call out as Theo starts towards me with buckets of tools dangling from each hand. In a royal blue t-shirt, sleeves cut off, and a worn pair of tan carpenter pants marked with small splashes of paint and stain, he's the kind of rugged handsome that would have women in L.A. dropping their designer panties. "You're here bright and early."

The slightest bit of interest sparks in the dark pools of his eyes when they skim across my silky pink blouse and cream skirt that falls past my knees before landing on my suede kitten heels. My heart skips a little when I take my turn in appreciating the thick muscles lining his arms and chest.

"Mornin'," he grunts back before stepping in past

me. He promptly squats in the center of the living room and begins removing tools from the buckets, arranging them in neat piles. When the coffee pot whirls to a stop, I pour myself a cup and begin to reach for another mug. "Would you like some coffee? I don't have any creamer, but—"

"Plumber's coming by later this morning," he says without looking up from the floor.

I laugh under my breath before taking a sip of the deliciously dark brew, briefly closing my eyes as it warms a path down to my stomach. "You're not much of a conversationalist, are you?"

"I'm here to work, not make conversation."

I snort in response to his stubbornness. Although he's clearly not interested in getting to know me, I refuse to let it deter me from somehow finding his softer side. "So much for that adage about Minnesota Nice," I say quietly. My watch vibrates on my wrist, reminding me it's time to leave if I want to arrive halfway early. I grab a travel mug from the cupboard and fill it to the top before securing the lid and reaching for my keys. I remove the extra key Carol gave me for the front door and slap it on the counter.

"I'm leaving you a spare key. I trust you won't use it to attack me in my sleep."

He tucks a strand of sandy brown hair behind his ear before glancing upward. Something cold and dangerous flickers in his beautiful eyes, causing a full-body shiver to ripple through my bones. "You shouldn't joke about shit like that."

"You're right. I'm sorry." Sheepishly lowering my head, I start for the door. "Have a nice day, Theo."

ALTHOUGH I'D PARTICIPATED in several video calls with my new supervisor, Megan, I take an instant liking to her in person. She's squarely built with no-nonsense, short white-blond hair and steely gray eyes that make me believe she doesn't miss a thing. She wears a gray suit jacket over a plain white t-shirt and black leather pumps that brings the top of her head to my eye-level, and she walks with the stilted movements of a former jock. It's not hard to picture her dominating either a volleyball or basketball court in her younger days—a stereotype that's confirmed when she leads me inside a well-orga-nized office with candid shots adorning the walls of her younger self in various stages of handling a basketball.

"I played for Mankato State," she says, motioning

to the collage of pictures. "I would've tried out for the WNBA if it'd been a thing back in my day."

I grin back at her. "My dad played ball in college too. I inherited his height, but not his coordination. Still never missed a home game in the four years I attended USC."

She tosses me a knowing wink. "Basketball wouldn't be the same without our fans." She then settles in a chair behind a laminated desk containing a keyboard, monitor, pen, and stack of Post-its. "Have a seat, Sterling."

As I settle into one of the two navy blue arm chairs facing her desk, my eyes gravitate to a flyer pinned to a bulletin board directly behind her desk. Below a caption in bold letters that reads, "LEAVE YOUR PORCH LIGHTS ON FOR THE GIRLS OF KATO SO THAT THEY MAY FIND THEIR WAY HOME," are faded pictures of several young girls. Printed in a heavy black, pixelated ink, it's difficult to distinguish their features. From their rigid poses and the plain backgrounds behind them, I'd guess they were yearbook candids. Based on what I can distinguish of their hairstyles and clothing, the photographs appear to have been taken in the 1980s. Not only that, the font was obviously created with a dot matrix printer.

A sensation of overwhelming dread pricks the base of my brain. "What's this about 'the girls of Kato'?" I ask, pointing to the flyer over her head.

"Kato is what the locals call the city," she explains, spinning in her office chair to study the flyer thoughtfully. "These girls started disappearing somewhere around a decade before I started working here...I believe around eighty-five, eighty-six."

"Did they ever find them?"

"You know, I'm not really sure. It's weird, because I never hear a single mention of these poor girls, and I wasn't able to find anything about them on the web. I inherited this flyer with the office, and I've left it up all this time because I was hoping it would spark a conversation with someone who knows something." She spins back around to face me with a puzzled expression. "I always said I was going to look into it, maybe check with the sheriff's office, but my caseload is so immense that I never seem to have the time."

The scent of freshly mowed grass drifts through the cracked window behind Megan as my eyes linger on the pictures. Feeling queasy, I wrap my arms around my middle. How could so many girls have been forgotten? Did they all run away, or did something more dire happen? If someone was kidnapping young girls in the 1980s, surely their whereabouts would be accounted for some 30 plus years later. As Megan launches into my new list of duties, I make a mental note to do my own research.

BY THE TIME I return home, exhausted and overwhelmed by my first day of training, there's a handwritten note on the front door instructing me to enter through the back. As I make my way around the house, an old tune I faintly recall from an 80s movie blasts from an open window. I giggle as I step inside the house, thinking the song is a bit whimsical for a tough guy like Theo.

I enter quietly, leaning against the kitchen cupboards and taking a moment to watch Theo work. Bent over on his knees in the center of my living room, he smooths a brown putty over a missing chunk in one of the planks. I rather enjoy the impressive way his muscular arms flex with every movement of the trowel before I notice he's barefoot. Even more surprisingly, I find his long, lean toes to be incredibly sexy. They're as deeply tanned as the rest of him, and his toenails are neatly trimmed.

"I feel like I should change into spandex and leg warmers," I call out over the music. "Maybe even crimp my hair."

Without so much as a flinch from my sudden intrusion, Theo calmly reaches out to silence the wireless speaker at his side before returning to his work.

"You didn't have to turn it off on my account." Clicking my tongue, I toss my keys and purse on the counter. "My day was awesome, thanks for asking. How was yours?"

"Productive," he says. "Plumber said he should have your pipes fixed by the end of the week."

I roll my eyes to the ceiling, surprised he even bothered with an answer. "So, Mr. Conversationalist, I have another easy question for you. Did you grow up here in Mankato?" I ask.

He twists around with a half-scowl. "Why do you wanna know?"

"Today at work I saw a poster for some girls who went missing in the eighties. I wondered if you were here back then and maybe knew something about it. My supervisor didn't seem to know much of anything, including whether or not they'd ever been found."

Expression blank, he turns away and quickly reorganizes his tools into orderly groups. "I'm heading out for the night," he says before rising to his bare feet. "Stay off this part of the floor until morning."

It would seem I've touched on a sore subject. But why? Did he know those girls?

"Do you want to stay for a drink?" I blurt as he's slipping into his work boots by the back door. I'm as surprised by the offer as he appears to be when his lips twist with a frown. All at once uncomfortable, I begin to ramble. "I have a bottle of white wine. If you're not into that, we could hit one of the local bars. We could even grab dinner somewhere... unless, of course, you already have plans. It'd be my treat."

With his back to me, he pauses. "I'll be back early tomorrow, same as today."

When the door slams shut behind him, disappointment weighs heavy on my shoulders.

I TAKE a chance on a clean-looking pub at the edge of the downtown bars that boasts a large selection of food along with local beers. A massive Craftsman-style bar stretches through the center of it, adorned in classic oak pillars similar to those in my new house. A handful of older patrons fill various stools as well as several tables scattered around the building. As I settle into one of the stools at the bar, a middle-aged bartender hands me a menu.

"Welcome to Pub 500," she greets me with a warm smile. "Can I start you off with something to drink?"

I immediately warm to her as she reminds me a bit of a friend back in L.A. with a punk faux hawk, ears filled with various piercings, and a full sleeve of black tattoos on her right arm with no clear theme. Plus there's a twinkle in her eye that suggests she's always ready for a good time. "I'll take your lightest craft beer and whatever's your favorite food item on the menu."

She quirks one brow. "You like pork?"

"Yes, ma'am."

Swiping the menu back out of my hands, she nods. "Perfect. I'll be right back with your beer." As I wait for her to return, I catch a few looks of interest from a group of lawyer-type guys in suits and ties gathered across the bar. Although a couple of them are cute enough and appear close to my age, I feel a major disconnect to every single one of them. At this point I'm more interested in friendship. *Unless it's Theo*, my conscience reminds me.

I scoff to myself as the bartender sets down my beer. Her dusty-rose painted lips twit with a wry grin. "Something funny?"

"I'm just thankful I'm no longer a single girl living in L.A. The guys here don't seem quite as aggressive."

"This place tends to attract a lot of older patrons and families." The bartender glances over her shoulder at the group of suits cheering over a soccer game on TV. "The single ones are generally pretty harmless unless they've had too much to drink. It doesn't mean we don't get the occasional jerk who thinks he's God's gift to women." Dramatically rolling her eyes, she offers her hand. "Beth Eichers."

I give her hand a firm shake. "Sterling Pruitt."

She releases my hand and laughs. "Ah. With a name like that, it's no surprise you're from L.A. What brings you to the land of ten thousand flakes?"

"I'm not really sure yet." Then my thoughts return to Theo and the missing girls. "But so far it's been pretty interesting." Wrapping my fingers around the cool pilsner glass, I narrow my gaze. "Where would you suggest I go to mingle with a younger crowd that isn't necessarily just out for a hook up? I'm mostly interested in finding a friend or two who'd be up for causal drinks to wind down at the end of a long day."

"I'm probably a handful of years older than you, but I could *totally* be one of those friends," Beth tells me in a scandalous whisper. She leans in closer, resting her forearms on the bar top. "I've lived here most of my life, and pretty much all of my friends are now married. Some even have *rug rats*. I personally haven't found a guy worth sacrificing my independence for, but I suppose I'm always keeping an eye out for The One." Smirking, she checks her smart watch. "If you can wait a little under an hour until my shift is over, I'd be more than happy to show you a few places."

I hold up my glass in salutation. "Here's to our new friendship."

5

JACKIE - 1986

I n the days that follow after J.R.'s argument with his dad, he spends every free moment of daylight at my side, as if afraid to be home alone. Although I'm glad for the extra time with him and wouldn't want him to be lonely, school starts soon and I'm running out of time to pick up the supplies I'll need from the church.

One Thursday morning as I brush detangler through my freshly washed hair, J.R. lays on my bed, paging through a *Tiger Beat* magazine Diane had borrowed from the library and left on the couch. "This is so lame," he tells me, turning the pages a little more aggressively. "Why do girls like this stuff?"

Giggling, I set down my brush and plop onto the

bed, peering over his shoulder to see an article about Corey Haim's new movie. "I have no idea," I lie, thinking Corey is actually pretty cute. I bite my lip thoughtfully. "There's something I have to do this morning. *By myself*. Wanna meet later at the river?"

He frowns. "Why do you have to go alone?"

"Because," I say with a dismissive shrug.

"Whatever it is, I'll come along and wait outside," he decides, tossing the magazine onto the bed. "It's not like I have anything better to do."

As I chew on my bottom lip, wondering if he wants to stay close to me because he likes me or because he's worried I'll disappear next, there's a flash of movement at my doorway. I look up to see Diane holding the Polaroid instant camera that had been our grandma Anna's.

"Smile!" she sings.

J.R. and I both look her way right as the flash goes off. My sister removes the film, fanning it through the air and giving me a mean look almost identical to the one my mom gives me when she's mad.

Sometimes it's obvious that Diane and me have different dads. Her straight, shoulder-length raven hair, sides pulled back and secured on top of her head in a scrunchie Madonna-style, couldn't be more opposite of my usually frizzy locks, and her face doesn't have a single freckle like the mess of them I got from my dad. Diane's tall and the bones in her shoulders stick out. I'm so short and chubby that one of the fifth grade girls once told me my mom should've named me Barney Rubble.

Diane's wide, sky-blue eyes staring a hole through me are the only thing that we have in common. "Mom would lose her shit if she knew there was a boy in your room!"

My heartbeat thumps like a rabbit inside my throat. I don't think my sister would tattle on me, but there's no promises with her. It depends on her mood. "Good thing she isn't here, *DeeDee*," I say, knowing my nickname for her when I was a toddler will get under her skin. "Aren't you supposed to be babysitting?"

"Mrs. Jackson came home from work with the flu. And don't call me that." She tosses the picture onto my dresser and places one hand on her hip while glaring at J.R. "Like, who even *are* you?"

"His name is J.R.," I snap. I'm suddenly aware that they're closer in age, and my sister's ten times prettier than I'll ever be. "He just moved here. He's *my* friend."

A harsh laugh shoots from Diane's lips. "You're

such a space cadet. Friends can be shared, you know." She lifts her chin at him, her eyes sharp. Although the bruise around J.R.'s eye has faded a little, it's starting to turn a gross shade of yellow. "Who'd you fight?"

"None of your business," he snarls at my side, fidgeting with the green and black Swatch watch on his wrist.

Diane's expression suddenly softens. "If it wasn't a fair fight...like, if an adult hit you for whatever reason, you should tell one of your teachers when school starts. They're trained to deal with that kind of thing."

An icky feeling tightens inside my chest when I remember what J.R. said about going to a foster home if his dad got into trouble. "Stop being a dweeb," I tell her in an annoyed tone. "He told you, it's none of your business. That means keep your big nose to yourself, *Diane*."

"Whatever," she says, rolling her eyes. "Are you two going to lay around here all day and suck face, or do you want to go do something fun?"

I draw in a sharp breath. Suck face, as in *kiss?* As I open my mouth to tell her she's disgusting, J.R. growls, "Whatever your sister and I do is also none of your damn business."

A nice kind of warmth spreads throughout all of my body and tingles at the tips of my limbs. I've had a crush on J.R. since the first time we met, and lately I've been starting to think that I might love him. Not in the way I love Diane or my mom, but the way a girl loves a boy. I've even dreamed about marrying him one day in a big wedding like Sam's sister in *Sixteen Candles*.

"Whatever you say." Laughing in a mean sound, Diane spins around to leave. "I'm outta here. You two are lame."

"Wait!" J.R. hollers after her. "What did you have in mind for fun?"

DIANE ARRANGES for us to hitch a ride to Skating World with our next-door neighbor when she reports for her afternoon shift. Karrie Schaumberg, a senior at West High School and one of Diane's best friends, lives in a trailer by herself and juggles even more jobs than our mom—although I'm not exactly sure how many jobs she has at any given time and how many of which she either quit or was fired. For as long as I can remember, she's had a shaggy haircut like Joan Jett and only wears something other than black when required for one of her jobs. She wears a lot of makeup too. Karrie is usually nice to me, but her rusty old Bronco stinks like mothballs and she drives like a maniac. For the hundredth time, I wish Diane would get another job so she could afford her own crappy car and we wouldn't always have to bum rides off her friends.

An hour before we're supposed to meet Karrie, J.R. and I head down the block to the Lutheran church. When J.R. asks what it looks like inside, I reluctantly lead him through the empty chapel, knowing from experience it's a shortcut to the gathering hall. There's something about the faint musty odor of the place paired with high-pitched ceiling, colorful stained glass windows that stretch as far as the eye can see, and long oak pews neatly arranged that always settles my nerves.

"This place is wicked cool," J.R. says, neck cranked back to study the glass art. "Do you go to church here?"

"No." I've always thought it would be nice to belong to a place like this, but my mom says people who go to church think they're better than everyone else. "Do you go to a church with your dad?"

"We stopped going when my mom left."

When he's done staring, I lead him the rest of the

way. My heart sinks down to my feet when we step into the large room filled with empty tables and folding chairs. There isn't a single school supply in sight.

"Can I help you?" a deep, friendly voice asks.

I spin around to face the man in black pants paired with a black button-down shirt, a little square of white tucked beneath the straight collar. With sandy brown hair cut short on the sides and wire-rimmed glasses that makes his hazel eyes pop, Pastor Babel possesses a welcoming look. His pale lips spread with a warm smile. "You're Jackie, right? I remember you from last year."

"Yessir," I say, feeling all at once painfully shy. I don't want to admit why I'm there with J.R. standing next to me, even though the pastor has been really nice to me in the past.

"Who's your friend?" Pastor asks.

"This is J.R.," I say. "He just moved here with his dad."

The apples of the pastor's cheeks rise, pushing his glasses high over his sandy eyebrows. "Nice to meet you, J.R. Are you here for school supplies as well?"

J.R. shoots him a questioning look and warmth floods my cheeks. "No, just me." I glance around the empty room. "Am I too late?"

His smile fades. "I'm afraid the drive ended yesterday. I'm not exactly sure what the ladies have done with the few items leftover, but they must be around here somewhere. If you care to return tomorrow afternoon, I'm sure I can scrounge them up by then." Hands clasped together, he glances between us. "You know, you could both come back on Saturday evening for the youth lock-in. We're watching *The Karate Kid* and *The Goonies*. There will even be a popcorn machine, loaned to us by one of our parishioners. If you don't own a sleeping bag, we can provide one." His wide smile returns, aimed at J.R. "Are you and your father planning to become members of a congregation in the area, J.R.?"

"My father's a man of science," J.R. replies, his voice unnecessarily rude. "He doesn't have time for religion."

Pastor Babel flinches, the smile melting from his lips. "That's no matter, son. We welcome teenagers from all walks of life to our gatherings."

J.R. hooks his arm through mine. "We have to go."

The minister glances back at me with a less assuring smile. "I look forward to seeing you tomorrow, Jackie. In the meantime, you should consider joining us on Saturday."

"Thank you," I call over my shoulder as J.R. yanks me away.

The second we're back outside on the warm asphalt parking lot, J.R. releases me and shivers. "That guy's creepy as hell. He's way too nice…like Mr. Rogers on Valium. Can you imagine sleeping in the same room as him for that lock-in? He probably does stuff to those kids in their sleep. My old man says the kind of people who are trusted by the public are often the most perverted."

I remain silent as we start walking back to my trailer. Pastor Babel has been one of very few adults to ever show me any degree of kindness. But what if J.R. is right?

J.R. nudges my shoulder. "You don't have to go back there tomorrow. I can help you get whatever you need for school."

"I'm not a charity case," I snap.

"I never said you were." He grips my elbow, pulling me to a stop in the middle of the sidewalk. "Look, Jackie. Every week my old man throws a wad of cash at me for groceries. I mostly just eat P and J sandwiches when he's gone, so I've saved up a big chunk of change…you know, just in case." His eyes slide away and he shrugs. "So don't worry about it." His gaze returns to meet mine and he smiles in a way that causes my toes to tingle. "I have enough games for my Atari. It's not like I'm home to play them anyway. We can swing by Woolworth's tomorrow. My old man took me there the other day to get my stuff—they had some cool Trapper Keepers."

Even though I'm still reluctant to let him buy my supplies, worried my mom would be angry if she discovered I'm taking handouts from a boy, it's impossible not to skip a little the rest of the way. The idea of having a brand new Trapper Keeper sends a thrill through me like it's Christmas—the kind normal kids with rich parents get in the movies.

―――――――――

LIKE COUNTLESS TIMES BEFORE, Karrie lets us into Skating World through the back door and snags 3 pairs of tan roller skates with orange wheels off the shelves, thrusting them into our arms before we exit through the concession area.

Even though I usually enjoy skating, I'm mad before our adventure even begins. The skates Karrie gave me hurt my toes, and I don't like how much J.R. talks to Diane as we're changing out of our sneakers. I catch Diane looking at him like Bugs Bunny with cartoonish hearts in her eyes. As we start for the rink I consider shoving her.

"I need some help getting started," J.R. tells me, gripping my arm as we enter the smooth surface inside the carpeted half-walls. I wish he'd hold my hand instead, like some of the couples already skating. "I'm usually pretty good at this, but my skates are too big."

"Sure you are," I tease.

His dimpled grin aims in Diane's direction nearby. "Your sister skates like Dorothy Hamill."

I don't say anything as we start to glide along with the other skaters. We come across a group of little kids skating in all directions, forcing us to split up. Diane stops to talk to a couple of boys she knows from the arcade and J.R. quickly returns to me on wobbling legs. He grabs my hand, making my skin tingle beneath my heart-adorned sweater like a thousand little pin pricks.

"We should rent something from Blockbuster tonight," he shouts over the opening riffs of Kool & The Gang's *Celebration*. "I think the second *Nightmare on Elm Street* is out."

"We don't have a VCR."

"I can bring mine over."

My insides clench as I remember the way his dad

struck him the other night. "What about the curfew?"

As his fingers tighten around mine, his eyes become a little darker. "My old man won't be around. He left early this morning, said a sixteen-year-old girl from Mankato was reported as missing. She was supposed to be driving back from an overnight visit with her grandparents in some little town called Blue Earth, but never returned home. I wouldn't be surprised if he's gone all night."

A rush of nausea stops me in me in my tracks, causing J.R. to crash into my side. "What's happening to these girls? Who's taking them?" I push the sudden visual of Becky's lifeless body from my thoughts. She can't be dead. She just can't. That kind of thing only happens in scary movies. "Why haven't they found Becky yet?"

"Maybe she doesn't want to be found," he tells me. "Didn't you say her dad is mean to her?"

When I think of how crazy Becky's dad sounded the other night, I wonder if J.R. could be right. Maybe she ran away because she couldn't be around her dad any longer.

"One time I was at her house when her dad came home from work early," I blurt. I've never told anyone this story and I'm still not sure I should tell

Becky's secret. But J.R. waits for me to continue, his eyes kind, so I lower my voice. "We heard him banging into things in the yard and swearing, his words all slurry. Becky got really scared and told me we had to hide before he found us. When I asked her why, she said he sometimes makes her do gross things when he's drunk." My stomach twists and bends with the memory. "We didn't have to sit in her closet for long before he started snoring. We snuck past him and went to my place. I was supposed to sleep over at her house for her birthday before she went missing. I know it sounds mean to say, but I'm glad I didn't have to go back there."

J.R.'s expression become serious when he grips my arm. "Jackie, that thing about her dad making her do things isn't cool. You have to tell my old man what you just said. What if Becky's dad killed her?"

I suck in a sharp breath, not sure how I could talk to the kind of man who hurts his own son. What if I say something that makes him angry? And what if Becky's dad finds out I tattled to a police detective?

My sister glides in on J.R.'s other side, draping her arm over his shoulder like they're old friends. "Anyone else notice that weirdo watching us?" She points beyond the rink to where a man around our mom's age sits alone at one of the party tables. He's chubby, bald, and his dark eyes bug out from his round face. I don't like the way he stares us as we glide around the curve. "He looks totally mental," Diane adds.

"That guy sold my old man a pair of dress shoes at Brett's last week," J.R. tells her. "He's a little slow, but I don't think he'd hurt a fly. He's probably here with his kid. Maybe even a niece or nephew."

For the rest of our time at the skating rink, I don't see the man interact with a single kid. Not only that, he never leaves that table.

And his creepy eyes are always on either me or Diane every single time we pass.

6
STERLING - 2018

Friday evening after running a handful of miles through my new neighborhood, I reluctantly return home. As much as I've vowed to stay out of Theo's way after our awkward exchange the other day, I've already unpacked everything that can be stored inside closets and cupboards, and there's only so much of the humidity I can handle.

Beth works double shifts all weekend, closing the pub each night, so she's unable to make any plans. While the atmosphere of the noisy bars we hit the other night made it difficult to bring up Theo or the missing girls, we forged an instant bond that made it clear there would be ample time in the future to pick her brain. *Someone* has to know *something* about those girls' disappearances, even though I spent my lunch hour on the public access computer in the County Court Administrator's lobby, scouring public records for any mention of it. The Deputy Court Administrator I spoke with was several years younger than myself, and didn't have any knowledge of past cases beyond what existed in the system.

My dreams about the girl with strawberry blond hair have become so vivid, it's like I'm becoming her. I last saw her rollerskating with the boy she has a crush on. I could actually smell a blend of popcorn and cotton candy, feel the sensation of wheels spinning beneath me, feel the boy's hand around mine.

I'm approaching the stone path leading to my front door when I notice a navy blue sedan parked two blocks away. I've seen the car parked in the neighborhood several times since moving in and assumed it belongs to one of my neighbors. When I realize someone is sitting in the driver's seat, I lift my hand to wave. The car's engine fires up and it promptly backs into the nearest driveway, taking off in the opposite direction.

"Hi to you too," I murmur, continuing toward my house.

Inside, I kick off my running shoes and strip out of my ankle socks by the front door. Theo's interested gaze takes its time sweeping over my peek-aboo style sports bra and short athletic shorts, warming a little more with every second it lingers. Although I didn't specifically pick out what to wear with him in mind—I'm always wearing freebies from the April Marie athletic line—I don't hate the appreciative reaction.

"Is the air always this thick here?" I ask. "You couldn't cut it with a samurai sword."

"Weather changes from day-to-day," he grunts, twisting the trowel around in his hand. "Beats the rigid cold when your lungs turn to ice." He pauses thoughtfully before glancing back my way. "Where you from?"

"California." I swipe a hand over my slick forehead. I'd considered Minnesota winters would be cold, but his description of the cold sounds downright unbearable. Guess I'm going to have to invest in some warmer clothes. "Not sure I'm ready for that level of cold," I grumble.

He huffs with a curt chuckle before returning his focus to the floor.

Grabbing two bottles of water from the refrigerator and my iPad from the counter, I set one of the bottles on the floor beside Theo before flinging myself into the only arm chair I brought from California. Although the modern style and blue velvet looks sorely out of place, I only brought it because I figured I'd need something to sit on until I found furniture that perfectly fit the space. "What does everyone around here do for fun?"

"I wouldn't know," Theo replies in a clipped tone. "Don't leave home much except to work or go on hikes."

"Why not?"

He glares up at me as I take a long swig of water. "Are all kids your age this inquisitive?"

"I wouldn't know. I haven't spent a lot of time around other *people* my age. I've spent most of my life hanging around older adults."

One of his brows lifts. "How much older?"

"What you *really* want to know is my age," I tease with a coy smile. "Admit it."

"I know better than to ask a woman her age."

I wing a brow back at him. "Are *you* single?"

"Now you're just being nosy."

"It's only fair. You asked mere minutes after we first met." I take my time crossing my legs and shifting my hips, hoping to appear seductive. The art of flirting has been lost on me after my pointless relationship with Stefan. "Is there a *Mrs.* Sullen waiting at home with a bunch of miniature versions of you running around?"

"No."

"Grandkids?" I tease.

"No kids *or* grandkids," he grumbles, rolling his eyes to the ceiling. "Never been married either."

Seriously? I decide he either has a commitment phobia, or he literally lives under a rock. There's no way all the single women in this city are that dense. Aside from being grumpy, he's hardworking and crazy attractive. I suspect there are far more favorable attributes I have yet to uncover.

"Are you into guys?" I push. The vibes he's been emitting since the first time our eyes locked leave no doubt in my mind that he's straight, but I'm not always the best judge of character. I once believed Stefan would make a great husband.

Hands held out at his sides, Theo gives me an exaggerated shrug. "I like to keep to myself, alright? Makes life less complicated."

"Do you have a problem dating someone a decade younger?"

A twitch of a smirk passes over his lips. "You think that's all there is between us?"

"Who said I'm referring to you and me?"

He shakes his head repeatedly and smooths a knife over a container of the brown substance. "You remember you're paying me to fix your house, right?

It's hard to get anything done with you asking so many questions. Don't you have somewhere better to be?"

"In this heat?" I drape my legs over the side of the chair and scroll through the apps on my iPad. "I'd rather catch up on my shows. Have you watched the second season of *Stranger Things* yet? A friend just told me about the series last week, so I've been binge-watching as much as I can. It's insanely good."

From the corner of my eye, I catch his gaze briefly flickering to my legs. "Stranger *what?*"

"It's only like the greatest show ever. Takes place back in the eighties. You know, back when you were in your prime." I figure if I keep needling him, he's bound to display a little personality...eventually. I hit "play" on the next episode in my queue and crank the volume once the theme song starts. "It's surprising how much I like your generation's music, considering you're so *old.*" I'm barely able to resist a burst of laughter when I catch the way he's scowling at the floor. "Or maybe you're even older than I think. What was popular when you were a kid? Disco? *Elvis?*"

The trowel clatters against the floor. When I look up, Theo tosses his hands into the air. "Why are you trying so damn hard to annoy me?" he demands, leaning back on his feet. "What do you want from me, Sterling?"

"I want you to take me somewhere!" I blurt, my voice raising an entire octave. "A bar, a movie, a museum of twine...I don't really care where we go. I just don't want to sit around in this empty house all weekend. My job is super stressful and I need to let off some steam."

Amusement lights his dark eyes. "You're harassing me so I'll take you on a date?"

"You're one of few people I know here other than Carol, and she's...well..."

His lips tilt with a smirk. "It's still a pretty unconventional way to ask a guy out. You could just ask nicely."

Electricity ripples through my chest and spreads down my limbs. The blinding urge to kiss the wolfish smirk off his lips hits me out of nowhere. "Will you *please* take me somewhere tonight? It can be anywhere. I mean, we could hang at the senior citizens' center, if that's where you'd be most comfortable."

"Don't push it," he warns, visibly fighting a deeper smirk. "Let me go home and clean up, then I'll come back for you. Do you own a swimsuit?"

"I'm from California, remember?"

"Wear it with a pair of jeans and sneakers."

"Seriously?" I tisk my tongue, realizing when it's too late that I'm starting to sound like my mother's clone. "It's like a hundred degrees out."

"Trust me. If you don't, you'll regret it."

There's no fighting the broad smile that passes over my lips. If nothing else were to happen between us, I'll forever be able to gloat in the satisfaction of witnessing Theo Davies doing something other than glowering.

I MUST TRY on a dozen different bikinis before I choose one that'll be sure to make Theo stop caring about our age gap. The jade green color makes my eyes pop, and the cut gives a provocative yet tasteful preview of the goods. I'm not camera-worthy by any means—another reason I'm grateful to be far away from L.A.—but I inherited my mother's envious chest and curvy hips. I complete my ensemble with a snug pair of blue jeans and a bright yellow halter top before adding a light application of makeup and curling my hair into soft waves. I'm misting my favorite perfume over my cleavage when I hear the roar of an engine outside.

By the time I open my front door, Theo is on my front step with a motorcycle helmet tucked under one arm. At least I *think* the guy in front of me is him. In a tight pair of blue jeans and a white vintage The Cars band t-shirt that highlights every generous muscle in his arms and chest, he's more irresistible than before. The most incredible part? His beard is neatly trimmed and he's sporting a crew cut with a considerably longer length on top. He somehow appears both more distinguished and temptingly younger without those longer locks framing his bearded face.

His intimate stare has the effect of an open flame against my skin when he says, "You look...damn good."

I can't seem to swallow past the tight band in my throat as I blink slowly back at him. "I'm sorry. Do I know you?"

Chuckling in the most delicious sound, he fingers his fresh haircut. "Figured it was time for a change. My neighbor's a beautician. She stopped me on my way home, offered to clean me up."

Where did he say he was going that would make his neighbor suggest such a thing? Did he admit he was taking a woman out on a date, or did he tell her he was headed to a babysitting gig? I need to both thank this beautician and check her out to ensure she's not any kind of competition.

He thrusts the helmet into my arms. "Ready to ride?"

All warmth drains from my face when I notice the monster-sized Harley Davidson parked in my driveway behind him. The last time I rode on the back of a motorcycle, I was sixteen and going through a rebellious phase. When my mother's Hollywood-heartthrob boyfriend had offered me a ride, I didn't give it a second thought. Now... I swear I can taste the eggs I fried ten hours ago.

"What's the matter?" he asks with an adorably crooked grin. "Should I've brought a permission slip for your parents to sign?"

"Funny guy." A little annoyed I'd spent so much time perfecting my hair, I wiggle the helmet down over my head and flip up the shield, forcing a smile. "Let's see what you've got, grandpa."

With another chuckle that vibrates against my bones, he steps in closer to nudge the helmet forward and secure the strap beneath my chin. When he's finished, he throws the shield back down over my face and slaps the top of the helmet—hard enough to make my teeth chatter. "Just need a riding jacket, and you'll be set. Come on—there's one in the saddle bag."

He hands me a black, lightweight jacket that's several sizes too big, but omits a heavenly combined scent of Theo and leather as I slip it on. Then he somehow coaxes me onto the back of the massive hunk of metal and tells me to hold onto his waist when he climbs on in front of me.

"Tighter," he commands over his shoulder before firing up the engine. I startle with the loud roar and vibration that follows, clinging to him for dear life.

Despite the heat, it's a beautiful day and the city is alive with others enjoying the weather. We come across entire groups of motorcycle enthusiasts, bicyclists, and dog walkers. Small children in swimsuits splash in plastic swimming pools and run through sprinklers in their frown lawns. We drive past a park where middle schoolers jump concrete ramps with skating boards and BMX bikes. Several older men on riding lawnmowers give a friendly wave as we roar past. Although the small-town vibe is something I've never experienced, it's both comforting and gives me the sense of being at home.

The way Theo steers the massive chunk of metal with confidence and ease is a major turn-on—especially when I feel the strength of his upper body beneath my grip with every corner he leans into. In no time he's navigated through every last winding street and steep hill in the city. Just when I've somewhat relaxed and lightened my grip, we emerge onto a 4-lane highway and Theo opens the throttle some more. I'm all at once grateful for the helmet's shield when we're blasted with a strong gust of wind.

When he eventually veers off toward a gravel road, I dig my fingers into his firm abs. Laughing in a tight sound, he pries my fingers loose and slows the motorcycle. Parking on a patch of grass beside a dirt road leading to a cluster of tall trees, he kills the engine before helping me climb off. After I remove the jacket, he pulls the helmet off of my head. The delightful smile that touches his lips will forever be burned into my memory.

"We'll walk from here," he says, setting the jacket and helmet on the motorcycle's front seat. "I hate getting my bike dirty."

He removes the stubby little key from the motorcycle's gas tank and slips it into his pocket before gesturing for me to follow. As I stride alongside him in silence, my entire body still vibrates from the rumble of the motorcycle's engine. When the back of his hand brushes against mine, I'm zapped with a surge of delightful electricity.

With the mid-evening breeze, wide-open fields of tall, golden grass bend and sway beneath massive oak trees. It's quiet and peaceful, giving the false impression we're a hundred miles from civilization. It's still plenty warm even though a passing cloud blocks some of the heat from the sun's brutal rays. The sharp, sweet scent of the wild grass gives me pause and takes my breath away. It both feels and smells so familiar, triggering something in the back of my mind.

"It's pretty here," I say after catching my breath. "Although I'm starting to wonder if I should've asked what you had planned. Walking with a stranger in the middle of nowhere...my mother would think I've lost my mind."

Theo's head snaps in my direction, eyes ablaze with anger. "I would *never* hurt a woman."

"Sorry," I say softly. "I didn't mean—"

"It's okay," he interrupts, shaking his head with a bashful look. "You're right. Guess I didn't really think it through either. I should've run the idea past you first."

I hear the rush of water a beat before we come across a steep bank beneath the trees. "This is why you told me to wear a swimsuit? Are you sure it's safe?"

"We aren't actually going to swim," he says. "I just figured you'd want the suit when we walk under the waterfall half a mile down." He turns to me, hand extended. "Come on. Take my hand. I won't let you fall."

I'm struck with a crippling sense of déjà vu.

Everything swirls around me in a haze of bright colors as my legs give out.

With my new Trapper Keeper adorned with three brown puppies clutched to my chest, I shuffle down the bleach-scented, sparkling white hallways lined with gray lockers and duck into my homeroom. Diane also had Mr. Kabe when she was in sixth grade, and she told me he's a pervert who only gives good grades to girls with big boobs and short jeans skirts. My stomach does a funny little dance when I notice Lori Matheson and Stacey Roberts, two of the school's most popular girls from last year, sitting in desks front and center. With mature, curvy bodies, Lori and Stacey could easily pass as sophomores or juniors, and they're wearing the kind of short jean skirts my mom sometimes wears when dancing.

Careful not to make eye contact with anyone, I claim a desk in the last row with the hopes of avoiding any unwanted attention from my classmates. Right before J.R. took me shopping, I found enough change in my piggy bank—mostly coins I'd found laying around town throughout the summer —to buy a brand new t-shirt from Woolworth's. It's pale blue with white polka dots and loose enough to hide my flat chest. Before Diane woke this morning, I stole one of her scrunchies and brushed my hair back into a ponytail on one side.

Although J.R. is attending West High School and Becky is gone, I feel a bit more confident this year since the older boys have gone on to high school, and at least one person on the planet doesn't think I'm totally lame.

Mr. Kabe enters the room just seconds before the first bell of the day rings. My mom has never taken either Diane or me to a single school conference, so it's my first time being in a classroom with him. He begins scribbling on the chalkboard before turning to face the low din of the classroom. Whenever I'd see him around school in past years, I thought he looked a lot like Pee-wee Herman, only with more of a square head. He's tall and slender with dark hair, oversized clear-framed glasses, and a stern face. His khaki pants continue for several inches above his bellybutton, and he's buttoned his dress shirt all the way to the top.

When his lips part, I half expect him to say, *"I know you are, but what am I?"* Instead he tells us, "Welcome to your new homeroom, sixth graders! Who's ready to open their brains and learn new things?"

As expected, no one raises their hand, but nearly everyone glances around the room with quiet, nervous laughter. I'm instantly annoyed by Mr. Kabe, thinking he's one of those adults who talks down to older kids because he thinks it's cool.

I'm even more annoyed when he makes each and every one of us stand up, say our name, and share our favorite part about this past summer break. A sinking fear rumbles through me once the introductions burn through our row. By the time it's my turn, I swear there are a thousand daddy long legs crawling through my skull.

"Jackie Tanner," I mumble, too afraid to look away from the ink stain on my desk. I can feel the judgmental stares of every one of my classmates. "My favorite part about summer was not having to come here."

My statement is met with a round of laughter that warms my insides. It's the good kind of laughter, not the usual sounds of older boys making fun of me. I tilt my head up to look around the room and release a shy smile. When my eyes land on Mr. Kabe, a slimy feeling runs through my belly. He's scowling, obviously displeased.

"That is enough, Miss Tanner," he scolds in a sharp tone. The classroom falls silent. "I expect your attitude to change if you want to succeed in my classroom."

My cheeks burn hot as I sink back down behind my desk. Mr. Kabe holds my stare for a moment, forcing me to absorb his disappointment.

For an entire hour, he speaks about anything and everything like he's the smartest man in the world. When the bell rings, announcing it's time to move to our next class, I want to cry tears of joy.

The way Mr. Kabe stares at me as I walk out with my classmates, I think it's going to be the longest year of my life.

———————

WHEN I WALK OUT of the school building at the end of the day, I spot J.R. waiting on the lawn and feel that awesome warm rush blossom behind my ribs. He stands out as a high schooler with a navy blue backpack hanging from one shoulder, acid jeans ripped at the knees, white Nikes with a red stripe, red flannel shirt tucked in, jean jacket slung over one shoulder. His dad wanted him to get a haircut before school started, but I'm glad his shaggy curls still twist around his ears. I just hope he didn't get into too much trouble for disobeying his dad.

Lori and Stacey, the mature girls from my home-room, also notice him and wave, then giggle and whisper to each other behind their hands. When J.R. rolls his eyes at my classmates, satisfaction bursts through me. I haven't been able to picture what kind of friends he's had in the past, but since he's been so nice to me, I can't imagine he was ever one of the popular kids who makes fun of others for being different.

Before I can get to him, Matt Jensen and Ben Callvin block my path. Ben's older brother Mark was one of the first boys to pick on me. Matt's on the skinny side with shaggy blond hair and widely-set googly eyes, while Ben's a husky kid, standing a head taller than the other boys in our grade, and is known for being a bulldozer in football. Heat drains from my face from their smirks alone. My fingers tighten on my Trapper Keeper, clutching it with all of my might. I wouldn't put it past them to break it.

"Nice hairdo, *Jackie*," Ben sings, making Matt snigger. "Did your mom do it? Did she borrow you some of her glitter panties too?"

With the sound of their cackling laughter, other kids begin to gather around us. A mountain of dread builds in my throat.

Ben then leans in to grasp my arm. "Do you think your mom would do *me*?"

Tears burn hot behind my eyelids. I know I should push them away or say something, but I'm unable to move a single muscle. Before he can say anything more, Ben is shoved sideways and J.R. appears in his place.

"Leave her alone!" he snarls, his brown eyes even darker than normal as he casts the two boys a look of warning. Ben and Matt take a step back, their faces ashen and eyes wide. My heart nearly leaps from my chest when J.R. pries one of my hands from the death grip on my Trapper Keeper and twists our fingers together before leading me away. "Come on, Jackie. Don't listen to these assholes."

I stumble to keep up with his clipped pace as we make our way past a sea of my gaping classmates. We're several blocks away from the school when I finally drop his hand.

"You shouldn't have done that!" I snap, briefly

glancing downward when we pass by a group of other students. "The kids at your school will give you a hard time once they see you hanging out with a sixth grader. You have no idea how mean the kids in Kato can get! When I was in second grade, I heard a girl my age from Washington Elementary had plastic surgery on her ears because older girls would surround her in the bathroom and call her *Dumbo*."

J.R.'s expression is serene when he shrugs. "I'm not scared of them. What's the worst they could do? Hit me? At least I'd finally have a chance to fight back."

I bite my bottom lip, barely resisting the sudden urge to hug him. His black eye has almost completely faded, but it doesn't mean his dad hasn't hurt him again in places I can't see. We walk in silence for a few moments before he nudges my shoulder and his dimples pop into place. I never fail to feel a buzz of comfortable warmth when he gives me that smile.

"How was your first day, other than dealing with those jerks?" he asks.

I puff out an irritated breath. "My homeroom teacher is lame. He made me feel dumb in front of the entire class."

"All teachers are lame. Don't let him get to you."

Once again I feel the need to hold my breath immediately after I ask, "What about you? Did you meet any cool guys to hang out with?" Now that he's in high school, I expect him to dump me as a friend at any moment.

"Why are you so obsessed about me finding other dudes my age?" he teases, tugging on the end of my ponytail. "Tired of me already?"

"Of course not." I swat his hand away with heat rushing into my cheeks. "Knock it off."

We aren't far from the trailer court when he asks, "Hey, do you think I could stay tonight for supper?"

I almost immediately blurt, "no way." My mom will be home between her shifts and would most certainly get angry if she found an older boy in the house. Then I think of him sitting all alone at home, eating a cold peanut butter and jelly sandwich, and I nod. It's not like we have anything a whole lot better than cold sandwiches, but at least he won't be by himself.

As LUCK WOULD HAVE IT, my mom calls to let us know she has to report to Mettler's early and won't be home for supper. Diane comes home from the arcade as I'm returning the phone back to its cradle and the long, stretched-out cord is winding back around itself.

"Mom just called. She isn't coming home."

Diane's shoulders roll inward. "Again? I haven't seen her in a whole week."

"Maybe she's having an affair with some married guy," J.R. offers from the couch. "My old man says that's usually the reason adults act weird—they're either hiding a secret lover or an unplanned pregnancy."

A funny feeling makes a wave through my stomach. What if he's right, and our mom is going to have another baby? She doesn't even have the time for us. Would Diane and I have to raise the baby? There's barely enough money for groceries and rent. Diane will leave for college in a couple of years. Would I have to raise the kid all on my own?

"That's dumb," I scold J.R. "Our mom doesn't have the time for that stuff. She's always working."

"What do you dweebs want?" Diane snaps, digging through the mostly-bare cabinets. The way she slams the doors, I guess she's also mad at J.R.'s idea. "SpaghettiOs, fried Spam, or tomato soup and grilled cheese?"

"We have the same old things all the time," I

grumble, sinking back onto the floral couch at J.R.'s side. He's busy clicking through the channels on our old Zenith TV. I'm embarrassed that we don't have cable, and wonder if he watches MTV all the time like I often overhear other kids say. I've only seen short clips of a few videos, and don't understand why watching a bunch of guys with long hair and weird outfits pretending to sing is so exciting.

Diane turns to me, her fists resting on her hips in a Wonder Woman pose. "If you want to get a job so we can afford filet mignon, *Jackie*, be my guest."

Sighing, I throw her my most dramatic eye-roll. "Bite me, *DeeDee*. You don't have to be so bossy all the time. Just make soup and grilled cheese then."

"What in the hell is fried Spam?" J.R. whispers, reaching over me to grab a handful of the Ruffles Cheddar chips he bought on our walk back from school.

"Trust me, you don't want to know." I reply, then tug on his arm. "Go back a channel. The Muppets are on."

"The Muppets are for babies!" Diane yells from the kitchen.

"I like the Muppets too," J.R. tells me with a grin.

"Really?"

"Are you kidding me?" His eyes light up. "Alice

Cooper was on there—Johnny Cash too! And the Muppets have a wicked sense of humor—especially Statler and Waldorf. Those two can get *dark*."

"My favorite was when Crystal Gayle sang about believing in magic," I whisper. "She's so pretty—I love her hair."

With the sounds of Diane banging around in the kitchen and, eventually, the sweet scent of buttered bread frying, J.R. leans against my side, giggling like a little boy when Bunsen launches pointed bananas at Beaker. It feels like we're boyfriend and girlfriend. I don't dare move a muscle, afraid to break the spell that somehow made a cute guy like me.

STERLING · 2018

I rouse to a set of haunted brown eyes hovering above me. As gentle fingers brush my hair away from my face, I realize I'm lying on the ground near the park, cradled against Theo's firm chest. *What the hell? I passed out?*

"You gave me a helluva a scare," Theo rasps. "I barely caught you in time. Are you all right?"

Cheeks burning with embarrassment, I release a nervous laugh. I've never fainted in my life. "I guess it's been a while since I last ate something. Between that and the heat…" I curl upright and pull in a deep breath. "At least we know your pacemaker works."

"And your humor's still in tact," he quips, helping me back to my feet. He holds onto me a moment longer than necessary, sparking something between us that I'm certain he also feels because I see the interest reflected in his eyes. "I probably should've taken you somewhere for dinner first. I guess I'm a little rusty at this dating thing."

If I wasn't completely mortified, worried he might have sprained something when he caught me on the way down, I would be tempted to lean in and steal a taste of his scrumptious lips.

"Was that pre-internet?" I tease, putting a safer distance between us. "Because they have apps now where you can meet women. I'm guessing you're unaware, considering you're still single."

The sullen carpenter returns with a dark flash of his eyes. "I told you, I like to keep to myself." He starts back in the direction of his motorcycle. "Come on. If you won't let me take you somewhere to eat, I'll take you back home."

Note to self: if you want to see Theo Davies relaxed and carefree, don't tease him about his dating history.

WE GRAB BURGERS, fries, and milkshakes from a quirky, retro-themed bar called Flask in the heart of downtown before Theo returns me to my front step. It turns out passing out on a first date kills any kind of playful mood, because he hasn't looked me in the eye once since we left the river.

"See you tomorrow," he tells me after I climb off the motorcycle behind him and hand him the helmet and jacket.

"Will I?" I challenge, setting my hands on my hips. "Or did my lack of gravity scare you away as my contractor too?"

He finally meets my gaze with a frown. "What's that supposed to mean?"

Shoulders relaxed, I glance back at my house. The previous owner left a small bench on the porch —a setting that could possibly re-spark the romance I felt brewing between us earlier—but the lingering heat is making me sluggish and cranky.

"I could use a good dose of air conditioning and something strong to settle my nerves, but I drank the only bottle of wine I had and I don't have AC yet." When he throws me a confused look, I roll my eyes. "I'm trying to invite myself over to your place."

He regards my house for a moment before grunting, "Fine. Get back on."

A handful of blocks later, he dismounts the motorcycle in the driveway of a Craftsman house twice the size of mine, and holds the front door open, inviting me to enter ahead. His house is neat and orderly, featuring high-quality walnut furniture and multiple stained glass windows in arts and crafts style. Everything, including the wood flooring, shines with newness. Most impressed by the cleanliness of it all, I wonder if he hires a cleaning lady. It's the complete opposite of a stereotypical bachelor pad.

In a U-shaped kitchen featuring stainless steel appliances and a cozy island for two, he retrieves two glass tumblers from a Shaker cabinet and begins to fill them with ice from the refrigerator's door dispenser.

"Are you okay with cinnamon whiskey?" he asks, distracting me from my search for a single ounce of dirt or dust. "Pretty sure it's all I have at the moment."

"I figured your drink of choice would be Ensure."

With an agitated scowl, he runs a hand through his wind-whipped hair. "How long are you planning to give me shit about my age?"

"Until you give me a number," I say, shrugging.

"Forty-six," he grumbles. "Satisfied?"

I throw him a dramatic roll of my eyes. "Fourteen years' difference is hardly enough to keep treating me like your daughter. Do you have any idea how many men in Hollywood date women more than *half* their age?"

"That town's a freak show."

"Tell me about it," I mumble as he pours us two fingers each. There will most likely come a time when I'll have to disclose the truth about my mom's identity, but I hate wondering if a guy likes me only because he wants to meet her or even because he wants to take advantage of my wealth. I'm convinced Stefan was holding on to hope that my mom could connect him with someone in the industry who wanted to use his weird-ass banjo music for a soundtrack.

When Theo hands me one of the glasses, I clink mine against his. "Here's to new beginnings." As he takes a drink, I sigh. "I'm sorry I fainted. I just had a weird...I don't know. It's hard to describe. I'm afraid if I tell you what really happened, you'll write me off as a whack job, and I'll scare you off for good."

One of his brows quirks in question. "What really happened?"

"I had this...feeling. Like I'd been in that exact same spot before."

He gives me a slow shake of his head. "I thought you just moved here."

"I did, but the sensation was *so* incredibly strong.

And I've been having these weird dreams ever since I was three that have only intensified after I moved here. I can't help wondering if they're somehow...I don't know...related."

One corner of his mouth lifts with a grin made sinfully hot by the accompanying dimples. "What are these dreams about?"

"Nothing perverted," I assure him with a scolding look. "They involve a blonde little girl who spends a lot of time down in a grass field—almost exactly like the one you took me to earlier. The similarities were...uncanny."

Theo knocks back the rest of his drink and slams the empty glass on the counter top—hard enough to make it crack against the granite surface. "I should take you home. It's late."

Watching him turn away, I huff out an annoyed breath. "I knew you'd react this way. You don't seem the type to embrace anything unconventional."

He stops dead in his tracks. "It has nothing to do with you or my beliefs." He turns back to face me, slowly shaking his head. "I have a lot of dark shit going through my head, alright? It's one of the reasons I prefer to stick to myself."

A wave of empathy seizes my heart. He reminds me more and more of some of the runaways I worked with in L.A. who desperately needed someone in their lives who cared. For whatever reason, I can't stand the idea of him sitting here all alone when he's upset. "Have you ever tried discussing that dark shit with someone?"

"Like a shrink?" he sniggers. "No chance of that."

"No, like a friend." I gulp the rest of my drink and set it down on the counter before I start for him. "I can be one of those friends you spill your guts to— I'm good at keeping secrets. It's not like I know many people here anyway."

His eyes widen as I tug on his hand. "That's what you want from me? Friendship?"

"In addition to other things." His warm, strong fingers tighten around mine when I lead him into his living room. A pleasant buzz spreads through my gut as I guide him down to sit in one of two walnut arm chairs. I'm two seconds away from climbing into his lap and ravaging the beautiful lips that have been taunting me all day, but I remain standing after I release his hand. "We can take it slow…see where things go once we get to know each other. Relax while I pour us another round of drinks."

He yanks me down into his lap. "What if I don't wanna talk?"

My breath catches with the feeling of his warm

thigh muscles beneath mine, and the severity of his dark gaze. He looks...ravenous. "Then we just hang out...enjoy each other's company."

"You're not hearing me," he says, fisting the hair at the nape of my neck. "The last thing I want to do with you is talk."

The room spins when his mouth covers mine, lips moving with an intensity that would've knocked my socks off if I hadn't already removed them along with my shoes at the front door. Something about the sensation of his kiss is extraordinarily warm and comforting. Familiar, even. When he draws back, his determined gaze making it clear he's far from finished, I'm unable to draw in a proper breath or placate the rapid beats of my heart.

"Old man has some moves," I gasp.

"You wouldn't believe the shit I learned playing bingo."

A brass peal of laughter falls from my lips. "He has jokes, too!"

He lowers his lips a second time, robbing me of both my wit and my sanity as my mouth yields to his. I become lost in the movement of his powerful lips and the way his hands grip my face as if I'm going to disappear. The intensity of his strong hold has me completely undone.

It's all too much. Too fast.

Reluctantly, I pull away to study his expression. "What is this, Theo?"

A smirk plays on his lips. "Do I really need to spell it out?"

"I mean, I know we just met and everything, but this connection between us...it's a little stronger than what I'm used to. Am I crazy, or do you feel it too?"

His coarse fingertip drags across my sore lips, adding to the fire already ablaze in my gut. "Told you I didn't want to talk."

"That's the problem," I say, disengaging myself from his embrace to stand and pace the room. "You say it's going to take several months to finish my house, right? I don't want us to get caught up in a quick fling that doesn't go anywhere, then have to suffer awkwardness around each other for how many hundreds of days after. If you can't open up to me about yourself...like at all—"

"Fine." His eyes meet mine, ripe with impatience. "What do you wanna know?"

I try like hell not to laugh, but I've never been with a guy quite this eager to get inside my pants. I stand in front of him, smirking as I study the hard lines of his jaw and the faint wrinkles forming around the corners of his eyes when he squints. "Well, uhhh…let's start with something easy. Like maybe your family. Are you an only child? Do your parents live here?"

"It's just me. My mom died a while back and I have nothing to do with my old man." He crosses his arms, studying me beyond the bridge of his strong nose. "What about you?"

"My parents are divorced. My mom still lives in L.A. where I grew up, and my dad recently moved to the northern Bay Area with wife number three."

"Why L.A.?"

"My mom's in the entertainment business," I say, pausing to briefly chew on my lower lip. If I'm going to get him to open up, I suppose it's only fair I reveal more about myself. "I'm guessing you've heard of April Marie?"

"She's your mom," he says, matter-of-fact like.

"How did you—"

"You look just like her." His expression remains even-keeled as he shrugs. "Something felt familiar about you the first time I walked into your house. It must've been that…I just couldn't put my finger on it until now."

Panic thickens in my throat. "Please don't tell anyone. Carol knows because my mom had to get involved in the purchase of my house, but I don't plan on letting anyone else know."

Theo grunts, gaze sweeping around the empty room. "Who am I gonna tell?"

"I don't know...you must have *some* buddies you like to hang out with and drink beer while watching football or whatever barbarian sport is in season. Isn't that what guys do around here?"

"Like I said, I prefer to keep to myself." In a flash, he snags my hand and pulls me back into his lap. It's impossible to breathe when his taunting mouth lingers so close to mine. "Your secrets are safe with me."

When he kisses me this time, I don't protest. It's been ages since I've experienced this degree of raw passion—since high school, to be exact—and Theo Davies is one exceptionally talented kisser. Besides, I'm satisfied that he was finally able to share something personal with me, even if it was barely a proper response to my questions. He didn't mention how his mom died, or if his father lives nearby. Hopefully, with time, I'll gain his trust and find a way to crack his stone facade.

J.R. adjusts the sling around his neck before holding his left hand out between us. "Come on, Jackie. Let's go. I won't let you fall."

This afternoon, a mere hour after school let out for MEA weekend, he appeared on my front step with his right forearm in a fresh cast. He claimed he tripped at basketball practice, and the doctor told him he fractured his radius bone. He was in a rotten mood and claimed it was because he won't get to play basketball for the rest of the season. He let me sign his cast, and now I kind of wish I hadn't signed my name with a heart. What if the other boys at school tease him because of it?

The fence he wants to climb to sneak into the

park is at least 10 feet tall. How's he going to scale it with one arm?

"You aren't supposed to get your cast wet," I remind him, shaking my head over and over. "And the water will be ice cold!"

"We aren't going to get wet," he promises. "I just want to see these waterfalls you keep talking about. Soon they'll be frozen and it won't be as cool."

I take his hand, still unsure, letting him guide me down the steep slope leading to the park. Relief slides through me when he pushes on a section of the fence and it gives way where it's been cut. I don't ask J.R. how he knew about the opening, although I do wonder if maybe he'd cut it himself on a different day. I slip through the opening ahead of him, then begin to lead the way down the path to the first waterfall. The park is quiet. We only pass two other couples walking their dogs.

"It's my birthday tomorrow," J.R. blurts.

"Really?" I turn to him with a thrill in my belly. Maybe I could bake him a cake, and we could sit on top of a table across from each other like Sam and Jake in *Sixteen Candles*. Maybe then he'd kiss me. Maybe he'd even ask me to the Albatross for one of their Teen Night dances. "We totally need to do something cool to celebrate. We could go to that new Tom Cruise movie everyone is talking about."

J.R. makes a funny little frown-face. "*Top Gun*? I don't think it's in the theatre anymore. We could always just hang out at your place."

My fantasy of going to the dance fizzles. Still, I could make him a cupcake, and stick a candle in the center. Maybe there's still a chance he'd want to kiss me. "It might still be playing at the drive-in," I tell him. "The movies there are always a couple of months behind. We can ask Karrie—she's working there all weekend and will let us in for free there too."

"Really?" J.R. throws me a lop-sided smile. "That would be rad!"

I glance down at his arm. "What about your dad?"

"What *about* him?" he snaps.

"Will he care if you're not home to celebrate?"

When he responds with a mean look, a rush of tears burn behind my eyelids. It's not too different from the way he looked at Ben and Matt after he came to my rescue. "You know, Jackie. Sometimes you can be really cool, and I think you might be the best friend I've ever had. But sometimes you totally act your age, and I wonder why I'm wasting my time with a sixth grader."

Tears dribble down my cheeks as I stand motionless, watching him walk away. I hold my breath when he pauses for a second like he's going to turn around and say he's sorry, but then he shakes his head and continues on.

LIKE EVERY OTHER SATURDAY, the drive-in theater is packed by the time the sun sets on J.R.'s birthday. Although J.R. didn't exactly apologize for the way he treated me the day before at the park, he's been extra sweet ever since he came to my house early this morning with my favorite donuts. I insisted we light a candle and stick it inside his, then I sang the birthday song before I'd let him blow it out. My mom didn't come home the night before, but my singing woke Diane and she's been clinging to us like velcro ever since. I spent the entire day wishing she'd go away, because there was no room for her in my plan to make J.R. want to kiss me.

When Karrie lets us in past the gate at the drive-in, she stops snapping her bubble gum long enough to give our trio a sly smile. "Hey, Diane. You're sure *babysitting* Jackie-O and the new kid a lot these days."

"It's J.R.," he tells her in a way that makes him

sound three years older. "And I'm fourteen. I don't need a babysitter."

Diane scoffs with a roll of her eyes. "*Someone* has to keep an eye on them."

Karrie pops a little pink bubble, dark eyes wide. "Speaking of babysitting, did you hear what happened to Karl's little sister?"

As Diane and Karrie catch up on gossip, I take the speaker from Karrie and head out with J.R. to find an ideal spot to camp out, an old blanket from home draped over my arm.

"Are you sure you're okay with seeing a scary movie?" J.R. asks as we maneuver around parked cars. "I heard this *Friday the Thirteenth* is more gory than the others."

When I'd asked Karrie was what playing, I almost lied to J.R. and told him it was a kids' movie. But then I reminded myself it's his birthday and he loves slasher movies, so I sucked it up and agreed to go. Now that we're outside in the cold, dark night, I'm not as sure I made the right choice.

Zipping my rainbow puffer jacket up to my chin, I shrug. "I'm not scared. It's just pretend." I glance around at the dark cars with a chill that rattles my bones. I'm more afraid that whoever took Becky, Shannon, and 16-year-old Heidi Thompson, is among those lurking nearby in the dark. If anything, it will give me a reason to snuggle a little closer to J.R. during the scary parts.

Once we come across an open lot in the back, I spread the blanket on the ground and J.R. begins to mess around with the speaker. "How does this work?" he asks.

"It'll come on once they start playing the trailers." I sit on the ground beside him. "I can't believe you've never been to a drive-in."

"My old man isn't into family time," he reminds me, tossing the speaker aside. He then throws me one of his dimpled grins. "Screw him. I'd rather spend my birthday with you anyway."

I brush my fingers over the heart I drew on his cast before meeting his warm gaze. "J.R.," I begin, my voice as soft as I can make it, "I think you should tell someone."

His smile fades. "Tell someone *what?*"

"About your dad. How he hurts you."

Lips curling with a frown, he bends in closer until his warm breath tickles my ear. "You want me to go away? Because that's what will happen if the courts get involved, Jackie. They'll stick me in a home for boys, unless of course my old man wipes me off the face of the planet first for ratting him out and probably losing his job. Either way, I'll never see you again. Is that what you want?"

"Of course not." I throw him a pleading look, wishing he'd take it back. "It would break my heart."

"Then let it go. I'm fine. I can take it."

"What are you kids doing here?" a gruff voice says. "This movie's rated R."

My spine tingles as I spin around and find Mr. Kabe standing behind us. He's an even bigger nerd than usual in jeans too short to cover his ankles, bright white sneakers, and a brown sweater the color of poop beneath a faded windbreaker jacket.

Embarrassment for being caught by a teacher quickly turns into a bolt of red-hot anger. He's been extra mean to me since the first day of school, calling me out in front of my classmates for not knowing the answers to hard questions and making me sit in the hallway a couple of times. Matt and Ben have left me alone since J.R. yelled at them, but I hear my other classmates laugh and whisper to each other when Mr. Kabe draws attention to me. Why does he have to pick on me outside of school, too?

"What are you, the movie police?" J.R. challenges without turning around.

"I'm Miss Tanner's teacher. She's far too young to be here."

J.R. sniggers at my side. "Ignore him, Jackie. He can't tell you what you can and can't do outside of school."

"That's where you're wrong, young man. I have an obligation to report any incident of juvenile neglect."

J.R. turns to him with a dark glare. "*Neglect*? How is this neglect? Her mom doesn't even know she's here!"

"That's exactly the point." Mr. Kabe tugs on the bottom of his jacket and juts his chin as if to remind us he's a person of authority. "Miss Tanner's mother fails to respond to my phone calls, and she failed to attend summer conferences. The fact that she's attending a movie intended for grown-ups is just one more reason to raise suspicion."

"Don't be a dick," J.R. says, taking a little longer to get back on his feet because of his cast. "Jackie's mom works her ass off so she can provide for them on her own. Jackie isn't the only latchkey kid in town."

Although I love that J.R. is coming to my rescue yet again, I begin to wonder if he should back off when Mr. Kabe's face turns a deep shade of red. "What is your name, young man?"

"John," J.R. answers.

"John what?" Mr. Kabe demands.

J.R. is barely able to contain his smirk. "Cock... tos...ton."

Among a growl, Mr. Kabe grabs a handful of J.R.'s jean jacket and yanks him close. "You think you're funny, stealing a joke from Chevy Chase like I'm some kind of an idiot?"

I jump to my feet, balling my vibrating hands at my sides. While I normally wouldn't hit a teacher, I could make an exception for Mr. Kabe. Especially if it meant getting kicked out of his class. "Let go of him!"

Diane swoops in among us, eyes hard. "What's going on here?"

For several moments after Mr. Kabe finally releases him, J.R. doesn't move an inch. I grab his hand and yank him back to me, afraid he's going to punch Mr. Kabe. There's no telling what his dad would do if J.R. did such a thing.

"Mr. Kabe is threatening to report Mom for letting me go to an R movie," I tell Diane.

My sister's face brightens with a smile as she turns to my teacher. "Mr. Kabe! I didn't recognize you at first!" She smooths the palm of her hand along his arm. "I haven't seen you in, like, forever! How have you been?"

I doubt anyone watching misses the way Mr. Kabe's eyes drop down to Diane's chest. "Well hello, Diane. It really has been a long time. I sometimes forget you and Jackie are sisters."

"That's because we have different dads," she pretend whispers.

My stomach roils when Mr. Kabe's eyes do another sweep of my sister's body. "You've certainly changed since you were in my class. You must be what...*sixteen* by now?"

"And a half," Diane sings with a corny wink.

With a shift of his weight, Mr. Kabe pushes his glasses up higher on the bridge of his nose. "It's perfectly fine that you're here, Diane, but your sister—"

"Snuck in," Diane tells him. "Our mom sent me here to find her. Jackie went missing after supper, and our mom's worried sick."

"What about this mouthy kid?" Mr. Kabe asks, motioning to J.R. "Is he old enough?"

"Don't you worry about him, Mr. Kabe. He's taking Jackie home with me." Giggling, Diane pats Mr. Kabe's chest. "We won't disturb your evening any longer. Good night, Mr. Kabe!"

"Good night, Diane," he replies, shooting me a stern look. "I won't be reporting your mother this time, Miss Tanner. But if something like this happens again, I'm afraid I'll have no other choice."

J.R. collects the blanket off the ground and tosses it at me to carry before he pulls me away with his good hand, keeping in pace with Diane. As we near the gate where Karrie continues to sell tickets, Diane shudders.

"Ugh, I need a shower," she grumbles. "I despise that perv."

"Me too," I say, crossing my arms over my belly.

"Me three," J.R. chimes in. Grinning, he bumps his hip against Diane's. "Thanks for saving my ass. I owe you one."

"You didn't have to act like that," I snarl at my sister. "It was gross the way you flirted with him while he stared at your boobs."

Diane releases a loud, nasally laugh. "Seriously? If I hadn't 'flirted' with him, someone from the county would've come to our house to see if mom was fit enough to keep us, and we'd both end up in a foster home. God, Diane. You can be such a baby." Bumping her hip against J.R.'s., she grins. "Come on, birthday boy. Karrie will go on break soon, and I bet she'll give us a ride to Baskin-Robbins."

They walk away, whispering to each other and laughing like I'm not even there.

10
STERLING - 2018

Following the breakthrough with Theo over the weekend, my supervisor loads me up on cases. On a daily basis, I'm called into multiple hairy situations involving abused children. The worst is when I'm forced to pull five young children from their home after their father, a repeat assault offender, violates the terms of his probation by skipping anger management classes to get wasted at the bar. The mother screams in my face, threatening to send her brother to "take care of me" as I'm strapping the newborn's car seat inside the back of the police cruiser. What was even more unsettling is the fact that I couldn't stop thinking about the girl from my dreams, and how she often fears someone equally violent.

By the time I return home after the incident with the five children and discover Theo kneeling in my bedroom, building a nightstand, I'm a tornado of raw emotions. I can't decide if I want to make him hold me while I cry, or rip my pants suit off and beg him to rock my world.

When his warm eyes meet mine, sharp with intent, I opt for the second option. He's been working over-time all week, trying to catch up on projects for clients, so I haven't seen him much since the other night at his place. Somehow he's managed to become even more alluring since then. I don't think it's because of the haircut, or the fact that he's not as much of an asshole as I'd first thought. Maybe it's because I now know he's an extremely generous kisser, and likely an equally generous lover. I'm eager for anything to remind me there can be an upside to the darkest of days.

"You look too damn hot to be a county worker," he teases as I kick my heels off near the edge of the bed. Setting the hammer down on the floor, he studies my grim expression. "Another bad day?"

"You don't want to know," I say, releasing my hair from the updo I'd spent far too long perfecting this morning when I couldn't sleep any longer because of my intense dreams. After removing my sports jacket,

I gesture to his project. "Whatcha got goin' there, big guy?"

"A housewarming gift. It just needs a few coats of stain and it's good to go." Grinning, he stands to admire the little table with what I perceive as pride. It's simple and classic enough to effortlessly match the style of my new home. "I don't know how you've managed living here this long without any furniture."

"I've lived too long without a lot of things." I unzip my trousers, letting them fall to the ground, before lifting my blouse over my head. Theo's tongue slips between his lips as he watches my dark waves of hair tumble down over my bare shoulders. The way his glassy-eyed gaze drinks in my pale pink bra and matching thong has my skin prickling with sizzling heat.

I rush to him and fist his blue t-shirt, dragging him close to ravage his lips. His thick arms wind around me as his lips reciprocate with an equal burst of enthusiasm. I nudge his shirt up and he yanks it over his head, giving me unencumbered access to bulging pectorals, an impressive 6-pack with a slight roll at his belly, and rosy nipples that bead when I dust my fingertips over them.

"Bed," I rasp between more kisses, nudging him in that direction. "Now."

Despite my urgency, he takes his time caressing my body. The way he touches me is like something out of my deepest, darkest fantasies. I feel treasured. Adored. I'm suddenly more awake than I've ever been in my life as my heart and mind soar to a blissful level of euphoria.

I try repeatedly to drag him closer, desperate to smooth my fingertips over his bunched muscles and run my tongue along his golden skin, but he remains out of touch, intent on learning how to play my body like an instrument.

Around the time I'm ready to tear his jeans off him, I completely come undone with a final well-placed stroke of his hand. He steals my raged breaths with more urgent kisses before sliding off the bed.

"Stay here," he orders in a borderline surly tone.

The sudden void of his warmth snaps me back to reality. "What...you're out of little blue pills?" I grumble back at him.

"I'm going to make you dinner while you relax."

A thrill blossoms through me, adding more pleasant heat to my afterglow. *A girl like me could easily fall in love with a guy like him*, I decide. "It's sweet of you to offer, but we have some unfinished business to attend to. Besides, I don't have much for groceries yet."

"Dinner's covered." His lips *split* with a dimpled grin. "We have plenty of time for business. I'll be around for months, remember?"

My body hums with satisfaction as I watch him stride out from the room, still shirtless. I almost gasp aloud with the discovery of a drawing of a beautiful angel inked across his back. Her wings stretch across his shoulder blades and her face is as serene as water. *Why an angel?* I wonder. *Could it have something to do with his mom?*

I can't help feeling a bit of disappointment by his comment about being around for months. Does he see this things between us having an expiration date? What if he considers this to be a fling, and nothing more? It's unnerving how effortlessly I accepted him into my life after he kissed me. I'm even more unsettled by the feeling of being home that I get when he's around. It's a new sensation—something I never experienced with Stefan or any other man.

Brushing my fingertips along the smooth wood top on the nightstand, I recall the way Theo had admired his own work. The man's still a mystery, but at least I know of one thing that seems to make him happy.

I slip into my kimono robe and pad barefoot into the kitchen, curious by his intentions. "You came prepared," I say, watching as he unfolds a deli package of chicken breasts.

"I stopped by the grocery store this afternoon. After that text you sent when I invited you to lunch, I figured you'd be too tired to cook." He glances my way with a hint of annoyance darkening his gaze. "Thought I told you to relax."

"This is far more entertaining." Shrugging, I boost myself onto the counter and watch as he prepares a coating for the chicken. Truthfully I'm watching the angel and the way his firm lats bunch and flex as he moves around the kitchen.

I've never felt so relaxed around a man. I don't even worry about the way my thighs jiggle when I swing my legs. It's as if Theo and I have known each other forever. "Now I understand why you have an awesome kitchen. Have you always enjoyed cooking?"

"Not always, no. My father was always working when I was a kid, and the only thing I knew how to make back then was sandwiches. It wasn't until after my captain made me a food service specialist while overseas that I learned how to cook."

"You're a veteran?"

Tossing a breast into an oiled pan on the stove, he nods. "Marine Corps."

Among the sounds of sizzling chicken, my pulse skips a little. It doesn't take a great stretch of the imagination to picture him in uniform, marching through rough terrain with an automatic weapon in hand. He definitely has the size and physique of a Marine—at least the kind portrayed by Hollywood standards.

As much as I wish he would keep sharing little tidbits about himself, I also don't want to accidentally ask something that will make him clam up again. "That's admirable," I merely say.

He shifts away, expression now solemn. "I enjoy grilling more, but I noticed you don't have a grill."

"Even if I did, I'm not sure my neighbors are ready for the kind of gun show you'd be giving them without a shirt." Smirking, I slide off the counter and head to my designated liquor cabinet. The prior evening, I'd swung by the liquor store on my way back from work for a bottle of the cinnamon whiskey he'd served at his place. I fill two glasses with ice and whiskey before handing him one. "Thank you for doing this. It was a rough day."

"Wanna talk about it?" He turns to me as he takes a drink, one eyebrow lifted.

From behind my glass, I shake my head. "Even if I could, I wouldn't want to rehash it. Let's just say there are some shitty people in this world."

"Don't I know it."

We clink glasses and simultaneously wolf them down. I relish in the burn of whiskey as it slips down my throat and into my belly. "That's so delicious."

He bends quickly, brushing his lips over mine. "Tastes even better on you."

I wrap my arms around his neck and kiss him back with a fire in my belly even warmer than the whiskey. The man is the equivalent of human cat nip —I don't know that I could ever get enough. He hoists me back onto the counter top and unties my robe, kissing my exposed skin before rejoining our mouths. What I wouldn't give to lock him inside my bedroom and do nothing but absorb his skillful kisses for months on end.

With the shrill wail of the fire alarm, we break apart. My senses were numb to everything except for the stroke of his lips, warmth of his tongue, and the scent of sawdust combined with his fragrant deodorant.

"Better turn the chicken, big guy," I tease, glancing over at the smoking pan.

He starts for the stove, chuckling. "Guess I better

get used to having tempting distractions while cooking."

With the wolfish grin that follows, my insides become the consistency of pudding. How will I survive falling for this once sour, now charming man if he plans to simply walk away?

WHEN MY FIRST HALF-FRIDAY ARRIVES, I try to convince Theo to take the afternoon off, but he's promised to fix an old widow's leaking windows, so I don't dare beg. I find it far too enduring that he's offered to help an elderly woman, free of charge. Instead, I manage to lure Beth downtown for drinks before her evening shift begins.

"There's something I've been meaning to ask you," I tell her before taking a sip of my cinnamon whiskey. It's not something I would've ordered before meeting Theo, but now it reminds me of kissing him. "Actually two things."

"Yes, they're real," she teases, cupping her large chest. "Both of them."

I nearly choke on my drink with a snort. "Now that we have *that* out of the way, I'm curious to know when exactly you moved to Mankato. Were you here when those girls went missing in the eighties?"

Eyes popping wide, Beth whispers, "How'd you know about them?"

"My supervisor had an old poster in her office."

"It's so weird," Beth says, continuing to keep her voice low. "I mean, no one likes to talk about it. Sometimes I forget they were never found." She stops to sip on her martini. "I moved here from New York in the late eighties to take care of my sick grandma. I'd spent my formative years immersed in the punk scene that was taking over Manhattan clubs, and people around here treated me like some kind of freak with the spiky blue hair I had at the time. It took almost a full year before I befriended someone halfway normal." She points to her face and laughs in a rich sound. "Well, normal in *my* world anyway. I was hired as an apprentice for K.C., a tattoo artist who worked for a studio a few blocks down from here. She eventually told me about the girls, said everyone had their theories on what happened. I guess most of the adults were convinced these girls had either run away to escape a bad family situation, or they'd taken off with a lover. K.C. said it made sense at first because most of them came from rough backgrounds and shitty families, but then the sister of one of her friends disappeared and the older sister-slash-K.C.'s friend was convinced her little sister wouldn't have run away for either of those reasons. K.C. thinks the mayor and whoever else ran the city at that time swept all the rumors under the rug and did their best to erase the girls' stories so people wouldn't be afraid to live in Mankato. They somehow managed to scrub any mention of it from public record, citing some bull-shit about the girls being minors."

"Do you think K.C. would be working tonight?"

Smirking, Beth arches a single eyebrow. "Han-kering for some ink?"

"No...I just...I think it's sad no one found these girls, and no one brought their kidnapper to justice. I'd love to talk to K.C. myself, see what other infor-mation I can get out of her."

"It's unsettling that no one seems to give a shit about them now," Beth agrees before taking a long sip of her drink. She then shrugs. "But K.C. left over a decade ago. She couldn't handle this town anymore."

My shoulders droop. "Do you know how I could get in touch with her?"

"Maybe. I haven't talked to her in a while, but last time she reached out, she had opened a studio in

White Bear Lake near St. Paul. I think she named it K.C.'s Touch. As in the letters 'K' and 'C', not C-a-s-e-y. I'm sure you could find her contact info online." Her straw crackles as she sucks down the remainder her drink, so she tries to get the bartender's attention. "You said you had two things you wanted to ask, Hollywood. What's the second?"

I pause. "Hollywood?"

"Seriously, do you own a mirror? I'd be an idiot not to see the resemblance. I didn't really put two and two together until after you mentioned you were from L.A."

Heat spreads down my neck. All those years I spent in hiding from the spotlight were apparently for nothing. "Please don't—"

"You don't have to ask. Your secret's safe with me," she declares, waving me along to the next subject. "Now what is this other thing you wanted to ask?"

"Do you know someone named Theo Davies?"

Beth's eyes squint. "Tall, crazy good looking guy with the personality of a troll?" With a hint of a smirk, she wiggles her eyebrows. "He comes around the bar every now and then, has a drink while he's waiting for his order of wings. No matter what I say, he keeps to himself. Why?"

"I was hoping you'd known him for a while since you've been living here for so many years. I hired him to fix up my house and I'm dying to know his story."

"I only know him from the bar, but *K.C.* brought him up a few times. I don't know what she saw in him, but I get the feeling they had something going back in the day."

Jealousy roils through my gut as I stab the ice cubes in my glass with the straw. "Deep down, he's nothing like he'd like the world to perceive him to be."

"You're flushed," she says, her eyes full of accusations. "Why are you flushing? Are you *hooking up* with the troll?" she practically shouts.

Embarrassed laughter bubbles from my lips. "Would you lower your voice? He's not a *troll*. He's just a complex person with complex emotions."

"Mmhmm," she replies with heavy sarcasm. "How in the hell did you manage to break a man as prickly as a cactus?"

It's a fair question, one I've even asked myself a few times throughout the past week, but I chalk it up to my determination and care-giver ways.

The college-aged bartender with pretty green

eyes approaches our end of the bar and motions to our drinks. "Another round, ladies?"

"Better make them both a double," Beth tells her. "My friend is about to tell me all about her latest conquest."

Still unsettled by Theo's connection to this K.C. person, I'm unable to laugh. I can't wait to return home so I can look up K.C.'s Touch in White Bear Lake.

The days following MEA break, Mr. Kabe treats me as if I'm not even there. I decide it's better being a ghost than being constantly picked on, and halfway through the week I'm actually in a really good mood because of it until I leave school on Wednesday and find J.R. and Diane waiting together on the lawn. He must say something funny because she throws her head back and laughs, grabbing his good arm.

My heart sinks. I sensed them getting closer after his birthday, especially when she offered him a lick of her ice cream cone. I glance at the other students in a hurry to leave the school grounds and wonder if I can sneak out behind them without being seen.

"Jackie!" J.R. calls out, waving his free arm high above his head. "Over here!"

I stomp over them, trying my best not to frown when J.R. takes my Trapper Keeper and tucks it under his cast. He's always carrying my things lately, and I thought it's because we were on our way to becoming boyfriend/girlfriend.

"Diane said the arcade just got Ms. Pac-Man," he tells me. "Wanna go check it out with us?"

Vomit burns up my throat. This isn't how it's supposed to go. J.R. and I are the ones who always make plans together, and sometimes invite Diane along.

"I guess," I mumble, kicking at a rock on the sidewalk.

J.R. slings his good arm around my neck. "Let's go get a pizza at Pagliai's first. I'm starving. It'll be my treat."

When we walk away, I feel a little better now that J.R. has attached himself to me and not Diane. Still, I want to trip her for tagging along.

HALFWAY TO THE PIZZA PARLOR, we pass the strange man who'd been watching us at Skating World. All three of us turn to watch as he continues down the sidewalk at a brisk pace, wearing dress clothes that look at least one size too small. His bright red tie with wide stripes stops in the middle of his round belly, and his tan dress pants swish around his ankles.

Diane grabs J.R.'s elbow. "There's that weirdo again!"

"He probably just finished a shift at the mall," J.R. decides with a shrug.

The man turns off the sidewalk and starts down a side street.

"Let's follow him," Diane tells us. "I wanna see where he's going."

I pull on the sleeves of my coat and scrape my teeth over my bottom lip. "I don't know, Diane. What if he sees us?"

She shrugs. "We're not doing anything wrong. It's a free country. Besides, for all he knows, we're walking home." She pulls on J.R.'s good elbow. "Come on!"

J.R. glances back at me with one of his dimpled grins and shrugs. "Let's just go. It'll be okay, I promise."

A boulder of dread settles in my gut as I shuffle behind them. I want to remind my dumb sister that three girls from Kato have gone missing, but I suppose no one would try to kidnap one of us when we're in a group. At least that's what I tell myself when my heart thuds hard enough to make my entire body shake. What if the man turns around and sees us following him?

The man continues for a couple of blocks before heading toward a tiny little white house on a corner. He removes a set of keys from his pocket and sticks one into the front door. We hide behind the neighbor's bushes, watching as he steps inside and the door closes behind him.

"That was totally lame," I grumble, turning back to the street. "Let's go, J.R. I'm hungry too."

"Wait!" Diane demands. "Now he's going into his backyard! Let's see what he's doing!"

Crossing my arms over my chest, I huff. "What's your obsession with this weirdo, Diane? Are you in love with him or something?"

"DeeDee and the weirdo sitting in a tree," J.R. sings with a wide grin. "K-i-s-s-i-n—"

Diane slaps her hand over his mouth. "Stop calling me that!" she whispers. "And be quiet! He'll hear you!"

Quietly laughing beneath her fingers, he pulls her

arm down. "Jackie's right. Why are you obsessed with this guy?"

"I don't know. He gives me the heebie jeebies. I wouldn't be surprised if he took Becky and the others."

Fear trickles down my spine. What if she's right?

J.R. shakes his head. "He's just weird, that's all. I don't think he's all there. He had some kind of speech impediment."

"Having a dad who's a police detective doesn't make you an expert on murderers," Diane scolds him. She turns back to the man's backyard. "He just went inside that creepy little shed. I'm going to get a closer look."

J.R. and I exchange an unsure look as she sneaks away, sticking close to the bushes separating the man's yard from his neighbor's. I glance behind us to the neighbor's house, waiting for someone to appear in one of the windows.

"We could get into big trouble for this," I warn J.R. "What if one of the neighbors calls the police and your dad finds out you've been spying on people?"

J.R.'s hickory-colored eyes dance around the neighborhood as he wets his lips. I can sense a fresh wave of fear vibrating off of him with the idea. "We'll wait here for her to come back…just in case."

I look down and kick a dead plant near my sneaker, happy he's at least on my side.

"What has your teacher been like this week?" he asks. "Has he said anything about last weekend?"

"He's been ignoring me," I say, meeting his gaze with a smile. "It's awesome."

"That guy is such a jerk. He's lucky I didn't knock his teeth in for threatening you like that."

Just when I'm floating above the clouds, knowing he wanted to defend me, he adds, "I didn't like the way he was looking at Diane, either."

"Do you like my sister?" I blurt.

His good shoulder lifts. "Yeah, she's cool."

"I mean…do you *like* her, like her."

His eyes dart away from mine. "She's a sophomore, Jackie. Why would she want to date an eighth grader?"

I turn away with hot tears burning behind my eyes. Life is so unfair. I'm going to lose the first boy I ever loved to my dumb sister, and I don't know how to stop it from happening. A dark thought slips into my mind.

I wish someone would take her next so I'd never have to see her again.

Diane comes running back to us a moment later, eyes wide. She stops to rest her hands on her knees, panting. "You...guys...we have to...go!"

"Why?" J.R. asks, setting his hand on her hunched back. "What happened?"

Her eyes skate back to the shed, spooked. "I don't know what he was doing in that shed, but there were these really weird noises. I heard pounding, then a chainsaw."

"So what?" J.R. says, crossing his arms. "He's probably making a project out of wood."

"That's not all I heard. There was a girl." When Diane looks at him, her eyes are wet. "She was screaming."

ONCE WE ARRIVE at Pagliai's, J.R. calls his dad from the payphone across the street to tell him everything Diane heard back at the man's shed. Diane chews on her fingernails as we watch him through the pizza parlor's window. I want to tell her she's selfish for insisting J.R. call his dad over something she probably made up anyway, just to gain J.R.'s attention. J.R.'s dad will certainly be angry to hear we followed

141

a stranger to his house. I'm positive his dad broke his arm. What will he do to J.R. next?

"You shouldn't have gone into that man's yard," I scold her. "If Mom finds out, she'll ground us both."

Diane releases a mean laugh. "What good will that do? It's not like she's around to make sure we stay home."

I would never think of going against our mom's punishment, whether she was around to see it or not. But when I realize she's right, our mom is hardly even around to take care of us, I'm all at once sad. "Do you think J.R. is right? Do you think Mom could be dating a married man, or pregnant with another baby?"

"Don't be stupid!" She bares her teeth like a wild dog. "God, Jackie! You're so stupid!"

"No I'm not!" I insist, feeling the burn of hot tears. "You have no idea where Mom is or who she's with, so don't act like you know everything! Why are you always so mean?"

The bell above the parlor's front door rings behind me. When I hear J.R.'s heavy sigh over my shoulder, I flutter my eyelashes to keep the tears from falling.

"My old man says they can't just go after the guy without some kind of probable cause. He said it's almost Halloween and you could've heard a horror movie playing on a neighbor's television." He slides into the booth next to me and glances my way from the corner of his eye. "He told me we're lucky they can't do anything because the guy would probably press charges against us for trespassing on private property."

Tension fills my entire body. He isn't able to look me in the eye because we both know he's going to get into serious trouble for making the call.

"That's bullshit," Diane grumbles, flicking a crumb on the table. "I know what I heard."

After the waiter comes to take our order, Diane heads to the bathroom.

"You shouldn't have called your dad," I tell J.R., turning to him in the booth.

He shakes his head several times. "But what if Diane's right? What if she really did hear a girl scream in that shed?"

I click my tongue and frown. "You don't know my sister like I do. She's always doing stuff to get attention. She probably only said that because she knew you'd worry about her." Softening my expression, I rest my hand on his sling. "I think you should ask your dad if you can stay at a friend's house tonight. You can stay in my room—my mom never comes in to check on me after she gets home. She'd never know you were there. We'll make you a bed out of blankets on the floor."

For a second, I think he's going to agree by the way his eyes light up. Then he glances out the window. "On a school night?" he scoffs, sounding more hopeless than anything. "He'd never agree to that."

The heat of tears return when I imagine his dad waiting in the doorway for him to come home. How was someone so mean able to get an important job working for the police?

"Say you have a big project to work on for school or something," I prod, refusing to give up the idea. "Whatever it takes." Panic clogs my throat. "Please, J.R., you have to somehow convince him to let you stay somewhere else. Maybe the night away would give him time to cool down before you had to see him again. Maybe he wouldn't be as mad."

With his dimpled grin in place, he reaches over his cast to wrap his hand around mine. "Jackie, you're a good friend to worry about me. But I'll be okay. I can handle whatever punishment the bastard dishes out."

Diane returns just then. Her eyes dart to J.R.'s hand around mine. "What'd I miss?"

"Nothing," J.R. says, dropping my hand and sliding away. "Jackie was just telling me about some of the jerks at her school."

"Maybe you should start by being less of an easy target," Diane tells me with a dramatic roll of her eyes. "They can probably smell your fear a mile away."

I wait for J.R. to laugh along with her, but his posture straightens in the booth. "Maybe *you* should be a good big sister and let those jerks know she's not fair game anymore."

Diane flinches then sips on her soda while watching a group of kids gathered outside.

In that moment, I actually believe everything is going to be okay, and we'll go back to being the best of friends without Diane. J.R. stood up to her, choosing to defend me instead of laughing the way she'd hoped. Maybe I don't have to worry about him falling in love with her after all.

12
STERLING - 2018

Saturday morning, I'm torn from a dream involving disturbing noises coming from a dilapidated little shed. I settle myself by scrolling through tattoos K.C. has posted on her Instagram account until my doorbell rings. I untangle myself from the new set of satiny sheets I'd found on sale at T.J. Maxx and squint out my window to discover the sun hasn't fully risen. Theo and I had planned to spend the day together, but we didn't specify an exact start time. I certainly hadn't expected him quite this early. Truthfully, I'd hoped he'd show up on my doorstep the night before and had sleep nude in anticipation of his arrival.

I throw my kimono over my naked body and shuffle to the front door. When I swing it open, I release a genuine scream with the sight of the beautiful brunette dressed from head to toe in white with a designer handbag slung over one narrow shoulder. "Mom!"

Giggling, my mother launches herself into my arms. The mystical scent of her Chanel perfume and clink of her signature gold bangles take me back to my childhood. She's become so slender that I worry I'm crushing her bones when I hold her tight. Between that and our remarkable height difference, it's like hugging a little child. But I know better than to say anything as her weight is an absurd requirement of her job.

"Surprise, baby girl! The director gave us the day off to work with the stunt crew, and of course there was only one place I wanted to spend my free time!"

"How long to you get to stay?"

"Only until this evening. My jet flies out of this town's little airport at six. I have to be back on set tomorrow at five a.m. sharp."

After she plants a kiss on my cheek, we release each other. I motion for her to enter my home. "Then you better come inside! We have a lot of catching up to do!"

As she steps in past me, I spot the same navy blue sedan that had taken off after I'd waved. It's parked far enough down the road that I'm unable to decide if anyone's behind the wheel. Unease rattles my bones as I close the door.

My mom pushes her oversized sunglasses on top of her head and seemingly scrutinizes every square inch of my house. "It sure is...old-world."

"It's a work in progress. I hired a carpenter."

My mom's steely gaze lands on me. "Is this carpenter any good?"

My cheeks grow hot as I recall just how good Theo truly is—at his job and other things. "He already fixed my floors. He plans to work on the kitchen, starting right away next week."

Not one to ever miss a single thing, my mother crosses her arms over her stomach. "Sterling Marie, why is your face suddenly so flushed?" Then she gasps, splaying the fingers of one hand over her chest. "You're sleeping with the help?"

"Don't call him that," I scold, removing her hand from her chest. "And stop being so dramatic. We're not *sleeping* together." A little smile tug at my lips. "At least not yet." Part of me wants to tell her how hard I'm falling for him, but it's still too new between us. I don't want to deal with any drama from her if things don't work out. Especially if my theory is right, and

Theo's only interested in having a little fun until he's finished fixing my home.

My mom squeals like a teenage girl. "Oh my god, *Sterling*! I want to hear all about this carpenter!" She starts for my kitchen, tossing her handbag onto the counter top, and begins opening cupboard doors. "Every last juicy detail!"

She doesn't make her own coffee at home, so I don't offer my help when I'm convinced that's what she's after. "Coffee grounds are in the container on your left," I say with a giggle.

"Screw coffee. Details of an affair with a sexy carpenter call for mimosas! Where are your champagne flutes?"

"I don't have any. I don't have any orange juice either. Or champagne."

Her jaw literally drops. "Please tell me you're joking."

"No jokes," I promise. "We can run to the market in a little bit." I check my digital watch for the time, realizing I'd failed to take it off for a charge in the night when it doesn't light up. "Shit. I need to go find my phone. Theo could be here—"

"His name is *Theo*?" my mom interrupts with a purr. She leans against the edge of my counter top, batting her surgically implanted eyelashes. "Do tell me more."

I release a heavy sigh, knowing she won't give up until I share some details. "He's not my usual type."

"You mean boring and mediocre looking, like Stefan?"

"Come on, Mom. Stefan was a nice guy."

"So's my gynecologist," she remarks in a dry tone. "Doesn't mean I want to become roommates with the guy for half a decade."

Unable to resist, I laugh. "There's something about Theo that I really like. I'm couldn't tell you why I was so drawn to him initially, because he was seriously grumpy and didn't want to engage in any conversations with me. But then he kissed me, and it was like the dam between us burst. The sparks have been intense ever since."

My mom claps her hands with the zest of a cheerleader. "Oh, Sterling! Maybe he's your soulmate!"

I tell myself it wouldn't be nice to laugh when I recall how many times she's declared a man to be *her* soulmate. I almost feel sorry for her, knowing she still clings to the hope of such a thing after she thought she'd be married to my father forever. "Mom, have you ever had an experience of déjà vu with such clarity that you couldn't deal with it? Like, you feel as if you've been in that *exact* same situation before?"

Swatting a hand through the air, my mother giggles. "Babe, my life is one big case of déjà vu. Especially now that I'm working with Aaron Sandwell on yet *another* film. Fans deemed us the ultimate power couple after *No Regrets*, so now they want more of us together."

"That's different. This was...just eerie. Theo took me to this park and I literally passed out when I felt as if I'd been in that exact same spot before. I almost wonder if...I don't know...maybe I'm somehow connecting with a real person...reliving their experiences."

"Sterling!" she scolds, her eyes growing wide. "This has something to do with that girl you used to dream about when you were little, doesn't it? Are you dreaming about her again?"

"I never stopped," I admit, tipping my chin downward.

She lets out one of her overly dramatic breaths. "This would be a better conversation to have with your aunt Constantine. She'd be able to tell you why those things happen. She spent time in India when she was your age, learned all about karma and that kind of thing from the Hindus and Buddhists. She may even understand why you would have a connection with that girl." With one hand on her hip, her gaze darts around the open space, landing on the blue velvet chair. "Sterling, where in the fresh hell is the rest of your furniture? Where do you and this captivating carpenter sit when he comes over? Where do you *eat*?"

Heat spreads down my neck as I remember sitting half-naked on the counter top while Theo fed me the remains of the charred chicken between steamy kisses. "I'm waiting until the house is finished so I can buy something that fits the space."

"That's ridiculous. Let's go pick something out. You can't except to maintain an adult relationship with a man when your house is more barren than a college dormitory."

As I try to come up with an excuse to turn her down, there's a blunt knock on the door. Eyes wide with panic, I resist the juvenile idea to tell my mom to hide. Instead I point at her on my way to answer the door. "Please try to behave. I'll never talk to you again if you scare him away."

Her green eyes sparkle with mischief. "I swear on my Golden Globe I'll behave."

I nearly forget I'm only wearing a robe until

Theo's eyes darken on my cleavage. "Glad I decided to come by early," he growls, wrapping his arm around my waist and yanking me closer before I can protest. I completely forget my mom is behind me when his lips meld with mine and his fingers slips beneath my robe to caress one of my breasts.

Then my mom clears her throat. "This must be the carpenter."

Theo jerks away like he's been electrocuted. Laughing, I tug my robe back into place before wrapping my fingers around his. I can't exactly blame myself for getting carried away, considering how he sexy looks in a black short sleeved shirt and khaki shorts.

"I promise you'll survive what I'm about to drag you into," I whisper before leading him inside.

When my mom greets him with a cat-like smile, Theo's expression turns blank. I know from experience her perfection can be intimidating. I didn't get a chance to ask if the director had released her after she'd already spent time in hair and makeup, although I suspect that's the case since her dark waves and bronzed cheeks appear camera-ready.

I coil myself around his bulging arm and giggle. "Mom, this is Theo."

She slinks over to him with her hands held out, expecting a hug. "I'm delighted to meet you, Theo."

He awkwardly bends long enough for her arms to wrap around him. "Ma'am," he chokes out when she releases him with a kiss on the cheek. His eyes snap over to me. "You didn't mention you'd have company today."

"That's because she didn't know," my mom tells him. "I wanted it to be a surprise. And don't you worry, I'm only in town for the day. You two love-birds can enjoy a quiet evening alone."

I squeeze his bicep and flash an apologetic smile. "I'll swing by your place after I drop her at the airport."

"That's not what I was implying, Sterling," she scolds in the same voice she used when I was a little girl. "I'd love it if Theo would spend the day with us so I can get to know the man who's apparently swept my fiercely independent daughter off her feet!" She tilts her head at Theo with one of her award-winning smiles. "We're going *furniture* shopping and could use the help of someone who knows a thing or two about good craftsmanship. We can go for a late lunch afterwards. It'll be my treat!"

I glance up at him, mildly amused by the way he squirms. "Sure," he grunts.

"Lovely!" My mom pats my arm, eyeing my robe like she's just realizing it's several seasons behind. "Babe, go get dressed. In the time it takes you to get ready, Theo and I will get to know each other a little better."

Part of me doesn't want to leave the room, curious how much information my mom can actually extort from him. But being the obedient daughter I've always been, I tug on his arm until he bends low enough for me to kiss his cheek. *"Sorry,"* I mouth with a sympathetic look before hurrying back to my room, knowing every second I'm away he'll be tortured.

THEO TAKES us to see a Desert Storm veteran who makes custom furniture superior to anything else we could buy in town. After we put in a large order, the three of us spend a leisurely afternoon in a chic steakhouse downtown called Number 4 where red velvet drapes, dark leather booths, and dim lighting afford us the kind of privacy my mom appreciates.

When Theo and I drop her at the airport, I release a deep breath, wondering when I'd last taken any kind of breath. My mom had spent far too much time drilling Theo with uncomfortable questions before I finally pulled her aside and warned her she was crossing a major line.

"But he's so much older than you," she'd said, cupping my face in her hands. "I don't understand how someone so talented *and* handsome has gone this far in life without any kind of partner the way he claims."

In the end, she respected my request and shifted the conversation to her hectic life and stories of my childhood. It was a chance for Theo to see her as the often flaky yet sometimes nurturing mother I know her to be. Thankfully she stuck to one glass of champagne since she had to report to the set early in the morning and didn't want puffy eyes. There's no telling how it would've gone if she'd been in a celebratory mood, like the night she won her first Oscar and called me the next afternoon, having no idea how she'd ended up in the Hawaiian home of a billionaire.

"I'm so, so sorry," I say as Theo merges my BMW onto the highway. When I comb my fingers through the thick hair on top of his head, I don't miss the subtle way he leans into my hand like a stray animal starved for attention. "I swear I had no idea she was coming today. And she's a lot to process, I know. I hated how she drilled you about your family. I should've stopped her sooner."

He doesn't say a word in response, doesn't look my way. Joining my hands in my lap, I press my lips together as tears of frustration and disappointment sting the back of my eyes. Although he was a good sport all day, flashing my mother deep smiles that showcased his enduring dimples, I sense he's done with me. I can't really blame him, considering we haven't even declared ourselves to be a couple and he was already ambushed into meeting my drama queen of a mother.

I decide to give him an easy out. "If you're too tired to hang out tonight, I totally understand. We probably both need to take a step back after today, slow things down a bit."

After a long stretch of silence, he finally speaks. "You and your mom are close."

Relief washes over me. With someone like him, a change of subject is usually a good sign. Maybe he's not quite ready to run yet. "We're not as close as you'd think. She was gone a lot when I was little, filming on far away locations like London and Greece. I usually only got to visit her on set during the holidays."

"Never really had any kind of relationship with

my mom. And my father..." He works his jaw with a mournful shake of his head. "Let's just say he was an asshole."

Pain crackles through my soul. As someone who has worked with juveniles for several years, I know all too well what he's implying. I remove his right hand from the steering wheel to kiss his knuckles, then twist my fingers around his. "I'm sorry, Theo."

"I ran away when I was seventeen," he continues, "lived with my mom's aunt in Seattle for a few months and finished school before I met with a recruiter. I vowed I'd never return to Mankato, never set foot in this state again. There are too many painful memories here. Too many ghosts."

Ghosts? I think, wondering if he means it in the literal sense. Squeezing his hand, I swallow the lump of emotion growing in the base of my throat and silently plead for him to continue.

His eyes dart between me and the road. "For the first time since I decided to move back, I can finally say I'm glad I did." His hand tightens around mine. "Being with you makes the dark shit hurt a little less."

13

JACKIE - 1986

The day after J.R. told his dad what Diane thought she heard in the strange man's backyard, J.R. isn't waiting for me after school like he's done every day since school started. I rush home to call him, but no one picks up at his house. I practically pounce on Diane when she finally arrives home from the arcade.

"Did you see J.R. in school today?"

She tosses her ratty old backpack onto the couch and glares back at me. "Why? Jealous that we go to the same school and you're still in elementary?"

"Did you see him?" I repeat in a growl.

"No. But it's not like we have any of the same classes."

I pace on the avocado green carpet in the living

room as I wonder what to do next. I could sneak over to his house and see if he's okay since his dad is probably at work. But what if his dad *is* home, guarding J.R. to make sure he doesn't leave? Maybe I could go to a public phone and call the police, say I'm a concerned citizen who'd heard yelling at his house. But it could make J.R.'s dad even more angry. What if he suspects J.R. called them?

Diane watches me with her hands on her hips. "What are you freaking about?"

"Someone needs to check on him. You don't know how mean his dad can get."

"Did you try calling him?"

"Yes, Diane," I snarl. "No one answered."

She begins chewing on her nails. "I'm sure he's fine." Her eyes strain with worry. "Maybe he has the flu or something."

For the first time in my life, I want to punch my sister. I want to see her cry. I want her to be equally as scared and angry as I am that J.R. is missing, and no one is doing anything about it. Sometimes she acts like everything's a big joke. She thinks she's too smart to have gotten J.R. into trouble.

"If something bad happened to him, it's all your fault!" I yell, storming off to my room.

I ignore her for the rest of the night and only

leave once to grab a slice of bread, and three other times to call J.R.'s house.

The last time I call, it's nearly eleven.

I'm greeted by his dad's deep voice, gruff with irritation. "Hello?"

I hang up.

ON FRIDAY, I walk around school like a zombie and have a hard time staying awake in my classes. I'd only slept a couple of hours after calling J.R.'s house. I was desperate enough for help that I waited for the sounds of my mom returning from work, but the trailer remained silent.

It ends up being the longest school day on record. To make it a little more painful, the fifth and sixth graders are called into the gymnasium for an assembly at the end of the day when I'm even sleepier from a second helping of the school's square pizza slices at lunch. I find a quiet spot in the far back corner of the bleachers where no one will bother me. Maybe the teachers won't notice if I doze off a little.

The thud of my heart shakes me wide-awake

when two city police offers enter the gymnasium with J.R.'s dad right behind them.

Just like when he'd been on the evening news, J.R.'s dad is well dressed in a suit and tie, and carries himself like he's someone of great importance. I hate that he's handsome and looks so much like his son. I hate the way Principal Fredrickson greets him with an excited smile and a big handshake, like he's some kind of famous person. I hate him for being here when his son might be all alone at home, and in pain.

It's the first time I've believed in real monsters.

An excited chatter echoes throughout the building until Principal Fredrickson steps in front of the crowd, yelling into a microphone for us to settle down. Eventually, it's quiet enough to hear a pin drop.

"Boys and girls," Principal Fredrickson begins, his shiny bald head reflecting the gymnasium's lights, "as everyone is all too aware by now, three young women from our community have gone missing. While we continue to pray for their safety, and hope they find their way back home, these police officers and this detective are here to tell you how you can help with their search as well as ways to stay safe."

He hands the microphone off to one of the officers. I'm unable to focus on what he's saying because

I'm too busy staring a hole into J.R.'s dad. It's the only time I can remember totally hating someone's guts before I've met them. I'm the only one in the gymnasium who knows his secret, that he's not as charming as he'd like everyone to believe. He's cruel to his own son, and all the adults in this community are trusting him to help save other kids.

The bitter taste of bile fills my throat when he takes the microphone from the officer. "I'd like to add to the stranger-danger bit," he tells us, gesturing with with his free hand the way President Reagan does on TV. "While it's certainly okay to ride with a family member or a trusted friend of the family, you should never get into a car with anyone else. Even if it's someone from the community you've seen every day of your life, or a neighbor you don't know all too well. Travel in groups and obey the curfew. Mayor Perkins put the curfew in effect for your safety. The young men in this room are tasked with protecting the young ladies of this community in any way possible. It's our hope that we can put an end to these unexplained disappearances, and keep everyone in this room safe."

The deep roll of his voice causes goosebumps to break out along my arms. I cradle my stomach, worried I'm going to lose my lunch when he continues speaking.

"As far as the old adage—'if you see something, say something'—goes, it's more important than ever that you contact local law enforcement if you observe anything unusual, or even if you remember anything you may have seen involving Becky, Heidi, or Shannon before they went missing. Someone knows something that can help us track them down and bring them back home to their families. Thank you for your cooperation. Be safe this weekend and make good choices."

My stomach lurches when he hands the microphone to Principal Fredrickson. How can he stand in front of us and say those things after he punished his own son for trying to report the very kind of thing he mentioned?

The only bit of comfort I get from seeing J.R.'s dad with my own eyes is that it means J.R. hasn't gone *missing*-missing like Becky and the others. Surely his dad wouldn't be here talking to us if, like with the girls, J.R. has completely disappeared without an explanation. Surely he's safely tucked in bed at home, hiding whatever injury his dad gave him this time.

I shudder when I wonder what exactly his dad may have done.

I may be in way over my head.

Once we're dismissed, I stay glued to the bleachers, watching J.R.'s dad talk with Principal Fredrickson and the officers. He says something that makes all three of them laugh. One of the officers even pats him on the shoulder like they're old pals.

It might be the perfect time to tell J.R.'s dad what I know about Becky's dad doing stuff to her with other responsible adults around. At least J.R.'s dad couldn't hurt me. And like he said, once they learn Becky's dad didn't treat her right, maybe it'll somehow help them find Becky.

But I can't find the courage to stand and walk over to the man who broke my friend's arm and gave him a black eye. I can't look him in the eye while he's pretending to be anything other than the monster his son knows. I don't know how to pretend everything is okay when I want to scream at him and demand he take me to his son.

No one notices me tucked away in the corner when the four men leave the gymnasium.

I'M sick with worry by the time I make it outside and J.R. is nowhere to be seen.

Tears sting my eyes as I run all the way home, gulping in icy air with every ragged breath.

Again, no one answers the phone when I call his house.

I can't wait any longer. Someone needs to check on J.R. I need to see with my own eyes that he's okay.

As I'm pulling my bike out from its hiding spot behind the lose section of tin leaning against the trailer, the wail of a police siren rings throughout the cool fall air. A second siren soon joins in. I stand still, listening as the sound becomes louder and louder.

Soon, I hear the unmistakable crunch of tires on gravel and the roar of engines. Two city police cars go racing past our trailer, leaving behind a big cloud of dust. I suck in a sharp breath when the cars slam their brakes a few trailers down from ours.

They're at Becky's house.

Dropping my bike, I race over to watch four officers climb out of their squad cars. They're wearing the same uniforms as the officers who'd been at the assembly, but none of them look familiar.

"Did you find Becky?" I call out to them as they're

starting for the front door of the trailer. "Is she okay?"

A skinny officer with a thick black mustache turns to me, face tight with irritation. He doesn't look much older than Diane. "Young lady, you need to go home," he snarls. "It's not safe to be here right now."

One of the other officers bangs on the trailer's flimsy metal door. "Police! Open the door, Mr. Myers! We have a warrant for your arrest!"

Chills trickle down my spine at the same time fear crushes my lungs.

They must already know about the gross things he did to Becky. Or maybe they know something even worse.

As the officers continue to bang on the door, Karrie shuffles over to stand next to me, her dark, shaggy hair sticking up every-which-way and her eyes only half open. Beneath a wool trench coat like I've seen adult men wear around town, she wears a pair of flannel pajamas. Sometimes, after she's worked a night shift at the pop factory in North Mankato, she calls in sick to school so she can catch up on sleep.

"What's goin' on?" she asks on the end of a yawn. Her breath stinks like cigarettes.

"They said they're going to arrest Becky's dad," I whisper, wrapping my coat around my middle a little tighter.

Karrie snorts with a smirk spreading over her puffy lips. "About time. That drunk bastard probably did something to his own daughter and doesn't even remember it because he was too blitzed."

I hold my breath as the mustached officer moves over to Mr. Myers's old pickup truck and sets his hand on the hood. He turns to the other three officers and nods once. The trailer's front door gives way after one of the officers kicks it with his boot. Karrie and I wait in silence as there's a bunch of shouting and commotion after the officers enter.

It feels like a lifetime before they appear in the doorway again. They lead Becky's dad down the steps to the trailer in his usual stained white tank top and filthy pants. Handcuffs force his hands behind his back, and his face is more red than a ripe tomato. He roars swear words I've never heard before and spits at the mustached officer like an angry cat.

As Becky's dad is being forced into the back of a police car, Karrie waves excitedly like she's greeting an old friend. "*Sayonara*, sucker. May you rot in a jail cell."

Shoulders relaxed, I let out a deep breath.

It's over.

I no longer have to worry about telling J.R.'s dad what I know.

Maybe Becky's dad was so sick in the head that he wanted to hurt other girls too. Maybe they'll find out where he's keeping Heidi and Shannon.

Turning to Karrie, I debate how much to tell her about J.R. I like her enough that I think I could trust her, but if she knew his dad was hurting him, she might tell. She has a habit of doing things she considers to be right, no matter the consequences.

"I have to go check on J.R. at his house."

Karrie's lips twist into one of her signature smirks. "J.R., as in the cute new kid we had ice cream with after he mouthed off to Kabe?"

I nod. "If anything bad happens to me, tell Diane where I went and tell her to have the cops question J.R.'s dad."

Her dark eyes narrow. "What are you talking about? Didn't you say his dad's a detective? Why would they question him? And what's wrong with J.R.?"

"Please, Karrie, just trust me. And don't repeat what I said to anyone unless it's after dark and Diane gets worried. Okay?"

Karrie's gaze studies mine for a moment, then she nods and holds up both hands. "Okay, Jackie-O. I won't tell a soul. Just be careful, alright?"

I return to my bike and pedal as fast as I can to the *Brady Bunch* style house nestled among the hills. As long as J.R. isn't hurt too badly, everything could still be okay.

14
STERLING - 2018

The moment we step foot inside my house after dropping my mom at the airport, Theo's lips are on mine. With the deepening of the kiss, we quickly become a savage tangle of tongues, limbs, and bodies. He hoists me into his strong arms and carries me into my bedroom, depositing me on the edge of the bed. My brain short-circuits when he holds my gaze while removing every article of my clothing, tossing everything aside without breaking eye contact. The way he unhooks my bra with ease, I wonder how many times he's done this. Jealously clouds my vision until he begins to remove his own clothing. I'm barely given enough time to appreciate his exceptional form before we're drawn back together.

"Sure you're up for this?" I ask between breathless kisses. Every touch of his fingers ignites tiny little blazes all over my body that turn my brain numb. "I'd hate for you to break a hip."

"It's not my hips you should be worried about, sweetheart, especially if this is your first time—"

"No more jokes," I decide, shoving him down to the mattress on his back. I can't wait a second longer to explore every crevice of the strong, beautiful body that's been taunting me for days. I climb over him, running my hands along the magnificent slopes and ridges of his long, hard torso. The slight roll of his belly makes it a little easier to expose my own imperfections, especially when I had previously assumed he worked out, and his body would be flawless. His bunched muscles become smooth under the caress of my fingertips, and he lets out a shuttered sigh.

"Are you okay?" I ask, my tone warm with sincerity.

"Haven't been touched like that in a long while," he admits, dragging me down for another taste of my lips.

He flips me over so our positions are reversed and captures one of my breasts inside his warm mouth. One of his hands slides down between us, applying the perfect amount of pressure to my center. Combined with the scrape of his teeth and flicker of his tongue, I'm unable to maintain any kind of composure. The world tilts, causing me to become the definition of dazed and confused—albeit it delightfully so. With a surge of warmth, I hiss through a clenched jaw before letting out a strained whimper.

Theo stops to watch me with a crooked smile pressed to his glorious lips.

"It's been a long while for me too," I manage. "Long enough that you can feel free to proceed without any precautionary measures—I'm covered."

Our greedy kisses resume as he looms over me, lining things up before filling me with sweet relief. Pleasure rocks me to my core, unhinging every last one of my inhibitions. I savor the tenderness he offers, the gentleness of his talented hands. He's generous in both his size and his slow, precise move-ments. Most importantly, I feel adored by the graze of his fingertips along the sides of my body, the unhurried strokes of his hips. The overwhelming connection between us has been set in stone, etched into my heart. It's so sudden, so severe, that I briefly wonder if this is what it feels like when one is on the brink of insanity.

By the time we've both been satisfied, we lie side-by-side, panting as if we've just completed a three-day marathon. "See, that was totally worth the wait," I say, lazily reaching out to dust my fingertips along his ribcage. "I'm curious how a carpenter maintains a body this amazing when I have yet to see you lift anything heavier than a drill. Am I interrupting your gym time?"

A deep chuckle runs through his throat. "I put on fifty pounds of muscle after joining the service and it just kind of stuck around...even after I quit loading my diet with protein and spending endless hours obsessing over different weightlifting programs." He pats the slight bulge of fat on his gut. "Can't say I've had an *amazing* body since developing a taste for whiskey and wings."

I hum in disagreement. "I think a guy with a little bit of imperfections is extremely sexy. Especially when he can own up to them with a dash of humor."

Straight faced, he maneuvers to his side. "What is it about you, Sterling?" he asks before briefly reuniting our lips. I suck on his bottom lip for an extra beat, releasing it with a loud *pop*. Temporarily unable to breathe, I'm incapable of telling him I was inexplicably drawn to him too, although I suspect I've done a decent job of showing him how I feel.

"I've wanted you ever since I first looked into those extraordinary eyes of yours," he continues. "What makes you so impossible to resist?"

"My youthful glow?"

Laughing, he gathers me in his arms and holds me tighter than I've ever been held before. Nothing has ever felt so perfect as the way we fit together. His heat and strength surround me like a second skin that I never want to shed.

I draw lazy circles across the smooth skin on his shoulder blade. "It's my turn to ask you something."

He grunts in reply.

"You told me you'd vowed never to return to Mankato. So why *did you* move back?"

A long beat of silence follows before he answers. "The only person that ever made me happy once lived here. I feel closer to her when I'm in this city."

I dust my lips across the dip in his shoulder. "It sounds like you loved her."

Another grunt of a reply.

"What happened?"

All at once his arms are no longer around me. He rolls away with a deafening sigh. "I'd rather not talk about it."

Silence stretches between us. I've discovered yet another one of his limits, and I have no intention of pushing him. Still, I can't help but wonder if this mysterious woman is the one who made him so sullen.

Then I remember what Beth said about K.C., the tattoo artist who may have valuable information about the missing girls, but couldn't handle living here anymore. Could she be the one who once broke Theo's heart and made him reluctant to enter into another relationship?

It's becoming clearer by the second that I'm going to have to make an appointment in White Bear Lake for my second tattoo. Or maybe even cover the first, a small rose on my ankle that I had done on a dare after turning sixteen.

Around the time I'm certain Theo has drifted off to sleep, he says, "In some ways you remind me of her."

AFTER SPENDING a leisurely Sunday at Theo's place that involves occasional sex and a movie marathon in his bedroom, we spend the next several days of living like newlyweds every minute I'm not at work. He often cooks our dinners naked because we're almost never dressed around each other anymore.

It's difficult to keep my thoughts focused whenever he's not around. I hadn't expected him to open up so soon after we'd met, but with every part of himself he reveals, I'm beginning to understand why he first had put up a wall between us. His heart has been stomped on by his parents, and possibly shattered by whatever woman made him want to return to Mankato.

Despite his reservations, Theo Davies is one helluva lover. I can only hope the short time in which we've become addicted to each other isn't something he's merely trying to work out of his system, because a girl could get used to more of these late night rendezvous with a man of his... stature. He doesn't express himself lightly. His kisses are always nothing short of bruising, especially with the stubbly beard he'd grown over the weekend.

On Wednesday afternoon, as Megan explains a volunteer program at the local high school in a staff meeting, flashes of the previous nights return in bits and pieces, making my cheeks warm and my entire body flush with pleasure. I shift in my seat glancing around to ensure no one is watching. I'm going to have to start meditating again if I want to regain any kind of focus.

Once the meeting is adjourned, I head back down

the hallway to my cubical and pass a tall, lanky police officer in the standard black uniform. There's enough gray around the temples of his thick dark hair that I suspect he could've been a young adult in the 80s. I spin around. "Excuse me, Officer?"

His wide smile reveals a perfectly straight row of blindingly white teeth. Presumably, dentures. He's mildly attractive with a friendly look that makes him approachable, reminding me of the kind of men that played supporting roles in my mom's hit TV show when I was young. My mom once told me it was the casting director's intention to make the men likable, but not too memorable. "You must be the new social worker," the officer says in a smooth tenor.

I accept his firm handshake as I introduce myself. "Sterling Pruitt."

"Chief Doug Nielsen. What can I do for you, Miss Pruitt?"

"How long have you been with Mankato Law Enforcement?"

His smile deepens. "Just about thirty-two years now."

"So you were on the force when those girls went missing in the eighties."

Hooking his thumb inside his duty belt just inches from his service weapon, he glances around the now empty hallway before stepping a little closer and lowering his voice. He seems...spooked. "I was fresh out of the academy when the first one disappeared."

"How many were there?"

"To the best of our knowledge, there were four."

Chills rattle my bones. "What happened?" I ask. "Were the girls ever found? Did you have any suspects?"

"Those are a lot of questions from someone who just moved to the city." Grunting with an unamused laugh, his wide-set hazel eyes narrow. "Why are you asking?"

"Because it's in my nature to care, and I can't seem to find anything about those girls online. Not a single newspaper article, police report, or court document."

"Then how did you know about them?"

I throw my hands up at my sides. "Why does that matter? Why does it seem as if these girls were merely swept under a rug? Why doesn't anyone seem to want to talk about them?"

"Because it's a sensitive subject, Miss Pruitt. That's all. They were daughters of the community...sisters, friends. It makes folks sad to think what might've happened to them and makes them feel helpless that there's nothing they can do about it."

"Are you sure that's all there is to it?" I persist, eyes narrowed and hands set on my hips. "Because it sure feels like their history was purposely erased."

His eyes sweep around us a second time before he guides me by my elbow a few feet closer to the short cove where the men's and women's restrooms face each other. "Folks around here don't like to talk about it—especially law enforcement. I think there's a deep sense of failure that's attached to the history of the investigation. I learned early on not to ask a lot of questions, but it never sat right with me."

I balk for a moment, surprised by his candor. "Any idea who took them?"

"A man named Darrel Heinrich was questioned at length, but they never found enough evidence to convict him."

A tick of irritation has me raising my voice. "What about *the girls?*"

Chief Nielsen hooks his other thumb in his duty belt and glances down at his feet. "I'm afraid they were never found." His gaze returns to mine, all at once sorrowful and utterly haunted. "Their death certificates were issued in the early nineties."

The sadness I've harbored for the girls since

learning their story becomes downright crippling. It's almost as if no one cared. Their poor families have had to carry on without any answers. I compose myself as best as I can when addressing the chief. "You may have been young and inexperienced when they disappeared, but you're in a powerful position now, Chief Nielsen," I reply grimly. "Those girls deserve justice."

His jaw slackens as I walk away.

THE REMAINDER OF THE DAY, I'm as unsettled as I've ever been. No matter how hard I try, I can't seem to shift my thoughts away from the missing girls and the feeling of hopelessness their families must still feel after so many decades. How would it feel to not have any kind of closure after losing your child so unexpectedly? Did the families hold memorial services for these girls, maybe even bury an empty casket to somehow appease their grief?

While Theo prepares something in my kitchen that creates a divine aroma, I pull up my laptop in my bedroom and return to K.C.'s Instagram page. She's unquestionably a stunning woman—jet black hair worn in a reverse bob, petite features, irises so dark they nearly swallow her pupils, and flawless pale skin—yet it's difficult to imagine her being Theo's type. The only part of her not tattooed appears to be her face, and she's sporting multiple body piercings above her shoulders. I consider it's also possible she could've been with Theo before she became invested in ink if they've known each other for as long as I suspect. Very few pictures posted involve much beyond her portfolio of work, but there's a selfie of her embracing an equally attractive, equally inked man.

I'm also beginning to suspect K.C. and Theo both knew the missing girls. It would explain his reluctance to discuss them when I first mentioned I'd seen the flyer at work. What if one of the girls was his sister? As much as I want to try revisiting the subject with him, now that he's beginning to reveal more of himself, I'd hate to see him regress to his former sullen ways. He's actually *singing* along to that old *Rio* song by Duran Duran as he prepares our meal in the other room.

Just as I'm ready to declare I'm only being paranoid, and K.C. can't possibly be the same woman who broke Theo's heart, I spot a familiar tattoo near the bottom of her Instagram feed.

From the muscular planes of the model's back, there's no questioning the man's identity.

It's Theo's angel.

I close the door to my bedroom and call the number on her page to book an appointment.

15
JACKIE - 1986

The crisp October air seeps through my sweatshirt as I push my bike a little faster toward J.R.'s house on the hill. Fallen leaves of red and gold crunch beneath my tires, and the woodsy scent of burning leaves surrounds me like a warm hug. It won't be long before snow begins to fall, forcing me to ditch my bike and walk in ugly red and white moon boots that give me blisters once I wear the thickest pair of socks I own.

Halloween is only a week away, but for the first time in my life I'm not concerned with Trick-or-Treating, or finding a costume at the secondhand store. With Becky, Shannon, and Heidi still missing, I doubt the adults in charge of the city would let us go without our parents this year anyway. And I'm sure J.R. would think dressing up was for babies since he's in high school.

I hold my breath as I walk my bike around to the backside of the house, glad to at least find the garage door open and no car inside. J.R.'s window is closed and is covered by a navy blue curtain. I press my ear against the windowpane, expecting to hear the robotic sounds of video games or maybe one of his dad's electropop records. It's dead silent. I shift my weight back and forth, trying to decide whether I should leave or wait to hear some kind of noise. I would hate to wake him if he's resting. I also don't want him to know I'm here if he happens to be crying like the last time I stood outside his window.

The curtains all at once part. I let out a little squeak of surprise when J.R. frowns back at me through the window, his dark sweat pants and over-sized t-shirt wrinkled. I'm glad to see for myself that he's where I thought he would be and he's alive, but he's cradling his torso with his good hand, dark shadows lurk beneath his eyes, and he's as white as a ghost. When he reaches out to tug the window open, I don't miss the way he winces.

Confusing emotions bubble up inside my stomach. I want to both hug J.R. and yell at him for making that stupid call because Diane made him. I want to hurt his dad for doing this to him. I want to run through the neighborhood, asking any other adult I can find for help.

"You shouldn't be here," he rasps in a way that makes the hairs on my neck stand straight.

"What's wrong with your voice?"

"*Nothing*," he grumbles. "Go home, Jackie."

Fat tears of anger and sadness blur my vision when I notice the angry red lines along his neck. "What did he do to you?"

"It doesn't matter. If he catches me talking to you he'll do worse."

"You can't stay here with him, J.R. What if next time he—"

His eyes briefly close. "I know. I'm running away."

Pain sharper than knives stabs at my stomach. I don't want him to leave. How will he take care of himself? I also don't want him to have to live in fear of his dad any longer. "You're only fourteen. Where will you go? How will you buy food? What about school?"

"I told you, I've been saving up. But I don't have a plan yet, and I don't really care. Just as long as I never have to see my old man another day for as long as I live."

"What about your mom?"

"I don't know how to find her. After she left, I have no idea where she went. She didn't have much of a family…just some distant relatives somewhere out West. She might've stayed in Ohio where we lived before my old man brought us back here, but I wouldn't know how to get ahold of her. Besides, she doesn't care about me any more than your mom cares about you and Diane."

His words sting like a million little bees. But he's right. Our parents don't care about us. "Maybe someone here in Kato could help you find a better way to leave, like Pastor Babel or one of your teachers."

"I told you, that pastor is creepy as hell. I wouldn't trust him any farther than I could throw him. And you remember how your jerk teacher treated me. Just because they were hired to teach kids doesn't make teachers good people, Jackie."

At this point I feel the overwhelming need to grab him through the window and never let him go. I swipe the damp corners of my eyes and attempt to calm my tight breaths. "There has to be another way, J.R. What if you hide at my place for a while until you come up with a plan? My mom would never know you're there. She never really knows whether or not Diane and I are—"

He reaches through the window, wrapping his hand around my wrist and shaking his head. "Jackie, stop. When I leave here, I have to get as far away as possible, and fast. It's my old man's job to track down missing people. I know he's doing a shit job of finding Becky and the others, but I think it's because they're dead and someone did a really good job of hiding their bodies. It's easier to track down someone who's alive and interacting with other people."

I wince with my eyes closed, sending a trickle of tears spilling down my cheeks. "You think Becky's dead?"

"I'm sorry," he says in a gentle voice. "I know she was your friend, but they would've found her by now if she was still alive."

"Becky's dad did it," I tell him. "They arrested him right before I left the trailer park."

He blows out a long breath. "Jackie, that's not—"

The slam of a door echoes through the house behind him. I gasp and J.R. pushes hard on my arm.

"Shit, he's home!" he frantically whispers, eyes wild. "You have to go, Jackie! *Now*! Meet me tonight at ten—at our spot by the park!"

As he begins to close the window, I want to beg him to change his mind and stay with me. Then I hear the deep roll of his father's voice calling his name, and I'm afraid standing here any longer will only get him into more trouble.

———————

THE BITTER COLD stabs my hands with pins and needles as I race away from J.R.'s house with fat tears streaming down my cheeks. The snot in my nose feels like balls of ice cubes when I bike through the quiet neighborhoods of fancy houses. It's also becoming dark, long after I'm supposed to be out alone. Every few minutes I glance over my shoulder, waiting for the same boogey man to come for me that came for Becky. Even worse yet, I fear I'll find J.R.'s dad.

My front bike tire hits something with a jarring thud. The rear end of my bike becomes airborne, flipping me off my seat and sending me down to the ground. I land hard on my hands and knees, skinning the palms of my hands on the concrete curb.

Bawling like a little baby, I kick my bike frame and plop my butt onto the curb, tucking my head behind my knees to hide my wet face.

If J.R. really leaves, I'll never see him again. If he stays, he might die.

He's the first friend I've ever had who stuck up for me and always wanted to hang out. I've never loved anyone the way I love him either. What's left here for me once he's gone? It's not fair that J.R. and I are forced to live this way—with parents who probably all wish we'd never been born. I bet it would take my mom a whole *month* before she realized I was missing.

Why couldn't I have been born into a nice family, to the kind of parents that love their children and go to their school conferences?

I don't remember the last time I saw my mom. Part of me wishes she'd just go away forever.

With the sound of an oncoming car, I wipe my tears away on the backs of my hands.

"Jackie Tanner?"

Pastor Babel leans out the driver's window of a newer blue car with four doors. His eyes shine with worry. "Are you okay?"

I quickly look away, worried his kindness will make me cry again. "Yes, I'm fine."

"Why are you out so late by yourself, Jackie? The curfew starts soon."

"I wasn't by myself. I was with my sister." I get the

feeling he didn't like J.R., so I purposely don't mention where I've been. "She was a few blocks ahead of me."

I glance back at him in time to see his lips pull tight. "Neither of you girls should be out this late." He shifts the car into park. "Why don't you put your bike on the lawn, and I'll give you a ride home? You can retrieve your bike in the morning."

"Someone will steal it if I leave it here," I tell him, shaking my head. "I'll be okay, Pastor. I can walk it the rest of the way home."

"Why were you crying, Jackie?" he asks in a softer voice. "Is everything okay at home? I may not be *your* minister, but you can talk to me in confidence. No one would have to know."

I want to tell him about J.R.'s dad, but J.R. would be mad at me. And what if the police didn't believe J.R.'s dad is really hurting him? What if they decide since he works for the police, J.R. must be lying?

Once I remember all the things J.R. said about Pastor Babel, I suddenly can't get away from him fast enough. "I have to go," I tell him, collecting my bike. I hook my leg over it and race away like the devil is chasing me.

LATER, the park feels alive as I bike down the familiar path of tall grass with a narrow sliver of moonlight marking my way. I've never come here alone this late at night. Somewhere above me an owl hoots and dark birds dart through the sky—possibly bats. Fear stabs my stomach as I come across "our spot" by the river. I've never seen the water glow the way it does now. Everything about being here is scary.

I lean my bike up against a tree and sit on the bank. As many minutes pass, I begin to worry. Why is J.R. late? Did his dad catch onto his plan? I don't own a watch, so I don't have any idea of the time. Maybe I biked faster than usual because I was afraid. Maybe it's still early.

The sudden rustle of grass behind me sends my heart into my throat. I turn around to find J.R. stomping toward me, his backpack hanging from one shoulder.

"Why are you so late?" I halfway yell. "You scared me!"

He shoves his hands into his jeans and looks down at his sneakers. "Sorry."

"I thought about the things you said earlier, and I've decided I'm running away with you." I point to the paper grocery bag hanging from my bike's handlebar, filled with a few changes of clothes and the only things from home that mean something to me—the picture I painted of this spot, and the Polaroid Diane took of me and J.R. that day in my room. "You were right. My mom doesn't care about me."

His dark eyes harden on mine. "You aren't going anywhere, Jackie! Don't be stupid!"

He's never talked to me in that mean of a voice. I hate it. Suddenly, I hate *him*. I let my hair fall around my face so he won't see the tears that rush down my face.

On a lough sigh he sits beside me, rubbing circles against my back. "I'm sorry I yelled at you. You're not stupid. But you can't run away. Your mom might not care if you leave, but Diane will. She loves you. I know you don't see it, but I do." He gathers my hair and tucks it behind my shoulder so I can see his dimpled smile. "You're lucky you have a sister like her. I'd give anything to have an older brother. At least then I'd have someone to run away with."

I turn to him, flinging my arms around his neck and burying my wet face against his chest. "You can't run away by yourself! What if I never see you again?"

"I'll be okay," he promises, wrapping me in his arms. "I promise I'll come back here some day to check on you. At least I won't have to worry, because at least your mom keeps you fed and doesn't hurt you. Whatever life throw at you while I'm gone, you'll survive it, Jackie. All this crap you're going through will make you a strong woman one day, like Sarah Connor in *Terminator*. You'll see."

I try really hard to control my trembling lips. "When are you leaving?"

"Now...after I leave here."

My heart gallops so hard I think it might shoot from my chest. "What?" I pull away from him and frown. "In the dark?"

"A train comes through downtown every night at ten thirty. I figure it'll get me away from here the fastest without anyone noticing. The boxcars will be warm and dry. My old man once told me that's how bums from the Midwest travel to warmer places."

"What if you trip and fall onto the track? What if the bums don't like you on there with them? What if—"

I'm silenced by the press of his cold lips over mine. A brief, warm rush of the best kind of happiness washes over me, making my heart pound a little harder. I've been wishing forever for this.

But I shove him away.

I hate him for choosing this moment to finally kiss me.

I hate him for leaving without me.

I jump to my feet and dash over to my bike.

"Jackie, wait!" he pleads. "Don't leave like this!"

As I pedal away, he yells my name louder, panting.

He's running after me.

I bike away as fast as I can until I can no longer hear his voice. It's almost impossible to see anything through the rush of fat tears when I make my way through the trail of tall grass and onto the gravel road.

A tall, dark shadow of a man steps out in front of me.

My bike tire wobbles beneath my trembling hands.

Maybe it's not a man after all, I decide with a harsh shiver running down my back. *Maybe it's a demon like Becky's dad said.*

16

STERLING - 2018

With the whirl of my coffee maker, I rouse to the land of the living early on Friday morning.

Theo's sound asleep at my side, spread out on his stomach. The tattoo of the angel stretched across his back taunts me—a reminder of all the things unknown about him.

As the details of my latest dream in the night slowly begin to return, I dust my fingertips over the angel's beautiful face and my heart thuds with urgency. Since moving here, I've relived the same scenario of the girl and boy arguing about him running away on an endless loop, but my dreams never went beyond their fight.

Until now.

Who was on that gravel road? What happened to her?

And why do I get the feeling she was in the same park where I fainted?

IN THE IDYLLIC heart of downtown White Bear Lake where there doesn't appear to be a shortage of charming boutiques or trendy restaurants, I enter a brick building with up-to-date furnishings and a stylish atmosphere featuring a clean black and white design. Tattoo artists in half a dozen booths surround the perimeter of the open space with quirky decor in various style hung from floor to ceiling. The hard beat of heavy rock only slightly mutes the buzz of tattoo guns and the din of customers conversing with their artists. Puffs of smoke from an electric defuser in the waiting area floods the building with the pleasant scent of lavender.

A female receptionist perched behind a sleek white desk greets me, her smile blindingly white. "Hi, there. Do you have an appointment?"

"Yeah, with K.C.," I tell her, all at once incredibly

nervous. I haven't sat down for a tattoo in over a decade. What if my tolerance has weakened?

"Sterling?" a deep female voice asks from behind me. When I turn, I almost completely lose the nerve needed to execute my plan. In person, K.C. has the aura of a supermodel with porcelain skin revealing only the slight presence of wrinkles that attest to her decade or more on me, wide eyes painted with dark eyeliner, and full, velvety lips stained cherry red. Even her not too slender, not too muscular figure is something most women spend their entire lives trying to achieve. I admire her simple black dress reminiscent of the 50s, and dark pin-up curls framing her face. "I'm K.C." Her smile rivals the brilliance of a shooting star when she hooks a thumb over her shoulder. "My booth is over this way."

As I follow her to a corner containing a stool on wheels, a square desk attached to the wall, and a leather reclining bed, the rough edges of panic begin to sharpen. I'm not always the best at lying. If she were to discover my true intentions, she might tell Theo, and that could potentially ruin the trust I've built with him. The part of my brain known for talking me out of less intelligent situations pleads me to abort the mission. My reckless side reminds me I drove a long way and had to lie about being sick to get the Friday morning off.

K.C. points to the chair. "Go ahead and have a seat, Sterling. I'm normally booked four to five months out, but someone canceled right before you called….it was kismet, I guess." While I'm reluctantly lowering to the edge of the chair, she crosses her arms beneath her large chest and eyes me up. "My receptionist mentioned you were thinking of getting a set of palm trees on the inside of your forearm, around two inches in height?"

"I want to pay homage to my home state," I say, feeling somewhat relieved than I can at least say something truthful. I hadn't bothered asking my supervisor about the office policies when I was hired because I hadn't planned on getting anything in the near future. At least I could easily cover something on my arm with a 3/4 sleeved shirt.

"Florida?" she asks.

"California."

"Ah…a Cali girl." Her cherry red lips pucker with a smirk. "What brings you to White Bear Lake?"

"Actually, I was just in town visiting a friend." I pause, watching her reaction as I add, "I recently moved to Mankato."

She opens her mouth to say something, then snap

it back shut before her eyes drift down to my arms. "Show me exactly where you want them and I'll sketch something up."

I point to the crook of my right arm. "Somewhere around here would be great."

"Perfect. Do you want black or color? Solid or an outline?"

"Black outlines," I decide.

With a nod, she perches on a backless stool and begins to sketch onto a wired sketchpad.

"I was looking through your portfolio last night," I tell her. "I absolutely *loved* the detailed angel you did on that guy's back. I've never seen anything so beautiful." It's another non-lie, but I only think that because it's on Theo's sculpted body.

"Thanks," she says, still scratching away on the paper. "It was my first back piece. A friend let me practice on him free of charge."

"Was the angel in memory of someone or something?"

"Or something."

It's safe to assume by her non-answer that the symbolism represents something she doesn't want to share. When she fails to offer any more information, I decide I can't push her on the subject without raising suspicion.

"So what do you think of Mankato?" she asks after a long pause, eyes still focused on her work.

"I like it so far. Sure beats the hustle of L.A."

"I grew up in Kato," she grumbles. "Stayed there too damn many years." She briefly glances up at me. "You should do yourself a favor and get out while you can."

"What's wrong with it?"

"The people there are what's wrong. When they can't fix something, they'll pretend it doesn't exist—try to rewrite history."

"Like the girls that went missing in the eighties?"

Her lips and gaze simultaneously harden. "Why would you mention them?"

"I work for Human Services and came across an old poster. When I looked into their disappearances, I realized something feels...amiss. And this is probably going to sound crazy, especially when I don't know what you believe in, but I think I have some kind of...*karmic* connection to them. It's hard to explain." My face warms as I decide to come clean. "I just happened to become friends with a bartender—your friend, Beth—who mentioned you were friends with the sister of one of the missing girls. She told me you had a studio here. I thought maybe you could enlighten me on a few things."

"And you decided the best way to find out what I know was under the guise of wanting a tattoo?" She sets down the sketch pen and shoots me a wicked glare. "Are you a reporter?"

"No, just a friend." My cheeks flush warm. "Of Theo's."

Her skillfully sculpted eyebrows the same dark shade as her hair rise high. "Oh, this just keeps getting richer. You came here to snoop because you're involved with Theo?"

"I know it might seem uncool, but he's a complicated guy. He's obviously hurting over something that happened in the past, and I can't get him to open up about it. It's killing me because I *really* care about him."

She gives me a look that I can't quite read. "You're in love with him."

The flush in my cheeks spreads down my neck. I can't admit anything to a stranger before I tell Theo how I feel, but I imagine the truth is written all over my face. "It's a little soon to know for sure, but I think the foundation is there. Once I chipped away at his icy cold demeanor, I realized he's a good man —the best I've ever been with anyway." A web of unease wraps around my center. What if they were lovers and she's still pining for him? I nervously glance at the array of sharp needles at her disposal. "Were you once involved with him?"

"Me and Theo?" she scoffs, stopping to release an abrupt laugh. "We were never anything more than friends."

Relief and disappointment twin through my core. I was convinced I had worked out their connection. "So you're not the one who broke his heart? You're not the reason he moved back home?"

For a moment she clasps her hands together and presses them to her forehead. "Listen, Sterling, you seem pretty cool and I can understand how you're frustrated with the big guy because of the way he closes himself off to everyone, but if you really care about him like you say, you need to *ask him* these things." Her hands fall back at her sides to reveal her irritated scowl. "It's not *my* place to disclose his complicated history." Tearing her drawing of palm trees from the sketchbook, she crumples it inside her hands, tossing it into the trash can at her side. "I think you should leave. Maybe you can call me again sometime in the future after I've cooled down to set up an actual meeting place instead of ambushing me at my place of business. Against my better judgment, I'm actually interested in this 'karmic' connection of yours."

Nodding, I slide down from the chair. At least she's not telling me to take a hike and never speak to her again. I stop to study her thoughtfully. "Can you please just tell me one more thing?"

With a flippant roll of her eyes, she rolls a hand through the air in a motion for me to continue.

"Was Theo close with one of the missing girls?"

Her eyes flutter closed like she's unable to believe I had the nerve to ask. "Goodbye, Sterling."

On my way out, I don't bother asking the receptionist if my deposit will be refunded to my credit card. I did a shitty thing to both K.C. and Theo, and I deserve to pay the price.

IT's dark when I return home from White Bear Lake. I catch Theo adding the finishing touches to my new kitchen island, dimpled grin deep in place as he watches me kick off my flats at the front door.

"It's Friday night," he says in a smooth rolling voice. His dark, suggestive gaze sets my body on fire. "I have you all to myself for an entire weekend."

With K.C. and the angel tattoo and the missing girls on the tip of my tongue, I can only stare back at him.

He crosses the room to gather me inside his arms. "Another bad day?"

I meld against him, savoring the warmth and strength of his body. My lips part.

Ask him, Sterling.

"You don't have to say a word. I know that look by now. Good woman with a good heart like yours has been taking a beating with the new job." He nuzzles the crook of my neck. "Pack a bag and we'll head to my place. I'm gonna shower before spoiling the hell outta you."

As good as his plan sounds, it's past time I disclose the details of my conversations with Chief Nielsen and K.C., explain how I believe my dreams are somehow connected to the missing girls and ask him to fill me in on the rest. But I'm unable to stomach the thought of him reverting to the quiet, sullen man who all but told me to take a hike. What if he leaves once I start asking deep questions, and never returns to me?

The moment his mouth claims mine, my thoughts are wiped clean. The need to let him possess me becomes overpowering. Everything about the man is incredibly addictive—his voice, his smell, his taste. Anything that doesn't involve his sinful body wrapped around mine can wait.

WITH THE HISS of the shower's spray from inside Theo's master bathroom, I rise from the sheets that still possess an intoxicating scent of sex and Theo, and slip into the Journey t-shirt I'd stripped off him once we'd arrived. He'd made the first move, but I'd already decided I needed him to quiet my unease, to silence my doubts and fears. When our bodies were joined I'd almost let it slip that I loved him, hoping he'd ruminate on that fact once my inquisition began.

Simply put, I'm a coward.

Now that he's temporarily occupied, it seems like a good time to snoop around. I've learned Theo's a meticulously neat person who doesn't have time for material things. Either that or he doesn't want to attach himself to anything of trivial meaning. Nearly every single piece of furniture inside his house was handmade by him, including the grand sleigh bed we've christened countless times. The rest of his belongings are sparse, and everything is in its place. His closet reminds me of a minimalist display in one of L.A.'s finest boutiques—what few items of clothing he owns are neatly hung, including his t-shirts and blue jeans. I imagine it's akin to getting a glimpse inside a monastery.

I slide out the top drawer on a tall dresser in the same craftsman style as the bed. Among perfectly folded socks and underwear, a small wooden box contains a gold analog watch and a silver tie clip adorned with black stones. It's more than I expected. Are the valuable items a gift from someone? Things he inherited? I can't imagine him buying anything from a department store. As he's pointed out numerous times, he doesn't like to leave his house unless he's working, or grabbing a quick bit to eat. When we'd gone to visit his carpenter colleague, there were moments he acted as if he was ready to crawl out of his skin.

Beneath a pair of boxers, I spy the white border of a square picture from an old-school instant camera.

When I slide it out to get a look, the room suddenly takes on an abnormal slant.

My eyes blink rapidly.

It can't be possible.

Gaping at the yellowed picture, I desperately attempt to find some kind of logic as to how I'm looking at irrefutable proof the boy and girl from my dreams are real, and not merely a lifelong product of my imagination. My head swarms, over-whelmed by the possibilities.

In the same moment I reach out to grab the corner of the dresser to stop myself from collapsing to the floor, Theo enters with a towel draped half an inch beneath his delightfully toned Adonis belt.

Noticing the picture grasped in my hands, his expression turns ice cold. "What are you doing in my dresser?" he snarls.

His sudden change of demeanor doesn't rattle me as much as what's grasped in my fingers. "Who are these kids?" I counter, holding out the Polaroid of the young teenagers sitting together on a Rainbow Brite blanket in a room that's all too familiar, thanks to my dreams.

Baring his teeth, he growls, "Why the fuck are you digging through *my things*?"

"It's what women do when they're falling for maddeningly mysterious men who are kind and beautiful inside and out, but are reluctant to open up about themselves." I step closer to thrust the picture at him. "Who are they, Theo? I need to know!"

"She's a friend from my childhood." He snags the picture from my grip with a tormented look that I feel in the depths of my soul. "And the boy is me."

PART TWO

17
STERLING - 2018

I n a moment that stretches on for an eternity, Theo and I both stare at the Polaroid gripped in his fingers as disbelief and confusion war through my thoughts. Before now, I've never believed in my aunt Constantine's faith in psychic connections and alternate universes. Yet it's hard to deny that something's at play that can't be easily explained. I've been dreaming about the blonde girl since I was three. How did a young Theo end up in my subconsciousness alongside her, especially when he looks nothing like the man scowling back at me?

"I think I'm going to be sick," I say, digging my fingers into Theo's warm forearm, still damp from his shower. Concern flashes through his dark eyes when I lose strength in my legs.

"I've got you," he says, wrapping his arm around me and assisting me back to sit on his bed. "Can I get you a glass of water?"

"I need something a lot stronger than water."

He squats in front of me with the Polaroid held up between us. "Why did this freak you out?"

"You won't believe me," I say, cradling my surging stomach. I take a slow, calming breath, but it turns into tight little huffs of panic. "Even *I* don't believe me."

"Try me," he pleads.

The way he tenderly brushes a lock of my hair over my shoulder and looks ready to gather me into his arms, I'm suddenly hopeful that he cares enough about me and our budding relationship to support the crazy things I'm about to say.

"This is the girl I've been dreaming about since I was three."

His jaw ticks. The Polaroid trembles inside his fingers. "That's not funny."

"Do I look like someone in the mood for jokes?"

He stabs his fingers through his wet hair. "It's probably just another girl who looked like her."

"Theo, I know without a doubt this is *her*. I've been dreaming about her for as long as I can remember."

Head titled, he studies me like he's convinced I'm certifiable. "There may be similarities—"

"No. She looks *exactly* like the girl in my dreams. And you…this *boy*…ever since I moved here, I've started seeing him too." Blinking back tears, I flatten the palms of my hands over the soft bristles on his strong jaw. How can that boy who'd been abused by his father be the beautiful man I'm growing attached to? He did mention he put on a ton of weight after he'd joined the military, and now I can see the similarities in his whiskey-colored eyes and the rare appearance of his dimpled smile. "I had no way of knowing it was you."

A conflicted look strains his features as he pulls my hand away from his face. "Sure you didn't see a photo of me at that age…somehow insert me into your dreams after?"

I glance around the tidy bedroom, void of anything personal. "Because you have *so many* photos of your childhood—of *anything*—just lying around?" I take a steadying breath, wishing he would accept the situation as it is so we could try to solve the mind-blowing situation together. "Why did she call you J.R.?"

"Christ," he chokes out, tossing the Polaroid onto the bed at my side. He stands and turns his back to me, taking a step away like he's going to leave the room. Then he says, "It was my mom's nickname for me as a kid. She liked it better than 'junior.' My old man's name was Theodore too."

"*Was?* You didn't mention he also died."

"He didn't," he amends, turning to me with his hands flexing into fists at his sides. "I try to forget that bastard is out there somewhere."

"Because he hurt you," I whisper with one lone tear spilling down my cheek. "You told Jackie you were going to run away."

A dark, angry cloud flashes through his eyes a moment before they dart away. "This is messed up, Sterling." Again, he stabs his fingers through his wet hair. "How could you possibly know these things?"

I wipe my face and reclaim the picture, pointing at the bedspread beneath the teenagers. "I've seen the pattern on this blanket a hundred times. It's in the girl's bedroom...she lives in a trailer park...with her mom and sister. Her mom's a dancer...you thought maybe even a stripper. She met this boy —*you*—the same place you took me—"

"*Stop it!*" he roars, bracing his arms out at his sides. His eyes shine with unshed tears when he adds in a less aggressive tone, "Please!"

"Am I right?" I ask quietly. "Did the girl in your

picture live with her mom and older sister in a trailer park?" His complexion becomes even more ashen, so I explain. "They come to me in my dreams. And they're not like other dreams. It's like...I'm living her life and the things I dream about are happening to me."

"This is bullshit." He readjusts the towel around his waist as he begins to pace the center of his room.

"I'm well aware how ridiculous this all sounds, but I'm just as clueless as you as to *why* it's happening, or *how*. But I hope you feel like you know me well enough by now to think I wouldn't have any reason to mess with you."

"We still don't know that much about each other," he scoffs.

"I know that you can go from temperamental to tender in an instant, and you're not only talented and kind, but you're incredibly passionate." I throw him a hopeful look. "I know that you're someone I don't want to see hurt because I care about you more deeply than I should considering the short amount of time we've known each other."

With a serene expression, he releases a gruff sigh in a way that makes me believe he's ready to give in. "What the hell is going on, Sterling? Why are you dreaming about me and a friend I knew before you were probably born?"

"I'd love to hear any theories you may have," I grumble, flopping back against the mattress with an exasperated sigh.

"The media could've leaked a photo of her...*us*... when you were a kid."

I lean on my elbow to study him, shaking my head. "That still wouldn't explain how I knew where she lived or what her mom did for a living."

"The kids at school teased her about her mom, and everyone knew she lived in a trailer park. It was all over the news after she went missing."

"You mean after the man abducted her," I say.

His lips tilt in a half-scowl, the way one would regard a rude stranger. "Why do you think a man *abducted* her?"

"Because I started dreaming about it—very recently."

He drops back down onto the edge of the mattress. "What did he look like?" With a shake of his head, he jumps back to his feet. "What the hell am I talking about? This is insane!"

"I wouldn't be able to describe him. It was dark."

He's pacing the room again. "You're sure a man took her?"

"Positive. I've had that same dream several times since I moved here."

"What happened after he..." His Adam's apple bobs with a deep swallow, "...took her?"

"I don't know." I stand and slowly cross over to him. "My dreams never go beyond the night you fought with her. It always ends with her abduction."

A pained look flashes through his eyes. "Do you think he—"

"I don't know what he did to her, Theo. There's no sense wondering, either. You'll drive yourself crazy."

He turns away, scrubbing his hands over his stubble. "Someone found a grocery bag on the gravel road leading into the park, filled with some of her things. That Polaroid included. The police never found any other trace of her, or the three other girls who went missing before her. My old man was a police detective—had brought us to Mankato to work on the case. Some people were convinced Jackie and the others had run away because they never came up with any viable leads except for some guy that had raised some suspicion."

"The man from the department store," I remember. "Diane pointed him out for being creepy at the skating rink. He's he's the one she spied on in that shed."

"Yeah," Theo confirms in a grunted response. Then he threads his fingers through his hair. "I can't believe you know these things. You *shouldn't* know them."

"What about Becky's dad?" I ask in a gentle voice, worried I'm pushing him too hard.

"He was arrested for threatening someone with a gun. They never found anything to suggest he was involved in Becky's disappearance."

"That's hard to believe," I mutter with dissatisfaction, remembering Jackie's story of having to hide from Becky's dad. "How about Jackie's teacher? He really seemed to have it out for her."

"He was an asshole, but he was questioned…had an air-tight alibi."

It seems with every one of Jackie's memories I tap into, another one reappears. I remember feeling the icy bitterness of the autumn air as she biked away from J.R.'s house, and the scrape of her hands on concrete when she fell.

"You can talk to me in confidence," the pastor had told her on that cold autumn night. *"No one would have to know."*

I run my hands up and down my arms, unsettled. "What about the Lutheran pastor?"

Theo flinches and stands a little taller. "What about him?"

"He gave you the creeps, right? He offered Jackie a ride on her way home after she left your house to check on you—just a few hours before you met her at the park to say goodbye. She turned him down because she sensed something was off. Was he ever considered as a suspect?"

"Not that I know of." His eyes blink rapidly. "Shit. We'll have to ask my old man...not that I'm dying to reach out to the prick. But you could be onto something. They probably didn't know she'd interacted with him that night."

The details of Jackie's visit to J.R. return in vivid detail...how she noticed red marks around his neck, the way his voice strained with every word he spoke. Jackie was terrified of his father, especially after seeing the sociopath pretend to be one of the good guys at the assembly. With the onset of a bone-breaking chill, I wind my arms around my middle. "What about your father? Do you think—"

"I'd considered it," he admits with a single nod. "But he was far too invested in the investigation. I saw it eating away at him. I think his frustration over not finding a viable lead was the reason I became more and more of a punching bag. I'm the only one he ever wanted to torture. Besides, we were still living in Ohio when the first girl and Becky were abducted."

The painful knot forming in my throat refuses to go down no matter how many times I swallow. "What did he do to you after Diane made you call him?"

Theo recoils with the force of a punch. "Jesus, Sterling!"

"Tell me what happened," I whisper, stepping in to stroke his arms with my fingertips.

Cursing under his breath, he breaks our eye contact and lifts his chin. "Things a man should never do to his son. Son of a bitch choked me, broke my ribs. Said I'd embarrassed him in front of everyone at the station. It's the first time I considered he might actually kill me."

"Theo…" I whimper. Overwhelming desperation and heartbreak make it difficult to breathe. As badly as I want to hug him, I sense something animalistic in the sudden flash of his dark eyes that stops me in my tracks. The strong scent of grass fills my lungs with my next breath. "You told Jackie you were taking a train to get out of town that night, but you told me you didn't run away until you were seventeen."

His shoulders coil with tension. "After she left the park, I went to her trailer and waited for her to return. I eventually convinced Diane to call the police, even though she didn't seem to want to at first. I had to stick around...had to help them find her. Her mom and Diane weren't of any use." He grips the back of his head with both hands, neck strained. "My old man discovered her mom had gotten involved in hardcore drugs shortly before Jackie went missing. On the one year anniversary of Jackie's disappearance, Rose OD'd. Diane mentally checked out after that, spent part of her junior year in a psych ward. I was all Jackie had left, so I couldn't leave. I returned to Minneopa park every single day for years, thinking she'd return to me."

I briefly close my eyes, squeezing a rush of tears out through my lashes. Jackie was convinced no one cared about her, yet her disappearance had destroyed her family and broken the heart of the boy she loved. The reality is almost more than I can handle. "You put up with your dad's abuse for three more years...for Jackie."

When I open my eyes again, he's watching me with a tender look. "It wasn't always bad. Once it was clear they weren't getting any closer to finding the girls, my old man took on other cases around the country. Sometimes he'd leave me alone in Mankato for weeks at a time. Those were some of my best days as a kid. At least then I was untouchable." He drops his grip on his neck and begins to rub the deep scar running through one of his eyebrows. "I tolerated him until the end of my junior year when he chucked a ceramic plate at me, took a chunk out of my nose and cut my head open. The ER doctor said I was lucky I didn't lose my eye. She suspected something was off, told me she wanted to help. I decided I'd finally had enough and took her up on the offer. She found a way to reach out to my great aunt in Seattle. Virginia took me in without hesitation—booked me a flight minutes after I called. She knew about my father's abusive ways, but had feared what he'd do if she'd tried to intervene." His gaze glistens as it holds mine. "By then I knew Jackie wasn't coming back anyway."

"Oh, Theo," I whisper, unable to resist touching him any longer. I frame his warm jaw in my hands, holding his tormented stare. "I'm so sorry they didn't find her. It isn't fair. For you or Jackie."

He drops his forehead against mine. "Why is this happening? How did you end up here...with *me*?"

"I wish I could tell you. It's freaking me out just as much that my dreams are based on actual events."

A set of his fat tears pool against my fingers. "It's my fault Jackie went missing."

Violent jolts of sadness and empathy nearly bring me to my knees. "What?" I tighten my grip on his face. "Why would you think that?"

"She broke curfew to come meet me that night." His eyes squeeze shut, forcing more tears to spill. "After we fought, she took off by herself. If I had let her run away with me like she wanted, or chased after her..."

On a gasp, I wrap him in my arms, nudging him down so I can press my lips against his cheek. In this moment, my feelings for him are more certain than ever. Without question, I love him. Not only for who he is, but for all he's been through. I love him for being a survivor. I love him for enduring his father's abuse all those years because he wanted to help Jackie. I love him for never letting his friend disappear from his heart.

"There's no way of knowing whether or not it would've gone any differently," I say, stroking a hand through his damp hair when he leans this head against my shoulder. "There's no sense in blaming yourself. That night was fated to go down that way, whether you'd told her to meet you that night or not."

Maybe it's like Aristotle believed, that all events in a person's life occur as a necessity.

I sense he's trying to keep it together, but his body trembles inside my arms. I continue to run my fingers through his hair, stopping every few seconds to drop kisses against his temple. After a few precious moments of silence, I tell him, "I know this is going to sound a bit strange, but my mom's best friend is a well-respected psychic. Constantine spent the better part of a year in India, studying different religions that believe in this kind of thing. Maybe she can somehow enlighten us. I don't necessarily believe in everything she does, even though there are times when she knows things she shouldn't, but I'm also desperate for someone to explain why this is happening to us. Maybe she can help me dig a little deeper into what happened to Jackie that night. Maybe we can somehow find justice for all of them." I squeeze him a little tighter and whisper, "Maybe she'll know something that explains how I found my way to you."

18

STERLING - 2018

Theo sucks down a glass of whiskey for breakfast while I call my aunt Constantine in California on speaker mode. She's full of questions, but doesn't offer much by way of explanation. Theo quietly listens in from his roost at his island, occasionally shaking his head and topping off his glass. He hasn't said much of anything since he cried in my arms, other than to offer to pour me a glass of whiskey too. At least he hasn't asked me to leave the way I'd feared.

Once I'm done telling my aunt everything, she's quiet for a long stretch. I worry the call was dropped until she asks, "How soon can you two come to California?"

"Aunt Connie, we can't," I say, meeting Theo's gaze. "Theo and I have to work on Monday."

"It wouldn't be necessary to stay any longer than the weekend," she says. "Have your mom book you a private charter today. You could be back in Minnesota by tomorrow night. I merely need to see you both in person to feel your energy, read your Tarot cards. Anyone who claims they can do that by video call is full of shit. It'll assist me in revealing who each of you were and are, who you are to become. It will aid us in putting your story into greater context, Sterling. You want answers? That's the only way I can give them to you."

"We'll have to discuss it and get back to you," I tell her.

"I know I'll hear back from you soon," she replies smartly. The double tone from my phone indicates the call has ended.

I grip the island and drop my head while taking a step back, inhaling deeply. The mention of "feeling my energy" and reading Tarot cards makes me second guess the decision to confide in my unconventional aunt. Yet I don't personally know of another living soul who would entertain our situation, or deduce we're anything other than delusional.

"I don't know what else we can do," I say, lifting

my head to eye Theo. "This all sounds crazy, but then again, so are my dreams. What do you think?"

"What the hell," he grumbles. His voice is quiet enough that I suspect he's speaking to himself. Then he gulps back the remainder of the liquid in his glass and slams down the empty tumbler on the island, meeting my questioning stare. "Let's do it."

SEVERAL MINUTES after we climb into the black town car my mom sent to meet the private jet once it landed in L.A., Theo finally looks at me in the affectionate way I'd become accustomed to before he learned I've been dreaming of him as a boy. We haven't engaged in any meaningful conversation since packing an overnight bag and hightailing it to the airport in Mankato for an 11 a.m. flight.

Nudging my hand out from beneath my leg, he interlaces our fingers. "I've been mulling over things since we left. Sounds insane, but I'm staring to believe Jackie brought you and me together. Wanted to apologize for the asshole way I reacted when you first told me about your dreams. It must be a lot for you to wrap your brain around, too. You're probably even a little scared." His fingers tighten over mine.

"You're the only person other than a friend of Jackie's sister who's offered to help me find answers. Karrie stayed in Kato long after I left. She could've afforded to move out of the trailer park by then, but she didn't in case Jackie returned. She was finally forced to leave when it was demolished in the early two thousands. Another ten years went by before she decided she couldn't deal with with the botched search for Jackie and the others any longer. She took the money she'd saved, opened her dream business in a suburb up by St. Paul."

A puzzle piece clicks into place, the figurative sound of it deafening to my ears. "She opened a tattoo parlor," I whisper. "In White Bear Lake."

I can't believe I didn't make the connection earlier. K.C. is *Karrie*—Jackie's fierce neighbor with Joan Jett's hairstyle who was always sneaking J.R. and the sisters into her places of employment.

Theo smooths his other hand over his forehead as if trying to absorb the lengths of my psychic knowledge. "Holy shit, Sterling. How—"

"Remember when I told you about Beth, the bartender from Pub 500 that I've been meeting for drinks? I asked her if she knew anything about the missing girls. She mentioned her friend, K.C., had known one of the girl's family. I didn't say anything to you because you'd gotten so upset when I first mentioned the subject. I did a little research on my own and discovered K.C. was the one who'd tattooed the angel on your back."

He laughs in a stilted way that hints he's relieved to hear no superpowers were involved in my deduction. Pulling his hand from mine, he tangles his fingers inside my loose waves at the base of my neck. "Sounds like you could give my old man a run for his money."

"It's not quite as innocent as it sounds," I sheepishly admit, wishing I had a better poker face when it begins to heat. "I feared K.C. was the one who broke your heart, the one who made it hard for you to enjoy life and stop tormenting yourself. So I called in sick to work yesterday and made an appointment to get a tattoo with her."

His eyebrows shoot upward. "You went to White Bear Lake yesterday?"

"I had to know whether or not there was a danger you'd leave me for her."

A small smirk toys at his lips. "I'm assuming you got your answer?"

"Not really. She wouldn't tell me anything, said your secrets weren't hers to share." My eyes flicker to the buttons on his white shirt as I'm overwhelmed with shame. "When she realized I wasn't actually there to get a tattoo, she basically kicked me out. She told me she'd be willing to talk to me again once she 'cooled down.'"

He laughs in a rolling sound. "That sounds like Karrie." Yanking me close, he slides my leg over his lap and lifts my hips so I'm straddling him. "Sweetheart," he begins, his voice husky, "let me clue you in on a little secret. Karrie, or K.C. as she prefers now, is not my type, and I'm sure as hell not hers. *You*, on the other hand..."

My mouth lags open. "But...but...there's a picture on her Instagram of her and a really hot guy. They looked really into each other."

"That's probably Travis, her business partner. They have a weird relationship. He's the only guy I've ever seen her flirt with." He bends for a moment, brushing his lips over mine. "It's hot to hear you were jealous enough to drive four hours to size up what you thought was your competition."

"I figured she was old enough that I could've easily taken her in a cat fight," I tease. "Lucky for her, she ended up being pretty chill." Smirking, I slip my fingers through the longer locks on the top of his head. "What about the woman who cut your hair? Do I have to pay her a visit next?"

A chuckle rumbles against his throat. "You're jealous of my neighbor, Vicky? She's more like a mother to me."

"That doesn't mean she's out of the picture," I tease, grinning while slipping open one of the buttons on his shirt. "You seem to thrive on dating someone with a considerable age gap."

"*You* pursued *me*, sweetheart."

Gazing into his beautifully deep eyes and finding the ghost of the boy who has pined for his missing friend all these years, I run my bottom lip through my teeth. "You're an amazing man, Theo. It must be the reason I'm falling so hard, so fast. I wanted to get a sense for your relationship with K.C. because I didn't figure there was any sense in both of us walking away with shattered hearts."

"I know what you mean about the falling thing," he admits, stroking a finger along my cheek.

A whirlwind of emotions takes flight inside my belly. There was no question he'd felt a strong attraction toward me, but I had assumed he regarded it as a bit of temporary fun to pass the time. With tears burning behind my eyes, I comb my fingers through his hair. "Wanna know what I was thinking during the flight? I know this is going to sound a little cheesy, but I can't help wondering if fate brought me to you. And if it wasn't fate, then maybe it was Jackie. Maybe she was tired of watching you torture yourself, so she sent me."

"You're saying you believe in ghosts?"

"I'm not sure," I admit. "I remember once hearing a theory that someone with a violent past might linger in the afterlife due to unfinished business."

His eyes flash to the window, watching thoughtfully as the industrial L.A. landscape rushes past. "I told you I figured she was dead by now, but that's not totally true." Exhaustion settles in the depths of his dark gaze. "She's been missing thirty-two years. In that time, I've come up with every scenario imaginable. The one I clung to is that someone took her, and she developed Stockholm syndrome. I wanted to believe she carried on to live an otherwise normal life." His eyes fall shut. "But deep down, I know better. Probably the reason I asked K.C. to tattoo that angel—wanted to feel pain...wanted to believe she'd gone on to somewhere better where she's being watched over."

Swallowing the lump rising in my throat, I smooth my thumbs over his cheeks. I've never experienced such a vast spectrum of emotions in such a short period of time. If there was any way I could ease even a minuscule amount of his sorrow, I'd do it in a heartbeat. I suppose that's the main reason I'm so eager to find justice for Jackie. "I think after thirty-two years, there's a good chance she's gone, Theo."

"Without a body..." he muses, forcing out a harsh sigh. "Until then, I refuse to believe there isn't some other kind of explanation."

"She loved you," I blurt, wanting to give him a shred of happiness. "She was hurt that you seemed sweet on her sister and that you waited to kiss her until you were getting ready to leave, but she still loved you more than anyone who'd ever been a part of her life."

His mouth becomes a hard line. "I know we've been through this already, but how could you possibly know how she felt about the kiss, or that she loved me?"

"It's hard to describe. In my dreams, I feel her every emotion...like it's happening to me in real time." I draw my attention to the tinted window. "It's almost like I *am*—

My heart thuds to a stop.

She's been gone 32 years.

I was born the same year Jackie died.

What if—

"You are *what*?" he prods.

Her, I think to myself, unable to utter the word aloud.

"Never mind," I say, dropping a soft kiss against his lips. "Just know without question that you meant the world to her." Glancing out the window, I maneuver down from his lap and sigh. "We're almost there. You better prepare yourself. My aunt is even more of a handful than my mother."

I'VE KNOWN my aunt Constantine since birth. My mom befriended her years before I was born, after my aunt predicted my mom would one day take the world by storm with her charm. Accordingly, I don't bat an eye when my raven-haired "aunt" with a surgically enhanced face, purple contacts, and silicon breasts greets us at the 20' front door of her Bel Air mansion wearing a jade green dress with more bling than decency. Theo, on the other hand, appears as if he's already regretting the trip to California when he throws me a wide-eyed look.

"My baby girl!" my aunt sings, drawing me against her stick-thin figure for a tight squeeze. "I know you haven't been gone all that long, but I still get to miss you!"

The combination of her floral perfume and weed clogs my throat as I pat her bony back. "It's good to be home," I say, even though we both know it's a lie. She coached me through my roughest teenage years, when I wanted to run far away from the madness of Hollywood. "I've missed you too."

She draws back, her grin for Theo turning devilish. "This handsome beast must be the literal man of your dreams." She offers him a limp hand, as if expecting him to kiss it. At 63 years of age, she's keenly aware that she's more attractive than most women in her age bracket—at least by L.A. standards. Accordingly she's incredibly flirtatious with all men, so I don't take her interest in him to heart. "I'm Constantine."

"Theo Davies." He gives her hand a quick shake before sliding his arm behind my back. "Good to meet you, ma'am."

"A pleasure, Theo," she purrs, fluttering her false lashes. "I can understand why my sweet girl might want to come back in another life to be with you a second time."

Theo stops mid-chuckle, as if misunderstanding the punchline of a joke. "Did you say *another life*?" he asks.

I hold my breath, waiting for him to turn and hightail it out of here as my aunt replies.

"The Buddhists believe in *samsara*, the never-ending cycle of life, death, and rebirth. A lot of it has to do with karma and whether or not a person has lived a life worthy of a second chance." Dark eyebrows shooting upright, my aunt grins brightly at both of us. "Based on what you've told me and what I learned from my studies with Tibetan monks, I believe Theo's Jackie has been reincarnated as our beloved Sterling."

Clutching Theo's arm, I nearly choke on a gasp. *She can't be serious, can she?* I look up at Theo to see he isn't moving, isn't blinking.

My aunt opens the massive door a little more. "Come on inside, kids. We have a ton of work to do in the short time you're here."

My head spins as we mutely follow her inside, each of us nearly stumbling over our own feet.

A part of me knows that no matter how impossible the theory may seem, she's absolutely right. I've sensed it myself, no matter how farfetched.

I was Jackie Tanner.

Theo quietly sticks by my side all afternoon as my aunt reads our Tarot cards and spews theories on how Jackie's soul was reincarnated so her death could be avenged. Whenever Theo's eyes connect with mine, they run through a plethora of emotions too intense to delve through individually. I keep hoping he'll snap out of it at any moment, and spar with me like usual. Truthfully, I worry neither of us will survive this without a skewed view on life.

My mom joins us for a late-night seafood dinner prepared by my aunt's chef, and decides she has time to stay a little longer once my aunt pops open a coveted bottle of Prosecco from her last trip to Italy. Theo relaxes after a couple of glasses, revealing to the two most important women in my life the part of him that made me fall head-over-heels in love.

"I knew there was something familiar about Sterling the first time we met," he tells my mom as I'm snuggled inside the crook of his arm. The four of us lounge in the sunken fire pit in my aunts lavish backyard on long couches the same deep shade of red as the stunning sunset that had stretched across the sky hours earlier. "I guessed you were her mom before she mentioned it."

"Maybe that's not why Sterling seemed so familiar to you, Theo," my aunt suggests. "Maybe your heart recognized Jackie's soul. Maybe that's why you chose to take Sterling to that park on your first date...the same one where you met Jackie."

"Let's ease up on the reincarnation stuff for a little while," I tell her, squeezing Theo's knee. "We're both exhausted by all of this, Aunt Connie. It's a lot to process."

With a faint smile that pops the charming dimples into his cheeks, Theo slips his hand over mine. "Don't change the subject on my account. The idea still seems a bit out there, but it's kind of nice thinking Jackie could be here with us—with me."

Although I suspect the Prosecco is loosening his inhibitions more than his beliefs, I mirror his smile.

Would it be so bad if he believed what my aunt's saying, even if it wasn't true? In the short time I've known him, he's never been this playful and light hearted. Based on what Beth and K.C. have said about him, I doubt *anyone* has.

His expression all at once becomes gravely serious. Regardless of the meaning behind my dreams and my purpose for reliving Jackie's final days, I'm beginning to understand the severity of my connection with Theo is lightyears beyond our control. Linking our hands together, he dips his head down and captures my mouth with a tender, meaningful kiss. For a blissful moment, I forget where we are and that we're not alone. I swear I can feel Jackie's heart burst with content from the gentle sweep of Theo's tongue.

My mom releases a dreamy sigh. "Just look at them, Constantine. I've never witnessed a love this pure firsthand."

With the reminder of our audience, I jerk away to throw her a warning look. "Seriously, Mom." Ignoring the flush of my cheeks, I regard my aunt. "You keep saying you think my purpose is to help Jackie avenge her death. How exactly do we go about doing that? My dreams haven't evolved beyond the moment she was abducted, and I wasn't given a clear view of the man's face."

My aunt taps on her lips with a blood-red fingernail. "Have you ever tried hypnotherapy?"

"Not in this lifetime," I quip.

Theo lets out a strangled chuckle, but my aunt Constance doesn't react. "I'm not entirely convinced it would help in your case, but we can give it a try in the morning after the effects of the Prosecco have worn off. Of course it's not exactly my forte, so no promises it will work. I suppose I could give you some peyote I received from a Dakota chief, although sometimes with that stuff it's hard to differentiate what the mind is hallucinating, and what it's recalling. If hypnosis doesn't work, the peyote could still be an option."

"Pretty sure that's a schedule one drug," I tell her with a firm shake of my head. "As much as I'd love to explain the complicated reason I failed their drug test to my new employer, I think I'm going to have to pass on that idea."

"Tell me again, Sterling," my mom says. "Which men stood out in your dreams as possible suspects?"

I settle back against the warmth of Theo's chest, drawing on his strength. "The chief of police told me they released Darrel Heinrich, the original suspect, because they didn't have enough to convict him, but I'm not completely convinced it still wasn't him. Jackie's sister was pretty certain she heard someone screaming in that shed." I stroke Theo's inner thigh, wishing he hadn't had to pay such a steep price for that call on Diane's behalf. "They didn't think Becky's dad was involved, but Jackie said he'd done 'gross things' to Becky, so I don't understand how he was so easily let off as a suspect. In addition to those two, Jackie was uncomfortable around her sixth grade teacher and, eventually, the Lutheran pastor."

"And my father," Theo adds through a clench jaw.

Swallowing a gasp, I pivot to face him. "You said you didn't think he'd done it."

"No sense in ruling him out this late in the game. A conversation with him will be necessary, no matter what." He drops a kiss against my temple. "I'm gonna head upstairs to try calling him, give you some privacy with your family." Then he bends in a little closer, brushing his lips over my ear as he speaks. "Don't worry about waking me, no matter how late. You and me are going to test the craftsmanship of that massive bed in the guest room...see how much it can take."

I'm easily the color of a tomato as he stands and shuffles over to my aunt, bending to kiss her cheek.

"Constantine, thank you for helping us try to make sense of this, and thank you for the best meal of my life. It was every bit worth the extra five pounds I'm sure I packed on."

My aunt takes his bearded face in her hands and returns a kiss to his cheek. "You are certainly welcome, sweet boy. We'll see if we can uncover something helpful about your dear friend's disappearance in the morning."

Theo moves over to my mom at her side, kissing her cheek as well. "Good to see you again, April. Hope everything goes smoothly with your movie."

"Thank you, Theo." She kisses him back, her lips landing a little closer to his than I'd like and leaving a smudged imprint of her scarlet lipstick. "I do hope you and my daughter will join me next spring for the premiere. You'd look positively *divine* in an Armani suit."

Theo turns to me with a brow raised in question. Giggling, I motion for him to wipe the lipstick from his face.

"Good night, ladies," he tells us with a curt nod, rubbing his fingers across his cheek.

"Good night," my mom and aunt chorus in sickly sweet tones.

We all three watch intently as he strolls back

toward the mansion. There's no question my aunt and mom are enjoying the view of his backside as much as I am, especially when an appreciative noise comes from the back of one of their throats.

I'm convinced he's still within earshot when my aunt grabs onto my wrist and tells me, "You're going to marry that man. I've been dying to tell you ever since you arrived. I sensed the unbreakable connection between you before he'd even opened his sexy mouth. The two of you are soulmates—a destiny that was set in place long before you were born."

My mom bobs her head in agreement. "I'm telling you, I've never seen a love so pure."

Heart pounding, I glance back to the house and watch Theo slip through one of the glass patio doors. "Would you two keep your voices down? This has been a lot for him to digest already! You'll scare him away!"

My aunt releases my wrist and shrugs. "There's no changing fate, baby girl. You and that man were destined to find that poor girl, and proceed with a long, beautiful life together."

I'd never really believed in fate or destiny before moving to Minnesota, but there's no denying she could be right. *Please, let her be right.*

Even if our relationship doesn't evolve the way

I'd like, I've never wanted anything as badly as I want to bring Jackie and the other girls home.

SUNDAY NIGHT, we return to Mankato in time to meet K.C. for a late dinner at a quaint little pizza joint downtown. I'm far too nervous to eat, but wouldn't have dreamed of turning the idea down once Theo told me it'd been arranged. I'm eager to connect with K.C. now that I know her role in Jackie's life.

"Check out that classic Bronco," Theo tells me before we enter the restaurant. He points at a sleek little 2-door SUV painted powder blue with large tires and white rims. Everything, including the tan leather benches in front and back, gleam with newness. "Karrie bought that hunk of junk when she was sixteen. She held onto it all these years, had it upgraded once she had extra cash. She never lets go of anything."

I sense the gravity of his words, appreciating how she'd never let go of her friends, either. Upon finding Jackie's old neighbor standing beside a booth in the farthest corner from the entrance, waiting to greet us, I'm overwhelmed with the compulsion to hug her. So I do.

"Whoa," she says, patting my back with mock enthusiasm. "Is asphyxiation how they say 'I'm sorry' in California?"

"Theo told me everything," I explain in a heartfelt rush. "How you stayed in the trailer park in case Jackie returned, how you left when you were upset with the failed search for her, how you were there for him through it all...I honestly can't thank you enough."

With a cackle of a laugh, she nudges me back. "Well this is certainly an unexpected development." She side-eyes Theo as if waiting for him to rescue her from the neurotic psycho. "Where exactly did you find this little bundle of energy?"

"It's a long story that's gonna require a lot of booze," Theo replies, nudging past me to wrap her in a brief, yet meaningful hug. "How've you been?"

"Apparently nowhere as good as you." She studies his face before pinching his cheek. "Dude, you're *glowing*. I've never seen you *glowing*."

"Knock it off," he growls, tugging on my hand and drawing me down into the booth at his side. "Let's order drinks."

Glancing past the booth toward the windows in the front of the building, my breath is knocked out of me. "This is where you went that day...with Jackie and Diane...after you followed Darrel Heinrich to his house. You made the phone call to your dad across the street in a phone booth." I clutch Theo's forearm. "This is where everything started to go to shit."

K.C. cocks her head at Theo, seemingly confused. "What's up with your girlfriend? Seriously. It's like we're in an episode of *Long Island Medium*."

He drapes his arm behind my back, nudging me closer. "This is what I was trying to explain to you when I called." He lets out the long, complicated sigh I'd guess he's been holding in since leaving California. "You have no idea what we've been through in the past twenty-four hours. Sterling was hypnotized this morning to see if she could help us find Jackie."

K.C. cocks her head. "And?"

"No dice," I reply, recalling the failed experiment with renewed frustration. My aunt had been unable to get anything out of me. She guessed it was because my brain refused to go under, which made me feel a little more broken. "Turns out I'm not a good candidate for that kind of thing."

"Maybe your brain is protecting you from trauma," K.C. suggests with a flippant shrug.

Baffled, I gape at her as a perky high school girl stops by to take Theo's order for a pitcher of craft beer. Is K.C. saying she believes us?

Once the girl's gone, K.C. leans over the table, holding my quizzical stare. "You could tell me aliens fed you this information through a butt probe and I wouldn't care as long as you know actual facts like that thing with the phone booth. It's past time someone does something about the pervert who took Jackie. Whatever you two have planned, I'm down."

Warmth spreads over me as I'm suddenly able to understand with crystal clarity why Theo valued their friendship for so many years. "I spoke with the chief of police last week," I tell her. "I asked him about the girls. He pulled me aside, said the department was embarrassed by their failure. He seemed unsettled by all of it."

K.C.'s heavily made-up eyes darken. "Chief Nielsen was one of the worthless cops that questioned everyone in the neighborhood after Jackie's disappearance. I remember wanting to rip that stupid mustache off of his pubescent face. He clearly didn't know what the hell he was doing."

I nod thoughtfully. "Probably because he was fresh out of the police academy at the time. But I reminded him that he has the power *now* do something about it. Maybe I got through to him. I'll call him tomorrow and see if he'll agree to meet me somewhere private."

"I'm going with," Theo insists.

"I don't think that's a good idea," I say, stroking his thigh. "I could tell he was paranoid about someone overhearing our conversation. You might spook him."

"You do have a spooky way about you," K.C. tells him, grinning. "Best let your little Nancy Drew deal with him alone."

Theo persistently shakes his head. "Cops can be dirty...same as detectives. Could be the reason no one was ever arrested."

"I can handle myself," I promise. "I worked with some shady characters in L.A. I'll carry mace if it will ease your concern." With a rush of embarrassment, I pat Theo's leg. After I'd joined him in the guest room at my aunt's, the passion that kindled between us was so intense that I forgot all about the call he said he was going to make. "Speaking of detectives, you never told me if you got ahold of your father last night."

"He didn't answer so I left him a message. Told him I had some questions about Jackie and wanted to discuss some possible suspects. It should get his attention."

"I'm going to dig a little deeper with Chief Nielsen, see what he knows about the Lutheran minister and Jackie's teacher. Maybe even learn some more about that Heinrich guy they once suspected."

K.C. crosses her arms and leans back in the booth across from us, eyes locked with mine. "There's someone else I think you should meet with, Sterling. Someone we've overlooked who might have insider information."

"You don't mean Diane," Theo grunts out. When K.C. makes it clear that's exactly who she means with a lift of her brows, Theo raises his voice. "She's still not all there! Mentioning Jackie to her could send her over the edge!"

K.C. holds a hand up between them. "Chillax, big guy. We could at least call the nursing home, see if they're letting her have visitors. If she's not on lock-down like last time, she might be doing better."

I slap my hand over my mouth in time to mute the sob ripping from my throat. Theo mentioned Diane had spent some time in a psych ward after Jackie disappeared, but I didn't imagine she'd still be in a state of mental decline after all this time.

"Diane's in a nursing home?" I rasp behind my fingers.

Theo's fingers nestle at the base of my neck, gently massaging as he answers. "She never really recovered from losing Jackie."

"We have to help her," I tell them, my eyes burning with tears. "We need to give her—*all* of you —closure."

"I have a wicked good feeling about you," K.C. says, grinning as she reaches across the table to grip my hands. "Maybe we can finally bring Jackie home."

20
STERLING - 2018

Monday evening, I'm forced to clock in an extra two hours at the office to process a last-minute emergency placement of an hour-old newborn after the father snuck drugs into the recovery room at the mother's request. I make it in time to meet Chief Nielsen on a back road of the warehouse district with mere minutes to spare. Theo still wasn't too pleased when I insisted on proceeding with the meeting on my own, and made me promise I'd call to check in the second it was over.

I'd half expected the chief wouldn't agree to the meeting when I'd called, and nearly cheer triumphantly when finding the black and white police cruiser waiting at the designated address.

Although I don't consider him to be any kind of threat, I slip my hand inside my handbag and wrap my fingers around the can of mace I promised Theo I'd bring along. This morning as I was on my way out the door, he vowed he'd take me to a shooting range later in the week. "Just in case someone doesn't like you looking into things," he'd said before silencing my protests with a deep kiss.

Even though the local kids will be returning to school in a few days, the air is still sticky and exceptionally warm, causing my satin blouse to stick to my damp skin. When I slip into the passenger's seat of the cruiser, I sigh happily with the blast of frigid air.

"Thank you for agreeing to meet me, Chief Nielsen."

He stares straight ahead out the cruiser's windshield, eyes fixated on the empty loading dock of an abandoned building. "After I spoke with you the other day, I couldn't shake the memory of seeing Jackie Tanner just hours before she was reported as missing. We were in the process of arresting Becky Myers's dad when Jackie came upon the scene, asked if we'd found Becky. She looked really scared. I told her to go home. I took an oath to serve and protect, but I was short with that frightened little girl, told her to go home." He turns to me, gaze strained and shadowed from what I assume to be a lack of sleep. He's also notably more pale than the last time we met. "Her case has haunted me ever since. I should've walked her back to her place. I should've ensured she was safe."

I respond with a firm shake of my head. "Jackie wouldn't have stayed home even if you'd locked her inside her room. She was worried about a friend, and determined to check in on him."

His keen gaze studies mine. "How do you know that?"

"I've recently befriended Theo Davies and Karrie Schaumberg. They've filled me in on every last detail they can remember about that fall."

He releases a rough chuckle and adjusts the screen on the laptop mounted between us. "That Schaumberg woman sure is a hellcat. She's been riding the department for decades. It always made me kind of glad when she refused to back down. She must've been close with the Tanner girl."

"She was. So was Theo."

He rotates in his seat to directly face me. "What did you want to speak to me about, Miss Pruitt?"

On instinct I brace myself, prepared to be met with resistance. After working alongside the officers out in Los Angeles, some of which had faced count-less allegations of neglect and corruption, I've become skeptical of the intentions of anyone in uniform.

"Did your department ever question a Lutheran minister in town by the name of Pastor Babel?"

"I don't recall there being any mention of a pastor. Why do you ask?"

"Jackie went to his church every year to collect donated school supplies. In the days leading up to her disappearance, she had several interactions with him—including one just hours before she went missing in which he claimed he was concerned that she was out too late by herself, and offered her a ride. She refused to get in his vehicle though. I think she sensed he was a little odd. He'd also offered to speak with her about her troubles in confidence, even though she wasn't one of his parishioners."

"The department's files on Jackie and the other girls have been sealed, but I can still request access to them." He blinks several times like something is hurting his head. "Hold on. How did you know he'd offered her a ride? I remember many details of her case, but nothing about that."

"We've been in touch with Jackie's sister," I say, following the plan the three of us had cooked up the night before over pizza and beer. "She's doing a little better these days—remembers little facts the police weren't able to extract from her before. The psychiatrists say she immediately went into a state of shock after discovering her sister was gone. She hasn't been quite right since." According to K.C. and Theo, the last part was based on 100% truth. It still hurts my heart to think Jackie's big sister lost her wits because of what happened.

With an absentminded bob of his head, the chief scratches his clean-shaven chin. "Maybe I need to interview this sister again, now that she's coherent."

"It goes in streaks," I tell him with a surge of panic. "Some days she's completely comatose. It depends on how many drugs they've pumped her with on any given day. And she doesn't open up to strangers. Karrie and Theo have been the only ones who've been able to get her to talk about her sister."

Guess I'm better at lying than I thought.

"Jackie's case rattled me more than the others," he tells me on a tired sigh. "Probably because she's the only one I'd met in person. For the longest time after her disappearance, I swore I'd never get married and have kids. I didn't think I could ever have a daughter and not fear for her safety every second of the day. For months on end I used to lie awake at night, trying to imagine what those girls' parents were going through. Can't say I was too surprised when Jackie's mother overdosed. I'll never understand how a parent survives a thing like that."

"Did you change your mind about having kids?" I ask, taking note of the silicone band on his left ring finger.

"Eventually." He glances past me with a wistful smile. "Had myself three strong boys who've since grown up to be good men. Two are in the military, and the third plans to follow in my footsteps. Probably was for the best we never had a girl. God only knows I would've driven myself mad with worry."

I'm beginning to wonder if half of the city remains rattled in one way or another by the girls' disappearances, even after three decades have passed. Why didn't the community stand up to law enforcement back then, and insist more was done to find them? "What about Jackie's teacher, Mr. Kabe?"

"I remember the chief sending us out to question Elroy Kabe because he may have known something that could've helped us find Jackie. He was never a person of interest, but he offered an alibi all the same, said he was with his wife and kids that night. Two of my boys had Kabe years later. Always had a hard time looking that man in the eye at conferences. He's a strange character. My boys didn't care for him all that much. My wife didn't either."

Bile trickles up my throat. I never would've imagined the pervert who'd all but drooled over Diane at the drive-in and favored young girls who dressed provocatively would have a family waiting back home. "He's still teaching?"

"No, praise the Lord. I saw something in the paper about him retiring a few years back. Maybe in twenty eleven or twelve. In the article it said he and his wife were moving to one of the nearby lakes where they planned to manage a bait shop. I wanna say the lake was Jefferson or Madison."

"You don't think his wife might've lied to protect him?"

"Sure, but it wasn't my call to make at the time."

"Who was your supervisor?"

"Chief Clifford Braunshausen. He retired a few years after the last disappearance with the onset of Alzheimer's. He was one of those who pushed to have these cases sealed."

"Who else wanted them sealed?"

"The mayor and one of the presiding judges. They've both passed since."

All dead ends. Blowing out a hard breath, I swing my focus back to the list of suspects. "The man you told me had been the only person of interest, Darrel Heinrich…did they ever search his shed?"

"We did, but only after your friends raised a fuss. The Davies kid claimed he'd told his father about some weird noises they'd heard, but there wasn't anything about the call on record. The shed was neat as a pin. That Heinrich character was the orderly type—had each of his tools outlined on a pegboard so they wouldn't get misplaced. He was an odd fellow all around…didn't know how to interact on a social level. Made rudimentary bird houses for friends and coworkers. His father had been a contractor, taught him the basics. But he let us search his property without a warrant. If he'd been guilty of something, I doubt he would've been clever enough to properly hide anything. He made a point of showing me his VHS collection, seemed some-what embarrassed that most of them were cartoons for young boys. The way he reacted, you'd think we were there to arrest him because of those tapes. The chief had me take them in for review to make sure they weren't anything more sinister, but they were exactly what they appeared to be—innocent shows for young kids."

A lack of social skills might explain the way he had openly gaped at the girls while they'd been rollerskating. Only somewhat satisfied, I decide to move on. "Karrie and Theo told me they thought Becky Myers's dad was molesting her. Was that ever brought into question?"

"An anonymous tip came in shortly after his arrest, but there wasn't any way to prosecute him for it without some kind of hard evidence, or a statement from a victim. The county prosecutor made the decision to dismiss the charges against him for possessing a firearm while he was on probation for stealing a car a few years prior— spewed some bullshit about how Myers had gone through enough with his daughter missing." He clenches his teeth with a seething look. "I heard that mean bastard died of liver failure a handful of years back."

While his death wouldn't rule him out as a suspect, it certainly narrows our search. I drum my fingertips against my knees, debating how much I want to disclose on the final suspect topping our list. "What was your impression of Detective Davies?"

He throws me a funny look. "I thought you were friendly with his boy."

"I am." A light flush spreads over my cheeks. "But Jackie's sister said there was something off about his father. Like maybe he was harboring a secret temper.

She told me Theo often came to school with unexplained injuries, like a broken arm and a black eye."

While I didn't exactly mention to Theo that I'd bring his father into my conversation with the chief, I doubt he'd protest. Especially since I'm using Diane as a scapegoat so as not to get Theo involved. He hasn't mentioned if his father is still an active detective, so I feel a need to tread lightly.

The chief shrugs. "Far as I knew, he was a standup guy."

The radio clipped to his shoulder crackles with static, then a woman's voice. "Dispatch to one-ohone, do you copy?"

He tilts his head and presses the button on his radio. "One-oh-one, go ahead."

"You're needed at ninety-one Kato View Road for a possible domestic."

His eyes briefly close as he blows out his cheeks, then presses the button again. "Ten-four. I'm enroute." He releases the radio and regards me with regret. "I'm afraid I have to take this. Repeat violent offender...wouldn't be surprised if this case ends up on your desk by morning."

Emotion clogs my throat as I think of Theo as a boy, and how no one came to his rescue. I clear my throat and nod in understanding. "I know you're taking a risk by meeting with me, Chief. Your time is much appreciated."

"I still don't understand your involvement in this case, but you've certainly given me a lot to chew on, Miss Pruitt."

When he reaches for the gear shifter, I rest my hand on top of his, waiting until his eyes return to mine. "I think it's time you consider reopening the investigation. Too many people are still in pain. They need to see these girls finally laid to rest, and their captor found."

His Adam's Apple dips before he nods and chokes out, "I'll be in touch."

ON MY WAY HOME, I park my BMW across from the same Lutheran church of which Jackie and J.R. had walked through all those years ago. It's a beautiful building situated in the middle of a residential neighborhood with well manicured lawns and a plethora of new construction. The church's structure hasn't changed much on the outside, except for a new steeple and updated siding. For a moment I consider going inside to see if the same pastor is still there.

Then, among the shadows of the oncoming twilight, I catch the bright flash of something metal across the street.

My heart goes still.

It's the same navy blue sedan that I've spotted parked in my neighborhood several times.

Someone is clearly following me.

Snagging the can of mace from my purse, I curl my other hand around the button on my phone that will summon the "Emergency SOS" slider, and step out into the street. Before I can get close enough to see the figure behind the wheel, the sedan's tires squeal and it roars past me in a blur.

Tuesday night as I'm sliding my aunt's chef's famous vegan lasagna into my new commercial-grade oven, praying it comes out edible instead of chewy like last time, Beth calls. "Hey," I answer after closing the oven door.

"Hey yourself," she says with a smile in her voice. "K.C. has been filling me in on your little Scooby-gang shenanigans, and mentioned you were questioning whether or not Jackie Tanner's teacher might've done something to the missing girls."

"There's something odd about him," I confirm. Then I remember how the last time I'd exchanged texts with Beth, she was annoyed that her boss had scheduled her to bartend every night this week and had threatened to quit. "Why are you calling about that? Aren't you at work?"

"That's the exact reason I'm calling," she says, all at once lowering her voice. "That dude is having dinner at the 500 as we speak. I'm pretty sure he's here with his wife or a girlfriend. They're awfully... cozy. And equally weird."

I draw in a sharp breath. "Are you sure it's him?"

"I've never met the guy, but one of the other girls commented he'd been her pervy teacher in sixth grade. She said she sucked at English but only had to wear short skirts and she'd ace every exam."

That's definitely him, I think to myself with a sickly shiver.

There's a muffled sound as Beth covers her phone to reply to someone calling her name. Then, "Sterling, I gotta go. But I wanted to let you know before they'd left. They've only been here a half hour or so and don't have their food yet."

I untie the apron I'd used to protect my white romper from my poor culinary skills. "I'll be right there."

As I set the apron on my newly installed quartz counter top, Theo emerges from my bedroom in a fresh Human League t-shirt and cargo shorts, rubbing his wet hair with a towel and flashing one of his delightful grins. "That smells delicious." His gaze darkens on the corded belt braided around my cotton romper. "You tryin' to kill me with that sweet little outfit? How the hell do you even remove it?"

"Wouldn't you like to know," I tease.

"Matter of fact, sweetheart, I do." He hooks a finger through the belt and drags me in closer. "How much time do I have before dinner's ready?"

A hot flush runs through me as I try to imagine exactly what's on his mind. Sometimes he's so slow and considerate with my body that I'm driven mad with yearning. Other times he's like a totally different person—rough and impatient as if he doesn't have the willpower to wait any longer. Either way, he always leaves me more than satisfied.

"I'm sorry, babe, but I have to run," I tell him, reaching for my handbag on the new island. "Check on the lasagna in forty-five minutes. Hopefully I'll be back in time to eat while it's still warm."

"Whoa." He tugs on my arm and drags his warm lips across my jaw. "Where you goin'?"

"Beth just called. Elroy Kabe is having dinner at the 500."

He draws back with a confused look. "What are you gonna do about it, Sterling? Follow him?"

It would seem an ideal time to tell him that I'm

being followed, but I can't make myself say the words out loud, knowing he'll only worry for my safety. Even if rightfully so.

I'll tell Chief Nielsen about the navy sedan the next time we meet. Maybe he can run through the list of suspects to see if any of them have a similar vehicle registered in their name.

"I don't have a plan," I admit, softening against the muscular planes of his firm chest. "But I'll be smart about it." Sighing, I reach back to stroke my fingertips over the cupped curve of his lower back beneath his t-shirt. Searching the depths of his soulful brown eyes, I wonder if there will ever be a time I'll be able to keep my hands to myself when he's near. "I only know he made Jackie uneasy too may times. Maybe I want to finally get a look at him myself. See if he's still just as weird."

Theo's body omits a vibration that echoes through mine. "I don't want you anywhere near that man on your own. Even if he's not a killer, he's still a royal jerk. I'm coming along."

I let out a tired sigh. "Beth is there along with probably a dozen coworkers, and who knows how many customers. It's dinnertime, so I'm sure the restaurant will be packed. There's nothing for you to worry about. Besides, I would be really bummed if my lasagna burned. I haven't made it in forever." I rise on my tiptoes to silence his doubts with a deep, intense kiss.

He cocoons me in his grip, lifting my feet off the floor and kissing me back until I'm breathless... tempted to cancel my plans to get lost in this blissful high for hours. Every time we're together in an intimate way, the connection between us runs a little deeper.

When he slides me onto the cool counter top the way I like because it gives me a position of power when looming over him, I grasp his head and hook my legs around his waist. My heart drums to a frazzled beat that quickens with the feeling of his fingertips slipping beneath my bra straps. It's far too easy to get lost in him.

I eventually wiggle free and shake my head. I've already wasted too much time. I'm afraid Kabe will be gone by the time I arrive downtown. "I have to go."

"Sure you wanna leave?" Theo rasps, dragging the tip of his nose down the sensitive skin on my neck.

"Don't let dinner burn," I say in a husky tone while sliding down from the counter top. "Things will get hot enough once I return and teach you the mechanics of rompers."

I feel a pang of guilt when I leave him breathless and flushed, eyes in a lust-driven haze. But I'll be back soon enough. More than anything, I want to see what kind of vehicle Elroy Kabe drives.

BETH TOPS off my glass of Moscato a second time as I continue watching Kabe and his wife from afar. They're notable a strange couple, especially because they almost look as if they could be siblings. They're both tall and sinewy with sharp noses and square jaws, thick black glasses, and narrow eyes. The biggest difference is her raven hair worn chin-length doesn't show a single inconsistency in color while his is peppered with gray. They're not overly cozy as Beth had suggested on the phone, but they do touch each other often in a non-sexual way as they carry on an animated conversation.

"He honestly gives me the willies," Beth says with an exaggerated shiver. "*Both* of them, really. They're almost...robotic looking."

"Jackie...uhhh, I mean, *K.C.* said he reminded her of that Pee-Wee Herman guy."

"I can totally see that."

As I'm studying the couple, the wife's eyes suddenly snap onto mine.

"Oh my god," I say, lowering my head and jerking my gaze back in Beth's direction. "The wife just caught me staring."

"Careful or she'll vaporize you with her robot eyes." Laughing wickedly, Beth rests her elbows on the bar top in front of me. "So I hear things are getting pretty hot and heavy with the grumpy carpenter. Are you some kind of a sadist?"

"Stop calling him that," I whine with a little smile. "His name is *Theo*. He's actually a really great guy. I was hoping you could formally meet him one of these days, but not if you're going to insist on labeling him like that. You'd like him."

"You're right, I'm sorry." She pours a tap beer for another patron at the bar, sighing dreamily. "Deep down I'm probably just jealous that you've only been in town for a hot minute and already you've snagged one of the only good ones around." She hands the beer off and throws a towel over her shoulder before heading back my way. "Don't look now, but the robot lady is on her way into the bathroom. Now's your chance to talk to her alone."

"What do I say?"

"You could try to catch her off guard by asking

straight out if she thinks her husband is into little girls." She leans forward to whisper, "Then again, I wouldn't be surprised to learn they're in on it *together.*"

Head tilted, I roll my eyes her way before chugging the rest of my wine. "If I'm not back in ten minutes, send a rescue party."

"Ten-four," she replies with a smart salute.

I enter the women's bathroom just steps behind Kabe's wife and wash my hands while she occupies one of the stalls. With the sound of the toilet flushing, I grab a handful of paper towels right as she steps out.

"Hi," I say to her, offering a cordial smile. "I'm sorry I was staring earlier. It's just...I swear your husband looks familiar. I feel like I know him from somewhere."

Her narrow face softens as she returns my smile. "He was a sixth grade teacher at one of the elementary schools here in town for a handful of decades."

"Roosevelt?" I ask.

"Yes, that's right." Her doubtful gaze flickers down to my romper and back to my face before she begins washing her hands. I'm starting to understand why Beth insisted on comparing the woman to a robot. Every movement she makes looks unnatural. Her wrists are stiff as she runs her hands beneath the water. "Did you go there?"

"My older cousins went to Roosevelt—Diane and Jackie Tanner. I must've recognized him from one of their yearbooks or something."

The smile evaporates from her face. "Oh, I'm so sorry to hear that." She stops the faucet with her elbow and stands with her wet hands held up like a surgeon. Water dribbles down her arms, pooling at her elbows as she sighs. "I'll never forget when we heard that your cousin, Jackie, had been reported as missing. We were in The Cities, taking our son and daughter to see the Globetrotters. My husband was distraught, said he'd seen Jackie leaving a school assembly less than an hour before we'd left."

The alleged timeline catches my interest. If I'm truly seeing Jackie's memories correctly, that assembly was several hours before Jackie met J.R. at the park. Maybe Kabe's alibi for that night really was air-tight, like Chief Nielsen said.

I tap my chin as if still trying to place her husband. "If I remember right, there was a search for her the day after she went missing. Maybe that's where I remember seeing him."

"That's not it." She reaches for the paper towels and gives a regretful shake of her head while wiping her hands dry. At last her wrists finally become mobile with the motion. "I'm sorry, but he wasn't able to be there. We'd left the afternoon she'd gone missing and spent the next two nights at a Holiday Inn, celebrating our son's birthday with friends and family. I know Elroy would've liked to have helped in any way possible. He was pretty shook up that one of his own students had gone missing." She tosses the used towels into the garbage and briefly touches my arm. "I'm so sorry they never found your cousin. You have my sympathies. My husband's too."

"Thank you," I say with a small nod.

I wait a beat to follow her back into the restaurant. Elroy stands beside their booth, rifling through his wallet.

"Well?" Beth asks as I return. "Did she try to shock you with her robot arms, or reveal what she looks like beneath her Scooby-style mask?"

"None of the above." Flashing her an apologetic look, I drop a twenty dollar bill on the bar and throw my handbag over my shoulder. "I have to run. I'll fill you in on everything later."

I remove my phone from my handbag and start after the couple when they exit through the front door. Although I'm parked in the lot out back, I stick close to the shadows the street lights cast, following them down South Riverfront with my eyes focused down on my phone in case they turn and notice I'm behind them.

From the corner of my eye, I watch as they veer toward a silver Jeep Cherokee parked at the curb. The wife slips in through the passenger's door, and Elroy climbs into the driver's seat.

While it's still possible they own a second car, something about my conversation with Elroy's wife makes me think he can safely be moved to the bottom of my list—maybe even crossed off entirely.

The following evening I swing by my house after work to pick up Theo and we head to a nursing home on Stadium Road. I'm constantly watching over my shoulder on the entire drive, paranoid that I'm once again being tailed. I still haven't mentioned the navy blue sedan to Theo, although I have good intentions to at some point.

The receptionist at the nursing home, a robust woman with bright eyes and round cheeks, greets Theo with a dazzling smile. I've noticed he seems to have that effect on all women. "It's good to see you again, Mr. Davies," she tells him as he's signing the visitor's log. "Diane hasn't had anyone come visit in a while. She's having a good day—I'm sure she'll be happy to see you. She's still in room one-oh-seven."

"Thank you," I reply on his behalf since he's suddenly gone mute. He hasn't had much of anything to say since K.C. called this morning to let us know the nursing home was okay with Diane having visitors. It's understandable that being around her would stir up too many painful memories for him, making it difficult to endure.

I take his hand and coax him down the sterilized hallway to room 107. The prevalent odor that nursing homes carry thickens around us along with the faint sound of distant conversations and the canned laughter from sitcoms. When I knock softly on 107's cracked door, we're greeted with a faint, "Come in."

Opening the door with the palm of my hand, I suck in a deep breath once discovering Jackie's big sister hunched in a wheelchair by the window. It's jarring enough to take in her snowy white, shoulder-length hair considering she's still in her forties, but she appears frail enough to break at any moment. Her chin lifts slightly as she regards us, her expression blank. It's as if we're witnessing an animated corpse at a theme park.

"DeeDee," I whisper, my throat tight. I drop Theo's hand and race over to kneel beside her, grasping her cool, bony hand in mine. Searching her beautiful blue eyes for a trace of the spirited big sister Jackie had known, I'm only met with a dull sheen of emptiness. "Oh, DeeDee, what's happened to you?"

Confusion settles in her gaze. "Jackie?" she asks, her other hand trembling as it reluctantly reaches out, as if wanting to touch my face. I guide her hand to my cheek and her skeletal face lights with a smile. "Jackie, where have you been?" She lovingly rubs her thumb along my cheekbone. "I've been so worried!"

Does she somehow sense the presence of her sister the way I do, or is her brain merely too confused to understand reality? Tears blur my vision when I glance over my shoulder to where Theo watches on from the doorway with hesitation.

Nodding in encouragement, he lumbers over to rest his hand on my shoulder. "I'm here too, Diane— J.R. It's good to see you."

"You've finally found her," she says to him with tears rolling down her cheeks. Her thumb continues stroking against my skin. "You found our Jackie."

"Not yet," he says quietly before bending down to whisper into my ear. "This is a waste of time. She's clearly *not* having a good day."

I reach up to touch his bearded face. "Let me talk with her for a little bit," I whisper back, panicked by the idea of having to leave her so soon. "Maybe she'll remember something if she thinks I'm really Jackie." I don't imagine he's down with the charade, and I feel a tremendous rush of guilt for even asking, so I add, "You can wait in the hallway if it's too much."

Jaw clenched, he bobs his head in surrender before bending to drop a kiss in my hair. "I'll be right outside the door if you need me."

I throw him an appreciative look before he slinks out of the room, gently pulling the door closed behind him. I slide the armchair out from the corner of the room, positioning it between her wheelchair and the simple hospital bed. The room is depressingly stark with the exception of a worn quilt folded at the foot of the bed and a framed picture on a nightstand of a preteen Diane embracing Jackie as a toddler. They're considerably younger than in my dreams, but their matching grins and bright blue eyes are unmistakable.

"My baby sister," Diane sings, taking a lock of my hair between her slender fingers. "Do you remember how Mom used to crank up the radio and dance with us? Those were the good days. We were all so happy back then...before she quit coming home at night and left us to fend for ourselves."

I nod somberly. "She liked the oldies."

"Sometimes it was random stuff, like The Oak Ridge Boys and Crystal Gayle."

"I loved it when Crystal Gayle was on *The Muppet Show*," I recall from Jackie's conversation with J.R. about the show.

"You always loved that stupid show," she says, scrunching her nose. Then her shoulders drop and she looks on the verge of tears. "I never should've picked on you for that. I shouldn't have picked on you over a lot of things."

"I still knew you loved me," I assure her, even though I'm suddenly reminded of some of the awful thoughts Jackie had when she feared Diane would steal J.R. from her. *I wish someone would take her next so I'd never have to see her again.* I gently tighten my fingers around her delicate hand. "Diane, what do you remember about the day I went missing?" I half expect to be struck down by lightening for impersonating her sister, but I suspect if she truly believes Jackie has returned, it could be the first bit of comfort she's felt since 1986. "J.R. tells me you were reluctant to call the police at first."

"I was starting to think Mom was involved in something illegal. I knew she'd be pissed if the cops came digging around. There was this creepy guy who kept stopping by, asking for her and wondering when she'd give him his money. One time she was actually home and he threatened to 'take the payment out' on me instead of her. Mom freaked, told me to hide under my bed if he came by again."

A shudder rips through me. "Why don't I remember this guy?"

"He didn't come over until after you met J.R. I didn't say anything because I didn't want to scare you. But I started hanging around with you and J.R. more to make sure you were safe from that guy." Her bird-like features tighten in anger. "Where the hell did you go, Jackie? Do you know how much trouble you caused?"

"I didn't leave willingly, Diane. I would never have done that to you."

Her gaze hardens. "We were better off when Mom never came home, like before. She was a totally different person after you left. I didn't know it was because she was on drugs until J.R.'s dad arrested her for making a fool of herself at that search party the cops arranged for you." With every word she utters about the past, a glimmer of the spunky sister Jackie had known slowly resurfaces. She sits a little taller when she continues and begins gesturing with her hands. "I'll never forget the time that guy came back and I heard them arguing. I snuck into the hallway to spy on them right as Mom slapped him and asked how he could say such a cruel thing when one of her babies was gone." Her teeth flash beneath her tense lips. "He looked her dead in the eye and said she better come up with the cash or he'd take the other one, too."

I let out a stilted breath. Was he claiming responsibility for what happened to Jackie? "Did you tell the police what he'd said?"

"Are you *nuts*?" she snaps. "When I first met him, he pointed a gun at me, threatened to shoot both me and Mom if I ever told anyone about his little visits. He told me he'd done time in prison for dealing and if they tried to send him back, he'd know I must've ratted him out. And he said if they locked him up, he had a powerful friend on the outside who would do anything he asked."

There's a deep ache in my heart knowing that she had to endure the man's threats all on her own. It was maybe even one of the factors that started of her mental decline. Although there doesn't seem to be an obvious connection between this lowlife dealer and the other girls who went missing, he clearly had the means and motive to do something unspeakable to Jackie.

I lovingly rub my fingers across the back of her

hand, wishing there was a better way to offer her something of more comfort. "Do you remember the man's name?"

"No. Mom only referred to him as 'that bastard'. He always had a cigarette dangling from his lips and I never saw him without a cowboy hat or boots, so I called him the Marlboro Man."

"That's good, Diane. You've been really helpful." Even without a name, it's possible Chief Nielsen could locate someone in the system from that timeframe who'd dressed like a cowboy and was on parole for dealing.

An orderly knocks on the door before entering. "Time for your meds, Diane."

As I reach out to embrace the broken woman who has lamented the loss of her little sister for too long, I shed a tear for them both. "I'll come back to visit again soon," I tell her, meaning it with all of my heart.

It's pitch dark when I park my BMW in my driveway. Theo remains still in the passenger's seat, staring at the lights reflected on the closed garage door. We'd grabbed fast food on the way back, but our greasy bags remain untouched on the console between us, and the call I placed to Chief Nielsen the moment we left Diane has yet to be returned.

Theo had listened intently on the drive back as I reiterated my conversation with Diane, but he wasn't equally convinced the drug dealer could've had anything to do with Jackie's disappearance. I sense seeing his old friend in such an advanced state of decline has messed with his head, so I bend over the takeout to kiss his bicep. "Come on, big guy. Let's eat, then take a hot bath together with that bottle of Prosecco my aunt sent back with us."

As I reach for the takeout bags, Theo's strong fingers clamp around my wrist. "The lights were off when we left," he says in a voice that's edged with caution. "I know for damn sure because I double checked."

I scan the house to discover he's right. Every single light inside has been turned on. My pulse pounds with urgency against my eardrums as I turn to survey the street. Although I don't see the navy sedan anywhere, it could still be parked among the deep shadows from the row of massive oak trees lining the curb.

"Should we call the police?" I ask, attempting to keep my voice even.

"Not yet." His demeanor remains calm as his eyes fixate on the house. "Pop the trunk and give me the keys to the front door. If I'm not back out here in five, you can call them."

Every last one of my instincts plead me to tell him it's ill-advised to go inside alone, but I remind myself he trained with the military, and acquiesce with a small nod. As he silently exits the vehicle to dig around inside my trunk, I type 9-1-1 into my phone's keypad, prepared to hit the green phone icon with the slightest hint of trouble.

Guilt for not disclosing the fact that I've been followed weighs heavily on my mind. What if something happens to Theo, and it's discovered the owner of that damn sedan is to blame? What if it's Jackie's killer? I can't imagine anyone else would feel a need to track my whereabouts for any other reason. Stefan, my ex-boyfriend, had no qualms about my move, and it's been months since I last clocked in at the shelter in L.A. If someone from California had issues with me, they certainly would've done something about it while I was still living there.

Theo slips inside the unlocked front door with a crowbar gripped in one hand. I don't dare breathe as his silhouette creeps past the blinds covering the front picture window. The urgent thud of my heart shakes my entire body as I glance down at my phone, confirming he's been inside for under a full minute.

Depending on how long and how often my stalker has been tailing me, they likely know by now that I've met with Chief Nielsen and Diane. They would know I've become close to both Theo and Diane's best friend from high school.

What's most disconcerting is the fact that they likely know my mom's identity, and possibly even that of my aunt. Would they have followed us to California? *Impossible,* I decide. We flew on a private jet. But whoever's keeping tabs on me likely knows by now that I'm the daughter of a famous celebrity, thanks to my mom's unannounced visit the prior week.

I erase the 3 numbers on my phone and navigate to my favorites, intending to warn my mom and aunt to stay alert. As soon as I've told them, I'll run inside and warn Theo next.

With the firm wrap of knuckles on the driver's window, I release a blood-curdling scream and drop my phone between the seats. I frantically reach for my purse, intending to snag my mace when a bright light over my shoulder floods the interior of my car.

"Sorry to scare you, miss," a deep voice rumbles,

slightly muffled through the glass. "Is this the residence of Sterling Pruitt?"

I'm utterly paralyzed by fear.

The voice sounds all too familiar.

The light's extinguished to reveal a man crouched outside my window.

Time has not been kind to the once handsome man. Deep creases line his forehead, hinting of countless worries in the past. Large bags beneath his dark eyes tell the story of a man who's spent the better part of his life hunting criminals.

My stomach folds over itself.

I'm staring into the cold, callous eyes of Theo's father.

23

STERLING - 2018

My short fingernails dig into the steering wheel as I glower back at the evil man who caused Theo endless pain. What is the bastard doing in my driveway? Why is he asking if this is where I live? How did I land on his radar?

Unbridled fear and seething hatred for the man standing in my driveway prevent me from opening the door. Theo has my keys, so I'm also unable to crack the window.

"What kind of car do you drive?" I ask through the glass. Although I doubt Theo's father will confess he's the one who has been stalking me, I hope the element of surprise will be on my side and his reaction will betray him if he's guilty.

"What?" he snaps, frowning and shaking his head.

"Where...is...your...car?" I shout, carefully annunciating each word.

Eyebrows drawn into a sharp V, he points across the street. "I rented the white Suburban parked over there."

I turn in my seat, squinting until I spot a shiny white SUV beneath one of the street lights. Why didn't I see his headlights? How long was he parked there?

"Someone broke into my house," I tell him, raising my voice enough to penetrate the glass barrier between us. I can hardly think straight beyond the frantic drumming of my heart. What if he's the one who broke into my house? *He could be Jackie's killer.* "The police are on their way."

"I'm a retired detective," he says like I appear naive enough to take him for his word and simply open the door. With a scraggly beard the same streaked gray as his short hair and deeply creased civilian clothing, he's a far cry from the proud man in an impeccable suit who'd commanded respect in my dreams. "Are you Sterling Pruitt? I'm looking for my son, Theodore. His neighbor told me he often stays over here with his girlfriend."

"Dammit, Vicky," I whine under my breath, fully aware Theo doesn't speak to anyone else in his

neighborhood. As I'm contemplating how to respond, Theo jogs toward us with an irate expression that could melt steel.

"*The hell* you doing here?" he demands, squaring up directly in front of his father. Not only is Theo of a considerably larger size, he's still gripping the crowbar in one hand. "How'd you know where to find me?"

I swing open my car's door, experiencing a slight lick of satisfaction when the edge slams into the old man's leg and shoves him aside. He should consider himself fortunate to have been struck with a door rather than the weapon I imagine his son would love to use on his skull. I'd be tempted to cheer Theo on if I weren't fearful he'd end up in jail for murder.

I step in between the two men and subtly remove the crowbar from Theo's grip, holding it behind his back as I nudge my way underneath his tense arm.

Theodore, Sr. throws me an irritated look before answering his son. "Your neighbor, Vicky, was kind enough to provide me with this address. Considering you haven't called me in nearly ten years, I assumed the call I'd missed from you yesterday in regards to Jackie Tanner must've been extremely urgent."

"You assumed wrong," Theo growls in return. He

tips his head back at my house. "Did you break into her place?"

His father scowls in a mannerism that reminds me too much of the first time I'd met his son. "Of course not."

"Either way, you're not welcome here," I tell him.

"You're not welcome at my place either," Theo adds, pulling me a little closer to prove we're united. "Go back to whatever hole you've been hiding out in since the government canned your ass."

His father was fired?

Arms crossed over his chest, Theo's father sizes me up with a stern look. "If you don't mind, *young lady*, I'd prefer to speak with my son in private."

In one long stride, I close the distance between us and lift my chin. "Why, so you can knock him around the way you did when he was a vulnerable child?" With his father's shocked expression, I release a maniacal laugh and grasp the crowbar in both hands. Since I have to keep my cool when dealing with abusive clients while on the clock, it feels liberating. "You'll have to get past me first."

Theo tugs me back beneath the shelter of his arm with a strangled chuckle ripping through his throat. "Ease up, Tyson," he whispers against my ear. "Message delivered."

Anger visibly vibrates through his father as I'm stabbed by his steely gaze. "Who in the hell do you think you are, speaking to me that way? Do you have any idea what I could do to you?"

Theo swings his fist, landing it in the center of the old man's face. The sound of bone-on-bone cracks through the air, more satisfying than anything I've ever heard.

Reeling backwards from the blow, his father winces loudly before attending to his nose. I slap both hands over my mouth to stifle my surprised laughter. I'm normally not a fan of violence, but that punch was a long time coming. Both Jackie and I had fantasized about doing it ourselves.

Theo flexes his fist before giving his fingers a gentle shake. "Did you really think I would just stand back and let you threaten the woman I love?" He looks ready to go after his father a second time when he yells, "I'm no longer that scared little boy you used as a punching bag!"

Twinned sirens breach the stillness of the neighborhood, sounding only a handful of blocks away. I toss the crowbar near my feet and bite down on my lips to stop myself from cheering. Not only did Theo finally fight the mean bastard back, he confessed that he loves me.

Theo Davies loves me.

Theo's father stands tall and wipes his bloodied nose on the crook of his elbow. "I guess the police will get to decide who's in the wrong in this situation."

"I called them from inside," Theo tells him with a firm shake of his head. "Someone with a serious vendetta trashed Sterling's home. Unless you want to spend the night answering their questions and explaining the reason you were forced to resign, I'd suggest you get the hell out of here."

The ecstatic high I'd experienced after Theo's declaration of love pops with the force of a needle piercing a balloon. *Someone trashed my house.* We must be getting closer to the truth than any of us realize.

Theo's father darts in the direction of the white Suburban, calling over his shoulder, "If you decide you want to carry on a civilized conversation, you can find me at the Courtyard hotel. I'll be there until Friday afternoon."

"Don't hold your breath," Theo snarls, wrapping his arms around my waist from behind me. As we watch his father drive off into the darkness in the opposite directions as the sirens, Theo's lips press against my head. "After the cops leave, you're coming back to my place where I have access to guns and ammo," he mutters with his lips still nestled in my hair. "We've officially pissed someone off. They left a note saying to 'keep your nose out of things you don't understand'."

Although rattled by the note and annoyed that Theo's carpentry skills may have gone to waste, I'd already suspected the invasion was directly related to our hunt for the killer.

The approaching sirens are nearly deafening when I spin in his arms to face him. "It seems a little convenient your father happened to show up at this exact moment."

"We'll tell the cops where they can find him...let them decide if he's a suspect."

A little smile curls the edges of my lips. "You told him you love me."

"Can you blame me?" With a quiet laugh, he gazes into my eyes with a look so sexy that if I wasn't better educated, I'd worry I was just impregnated. "Sweetheart, I don't take anything lightly. I already had a feeling that's the direction this thing with you was headed, but when you told my old man he'd have to go through you before he got to me, I swear my heart did a somersault."

As two squad cars pull up to the curb, Theo

draws me in for a kiss far too passionate for the officers' eyes. I don't stop him, however, because I'm all at once fearful our time together could be cut short.

I can't stop wondering how far the invader will go to try to stop us.

———

THE NEXT MORNING, Chief Nielsen asks me to stop by to see him at the public safety center before checking in for work. We agreed there's no longer a need to sneak around now that he's officially investigating the break-in. Mere minutes after the two squad cars pulled up to my house, he'd arrived in plain clothes. He spent the better part of two hours cataloging the damage to my house and taking notes as I filled him in on our interactions with Diane and Theo's father, and the instances in which I'd been tailed.

Crossing his arms, the chief settles behind a wide industrial desk. Countless awards and framed pictures of him shaking various dignitaries' hands line a bookcase over his shoulder that's otherwise overflowing with binders. "I ran through the DMV records like you asked," he informs me. "None of the men on your list have a navy blue sedan registered in their name.

That doesn't mean one of them hasn't been driving a stolen car or borrowed something from a friend or family member, and I'm unable to check for any rental charges made to their accounts without a warrant." His brows lift. "However, I was able to confirm both Darrel Heinrich and your Pastor Babel are still living in the area. It's a little odd, because usually ministers move on to another perish after so many years."

Maybe this minister wanted to remain close to his victims' remains. I crack my knuckles, a nervous habit I thought I'd kicked after college. "Have you had a chance to look into Diane's Marlboro Man?"

His eyes are notably shadowed from exhaustion when he nods. "A man by the name of Dicky Peterson fit within the perimeters of my search."

"You've been busy. Did you sleep at all after leaving my place?"

Grunting, he shuffles a small stack of papers on his desk and tosses one out in front of me. "Dicky was released on parole for dealing coke three weeks before Jackie went missing—same drug of choice consumed by Jackie Tanner's mom. His P.O. confirmed he dressed like a cowboy."

"Three weeks," I repeat, scanning over the man's mug shot and long list of drug-related convictions.

"That means he would've been in prison when Becky and the other two girls went missing."

"Doesn't mean he didn't do something to Jackie like you said. He's living up by Brainerd, so his P.O. told me he'd arrange to have someone pay him a visit, see if he can account for his whereabouts last night and if he can produce a solid alibi for the night Jackie went missing. Hard to say what he'll come up with considering it was so long ago."

I shove the paper away as my frustration rises. "What about the note left inside my house? Did you find any fingerprints?"

"The lab tech assured me he'd have it processed before noon. My guess is whoever's trying to rattle your cage is too smart to leave any prints behind. Theo's are probably the only ones we'll find." He leans forward with a thoughtful look. "Speaking of Theo, I got to thinking it over last night and I'm not convinced he shouldn't be on your list of suspects." His eyebrows lift. "Now would be a good time to let me know if you think your boyfriend could be the one behind all of this."

I respond with a humorless laugh. "You think *Theo* would've killed his best friend?"

"He was the last one to see Jackie alive. He could

be lying about how things went down between them that night."

"He's not lying."

"Now, Sterling, I understand how you may have been easily charmed by an older man, but—"

"He's not lying!" I insist, bolting to my feet. I shake his accusation from my thoughts before it festers. "I know he's telling the truth because I was there!"

His shrewd eyes narrow. "We both know that's not physically possible."

"Maybe not, but I've seen things that should also be impossible for me to know, like the fact that you had a mustache the day you arrested Becky Myers's dad, and how you touched the hood of his truck to confirm it was still warm. I saw the terrified look in your eye when Becky's dad spit on you."

He pauses as if to entertain the thought, then shakes his head. "Karrie Schaumberg was there. She could've told you all of this."

"But she didn't have to. I'd already seen it in my dreams just like I witnessed that pastor offering Jackie a ride, her teaching giving her a hard time, and Diane saying she'd heard screams inside Heinrich's shed." I tug at fistfuls of my hair, wishing there was a faster way to make him understand. "I know how crazy it sounds, but I swear I'm not making any of this up. I'm telling you, Chief, one of those men is a monster hiding in plain sight."

There's a sharp knock on the door before a young, bright-eyed female officer in uniform enters. "Sorry to interrupt, Chief, but we have a situation," she tells him, breathless. The officer and I assess each other before she nods and smiles with recognition. "Hi, Sterling."

"Hi, Sierra," I reply with a similar smile as I fondly recall how she'd prevented an angry father from coming after me the previous week. We'd grabbed lunch together after.

"What do you need, Officer Hicks?" Chief Nielsen asks sharply, still eyeing me with skepticism.

"There's a frantic mom at the front desk, demanding to speak with you," Sierra reports. "She claims her eldest daughter was supposed to be watching her younger siblings last night, but they didn't realize until this morning that the twelve-year-old never came home from a friend's house. The mom called the friend, friend says the daughter blew her off to meet someone at Minneopa park. They found the daughter's bike this morning...abandoned on the gravel road leading up to the park's front gate. Her overnight bag was left behind too."

Bile snakes up my throat as I exchange a knowing look with Chief Nielsen.

The circumstances are too similar to ignore.

Either there's a copycat on the loose, or Jackie's killer has struck again, and is taunting us.

Taunting *me*.

24

STERLING - 2018

As I race up the hill toward River Hills Mall, dodging slower cars as if they're standing still, my phone buzzes with an Amber Alert. I don't bothering looking, knowing the emergency alert is in regards to a possible abduction of the 12-year-old girl who'd gone missing at the park. I'd briefly considered calling Theo and asking him to meet me, but Chief Nielsen has planted an ugly seed of suspicion inside my head.

What if Theo isn't grieving over Jackie's disappearance like I've always assumed? What if he's feeling remorse for what he's done? He could've doubled back to the gravel road that night after they'd argued. What if he snapped after Jackie rejected his kiss and channeled the resentment he'd been harboring for his father? Last night he'd unleashed an anger on the old man that seemed beyond his control.

"No way," I tell myself. Theo's involvement wouldn't justify the presence of the navy sedan, or explain how my house had been trashed while Theo was with me at the nursing home. Besides, I've been given more than a brief glimpse of Theo's intentions, and I know his heart to be pure...so pure that I don't want to get him involved in my plan in case one of my theories on the new girl's disappearance is right. By reopening this case, we may have poked an angry bear—or literally reawakened a serial killer. I can't stomach the thought of Theo coming to my rescue and becoming injured...or worse.

My mind races as I accelerate my BMW through a yellow light in front of the entrance to the mall, narrowly escaping getting sideswiped by an angry driver of a pickup truck. I suppose I could apprise K.C. of the situation since she's a full 2-hour drive away. It would be safe to alert her of my where-abouts...just in case. At least she wouldn't get here soon enough to stop me. As I park in front of the hotel among a row of cars, I dial the number she gave me the other night at the pizza parlor.

The moment I hear her intake of breath in preparing to answer, I blurt, "Another twelve-year-old girl in Mankato was just reported as missing, K.C. It was the exact same situation as mine—um, I mean—*Jackie's*. They found her bike and an overnight bag on the gravel road leading up to Minneopa park."

"Oh, shit. I saw the Amber Alert."

"After we returned from visiting Diane and found my house ransacked with a threatening note, Theo's dad just happened to stop by for a visit. I think it's too soon to rule out anyone else as the killer, but the recent turn of events seems too coincidental to *not* be his father. I mean, a girl went missing the same night he returned to Mankato, and he mentioned he hadn't spoken with Theo in a decade. So I'm on my way to ambush the son of a bitch, see if he's even where he told us he'd be. Even if he's innocent, I still have some questions for him related to the girls. I don't want Theo to worry, so I'm only telling you in the event that something happens to me."

"You're going to confront Theo's dad on your own?" She makes an exasperated noise. "That *can't* be a good idea. Theo told me little snippets of what went down last night—he said you were ready to bash his old man's head in with a crowbar." The ding of a car alerting to an open door echos through the phone. "Where are you? I'm already in Kato for a funeral."

"Shit," I hiss, annoyed by the wrench in my plan. "It's too late, I'm already outside his hotel. But in the event I don't check in with Theo in the next hour, he'll know where—"

"Sterling, listen to me," she pleads, her voice all at once thick with emotion. "This déjà vu bullshit is too much for me to handle. You probably know Jackie told me nearly the same thing the night she went missing—to let her sister know if anything happened. I couldn't live with myself if you suffered a similar fate. Theo wouldn't let me live if he knew I didn't try to stop you anyway. So please, I beg of you, tell me where I can meet you and I'll be there just as fast as I can so we're both able to live another day to see Theo ridiculously happy with your weird ass."

I hang my head and sigh. "I'm in the parking lot of the hotel right behind Scheels."

"Perfect. Stay right where you are. I'm just a handful of miles down the road."

The call ends and my phone immediately vibrates with a call from Theo. Staring at his rugged features on the screen, captured in a candid I took one night while we'd snuggled naked in his bed, I reject the call and scold myself for being stupid.

Stupid or cautious?

Although Theo certainly hadn't "charmed" me as Chief Nielsen suggested, I was initially so drawn to him that it would've been almost impossible to simply walk away. But it's not like he sought me out, nor would he have had any way of knowing I had a connection to Jackie. And he was just a kid himself when the four girls were abducted. *A kid with ample insider information because of his father's involvement with law enforcement.*

The biggest flaw in Chief Nielsen's suggestion is glaringly obvious—Theo was with me from the moment I got off work last night until we crawled into bed at his place a little before midnight. But I slept hard, not stirring until my alarm went off this morning. And it's not clear if they know an exact time the girl went missing. For all I know, it was late afternoon.

Unable to entertain such ridiculous thoughts any longer, I spring out of my car and start for the entrance of the hotel.

"Oh no you don't!" I hear, turning to find K.C.'s

head protruding from the window of the light blue Bronco from the other night. Without taking her eyes off me, she parks in an open space two down from my BMW and jumps out, slamming her door. In a black tank top that shows off her brightly colored tattoo sleeves, black jeans and combats boots, oodles of necklaces, and ponytail styled in a Mohawk fashion, she may very well be my new favorite fashion icon. "You were told to wait for me, young lady."

"I waited!" I snap, half stomping toward the hotel's entrance. She hurries ahead and holds the door open with a smug look, motioning for me to enter.

The college-aged woman behind the front desk gathers her luscious blond hair behind one shoulder and flutters her false eyelashes. The poor girl looks utterly exhausted, as if it's physically hurting her to sit upright. Her eyes flinch when she plasters on a wide smile. "Good afternoon, ladies! What can I do for you today?"

"We're here to see Theodore Davies." I say.

Her light green eyes flicker back and forth between us. "Us, as in...?"

"As in he's expecting us," K.C. clarifies, slipping a

hand inside her back jeans pocket to produce a $100 bill. She holds it precariously beneath her fingertips on the desk between her and the younger girl. "When did your shift start?"

The receptionist's eyes widen on the bill before she glances over each of her shoulders. "I'm on the tail end of a double," she tell us with a snarl. "I've been here since five last night."

"Were you here when Mr. Davies checked in?" I ask.

"Yeah," she snorts, her eyes all at once dull. "He was a total prick. Talked down to me like I was five."

I snort in a similar way. *If she only knew.* "Do you remember what time he checked in?"

"It was just a few minutes after I got here. He was my first guest of the night."

"Did you see him leave the hotel again at any point?" I ask, vaguely wondering if I should've insisted Chief Nielsen or one of his officers accompany me on this mission. What if there's a glaringly obvious question I forget to ask?

The blonde bobs her head in confirmation. "He went out for a short while right before it got dark, like for half an hour, then he came back and ordered dinner at the bar. He got *super* wasted and refused to leave at closing. The bartender had to call security to help drag him up to his room. He took a swing at the security guard—one of State's star football players. It wasn't pretty."

If he was only gone for half an hour, it would've been just long enough to stop by my place. A round trip to Minneopa would've taken an extra 40 minutes minimum, and that's not taking a kidnapping into consideration. "Did he leave again after that?"

"I haven't seen him again since. The security guard said he'd passed out cold before he'd left the room." Her eyes flicker back to K.C.'s bribe. "But some guy came to see him a little bit ago. He's still up there."

K.C. and I exchange a glance. "What did the guy look like?" I ask.

Her eyebrows wiggle. "Bearded dude...super fit and crazy hot, but kinda old and a bit cranky."

Cramps of worry spread through my stomach. "Was he wearing tan cargo jeans and a plain black t-shirt?"

"That sounds right."

"What's the room number?" I demand with urgency.

Her long, manicured fingernails snag the bill from K.C.'s fingers and she gives K.C. a sideways look. "Hmmm…I'm not sure I remember."

Rolling her eyes, K.C. retrieves a twenty from her other back pocket and throws it onto the desk. "That's all I have, you conniving little shrew. *What's the number?*"

The receptionist grabs the twenty and sticks it into her pants pocket along with the hundred before throwing K.C. a satisfied smile. "Five ten."

K.C. and I race to the elevators where I repeatedly stab the up arrow button. "Theo might not be able to contain his anger for him on his own," I say to her.

"Probably the reason he came here without telling you," K.C. agrees, nodding with a distant look. "Either that or he saw the Amber Alert and came to the same conclusion as you."

"He tried calling me a few minutes ago," I admit. "But there's no way he made it here that soon after the alert was issued. I was already halfway here when it went off."

The elevator doors open with a ding and we simultaneously step into the empty car. I bite my lip as K.C. presses the number 5 and the doors close.

She tilts her head. "Why are you looking at me like that?"

"Earlier this morning, Chief Nielsen said something ridiculous that I can't erase from my thoughts. In my heart I know it can't be true, especially because I've spent so much time inside Jackie's head, but the logical side of me that knows sociopaths are skilled at hiding in plain sight can't stop processing the facts." Eyes locked with hers, I let out a stuttered sigh. "Do you think there's any chance in hell Theo would've done something to Jackie?"

Right as she opens her mouth, the elevator dings and the doors open. Theo and his father stand waiting on the other side. Their reactions of surprise are nearly identical, giving me a new sense of unease. *How many of his father's undesirable traits did Theo inherit?*

"What are you two doing here?" Theo asks, taking on a cautious posture.

I'm unable to form a coherent answer once I get a good look at his father's face. In addition to a swollen nose and the start of two black eyes, a deep cut slashes through his bottom lip and another slices parallel with one of his eyebrows. Confusingly enough, the wounds are as congealed as the damage Theo inflicted upon his nose.

Theo notices my expression and grunts, "Wasn't me. He went a round with hotel security."

"They're fools if they don't think I'll sue," his father grumbles, glancing off into the empty hallway.

As K.C. holds the doors to prevent them from closing, I bite down on a smirk, wishing I'd been there to watch. "Why are *you* here?" I ask Theo.

His lips twist with a scowl. "Wanted a chance to tell him about your theories, see what he had to say."

"And?" K.C. asks, eyeing his father.

Theodore, Sr. raises his chin. "I'm headed downtown to speak with Chief Nielsen."

"He remembered Pastor Babel drove a blue four-door back in the day," Theo explains. "It was registered under the church's non-profit corporation."

A brief flash of Jackie's memories returns to the night she went missing. "That wasn't the same kind of vehicle," I say with a firm shake of my head. "They were different shades of blue, and the pastor's car was already old back then. The one that's been following me is maybe only a few years old."

"How would you know what he drove in eighty-six?" his father sneers with arrogance.

"Wait for me in the lobby," Theo tells him, his tone sharp with malice. "I'll be down in a few." He then takes my hand and leads me out from the elevator. I flinch from his warm grip, tempted to pull away even though it sounds as if he's genuinely trying to aid in the search for my stalker.

"Come on, K.C.," I call to our friend, knowing she also can't be trusted alone with the abusive prick any more than the rest of us. She steps out of the elevator, casting Theodore, Sr. a deadly glare. The three of us watch him step inside, not moving a muscle until the doors close in his face.

"I really wish you still had that crowbar," K.C. says, flashing a middle finger at the doors.

I turn to Theo. "You know about the missing local girl?"

"The alert went off while I was with my old man in his room," he confirms with a nod.

"I don't think he could've taken her, even though it's strange that he happened to pick the same night to return. Sounds like he came back here after he left my place, then proceeded to get wasted before passing out for the night. The woman at the front desk kept a close eye on him after he checked in." I rest my hand on his chest, telling myself he's still the man I fell in love with and isn't capable of anything dark. "The girl that went missing—Theo, her circumstances were almost identical to Jackie's. Either someone's trying to send us a message, or we've made the killer nostalgic."

Theo grunts in response and digs inside his pocket. My throat goes dry when his shirt inches upward with the movement, revealing the grip of a handgun tucked into his jeans. He removes a folded piece of paper from his pocket and holds it up between us. "My old man called a buddy still with the bureau, got the addresses for the pastor and Darrel Heinrich. You may not be able to convince Chief Nielsen to act on what you know, but we can tail them for a while...see what they're up to."

Belatedly, I remember there's one thing Theo failed to mention in our conversation with Chief Nielsen the night before. I stroke my hands over his t-shirt. "Why was your father fired?"

He releases a deep sigh. "A handful of years back, he pulled a crucial suspect over in a kidnapping case, let him go without making an arrest."

"Did he say *why* he let him go?" K.C. asks.

"No, but there was an internal investigation." His gaze darkens as it falls back on mine, filled with an air of distress. "They found the suspect's abandoned car half an hour later with a little girl's body in the backseat. She'd been dead for hours, and there wasn't anything to suggest she'd been anywhere other than in that back seat, in plain sight." His eyes shift away. "The bureau believed my old man knew she'd been there when he'd pulled the suspect over."

The whirl of a state patrol helicopter buzzes high above my BMW as Theo and I continue to monitor the minister's little rambler on the north side of Mankato. The quaint house with a one-stall garage is outdated and rather modest compared to the other homes in the neighborhood, most of which are at least two stories high and feature 2-3 garage doors. We'd seen movement in front of the bay window after we first parked and haven't witnessed anything since.

Theo's father had told him that the minister has been a widower for three years and now lives alone. For whatever reason, Theodore, Sr. seemed convinced the elderly minister was involved despite the discrepancies in vehicles. I'm convinced we're wasting our time, and worry I won't have a job by the end of the day. When I'd called Megan to let her know I had a personal emergency that needed my attention, I detected a trace of disappointment in her tone. After all, I had called in sick last Friday. Maybe she's starting to think I'm not as valuable of an employee as she'd first thought.

From the corner of my eye, I watch Theo shift around in the passenger's seat, clearly uncomfortable from sitting for so long. At first I was a little reluctant to be alone with him, especially knowing he's carrying a deadly weapon, but he refused to allow me to conduct the surveillance without him, and K.C. was okay with tailing Darrel Heinrich on her own. Before we'd parted ways in the hotel parking lot, she'd patted me on the backside and assured me I had nothing to worry about. From the determined gleam in her eye as she held my stare for a beat longer, I sense it was a delayed answer to my question of Theo's involvement.

The explanation behind Theodore, Sr.'s dismissal from the police force hasn't sat right with me ever since Theo disclosed the details. Although Theo had told me his father vehemently denied the allegation, Theo agreed the circumstances were unsettling.

I drum my fingers on the steering wheel. There's so much I still don't know about Theo's family and his childhood. "When you met Jackie, you told her that your father had brought you *back* to Mankato." I turn to him, eyes narrowed. "How long did you live here the first time?"

"When I met Jackie that *was* my first time living here," he clarifies with a slow shake of his head. "My old man was born and raised in Mankato. He met my mom in Connecticut while he was attending a police academy and she was going to college nearby. I was born there, then we moved around a few times after that."

"Did you meet any of his friends after he moved you here?"

He lets out a curt laugh. "Not sure he had any. I get the feeling he was a loner as a kid. He wasn't into sports or clubs."

"How old is he now?"

"Sixty-something, I guess." He grunts, clearly irritated. "Don't really know, don't really care."

"Can you at least guess?"

"Probably closer to seventy. My parents were both young when they had me...maybe twenty, twenty-one."

After doing a little math in my head, I pull up a

web browser on my phone and type in "Mankato high school 1969." I receive over a million results, the very first of which is a website created for the class of 1969's upcoming 50th reunion and includes a link that lists the classmates' names. I scroll down to the 'D's and promptly locate Theodore, Sr. When I click on his name, I'm asked to create a login profile.

I rub circles into one of my temples, sensing there's more behind the old man's history that Theo doesn't know. "What about hunting? Was he into that?"

What I'd really like to know is if he had any kind of obsession with dead animals.

"Couldn't tell you, but I remember him once mentioning that people around here take deer hunting season seriously. Now that I live here, there's no denying he was right." His fingers begin to toy with the end of my side braid resting on my shoulder. "Listen, sweetheart. I get that you're worried about this girl, but you've been...distant. If you're afraid of me after I punched my old man, you should know I've never hit a woman, never will. I'd let one beat me to death before I'd raise a hand."

I close my eyes, sensing with every bit of my soul that he's speaking the truth. "I trust you," I say quietly. "It's just—"

"Hold on," he grunts. "The minister's garage door is opening."

We silently watch as a slender, gray-haired man in a cardigan sweater who possesses a hunched back and wears wire-rimmed glasses lugs a black trash bag from the door separating the house from the attached garage. Behind a shiny red crossover, he drops the bag at his feet and leans against the trunk, panting.

"What if that's a body?" I ask Theo, nauseated by the thought. Before I've turned to him, he's out the passenger's door and crossing the road. Swearing under my breath, I spring from my car and run to catch up.

"Sir, that bag looks heavy," Theo calls out from the edge of the sidewalk. "We were walking by and saw you struggling. Can I help you lift it into your trunk?"

The man's eyes glisten with a sweet smile, producing a network of wrinkles that deepen across his face. "That would be mighty kind of you, young man. Thank you." He shuffles away from the trunk and starts for the passenger's door. "I'll pop the trunk."

It's difficult to envision the elderly minister as anything other than a caring man, especially considering how many times he'd offered to help Jackie. I'm beginning to sense Theo's prior aversion to him had more to do with the fact that Theo was simply weary of religion as a kid.

Exchanging a similar look of doubt, Theo and I advance inside the garage. Garden tools hang from an organizer beside the vehicle and a few plastic tubs are piled on the far end, otherwise the space is barren. It's immaculate with floors so shiny that I'm surprised the minister parks his crossover inside.

The trunk releases with with a dull click as Theo bends to retrieve the bag, massaging the contents with both hands.

"My sister came over and helped me go through my wife's things," the minister explains as he comes back around to join us. "I've been putting off a trip to the salvation store."

Theo throws me a look that promises nothing sinister is inside the bag when he drops it into the spotless trunk. "Wait for them to come help you unload this at the store. Must be several dozen books in here."

"My sweet Tabby was an avid reader," the minister digresses with another fond smile. "She mostly enjoyed religious non-fiction, but there were a few romance novels sprinkled among them."

The minister shades his eyes with a liver-spotted hand to watch the helicopter whiz past again. "What on earth are they doing? They've been buzzing around for hours."

"They're searching for a missing young girl," I say, stopping to gauge his reaction.

The wrinkles on his face stretch with his frown. "Another local girl is missing?"

"My mom's pretty upset over it," I tell him with a sullen nod. "She said it reminds her of when she was young and Jackie Tanner went missing."

After a moment, he covers his face with his hands before a loud sob slips from his lips. "I'm sorry...I'm so, so sorry! I can only hope God will forgive me!"

There's no way, I think with a bolt of shock. He couldn't have kidnapped that girl last night. I doubt he could carry a gallon of milk. Theo's eyes widen on mine as if he's thinking the same thing.

"I should've insisted on giving that poor Tanner girl a ride that night!" the old man cries. "I'm a mandated reporter! I should've called law enforcement and let them know something was amiss! Had I done something, she would've been safe and sound!"

I wrap my arm around him in a side embrace, partially relieved yet mostly unsurprised. He's too feeble to have recently overpowered a 12-year-old, and he's clearly still distraught about Jackie. He may have been a bit strange back in the day, but he's no killer.

"I'm sorry to have upset you," I say, giving his geriatric bones a light squeeze before releasing him. "It sounds like a lot of people who knew Jackie are upset they couldn't have done more to save her." I eye Theo with a sympathetic smile. "You're certainly not alone in feeling that way."

The minister removes his glasses to wipe his wet eyes on his sweater sleeve. "That's alright, child. I imagine Jackie's in the Lord's loving hands by now." He sets his glasses back on his nose before he pats Theo's elbow. "Thank you again for your kindness. I hope you both have a lovely day."

We both tell him goodbye before Theo takes my hand. As we descend the driveway and re-enter the quiet street, I release a heavy breath and slip my hand out from his. "That went the way I imagined. There's no way he's involved. At least not with the newest abduction."

Theo gives me an agreeable nod. "We should meet up with K.C., see if she's had any luck." He gently nudges my arm. "Give me the keys. I'll drive."

I pass the fob over and slip into the passenger's side, grabbing my phone before securing my seatbelt. The website from Theodore, Sr.'s reunion is still up when I wake the screen. I scroll through it again, freezing with the sight of a familiar name.

I blink several times to make sure I'm truly seeing the teacher's name and not imagining things. "Your father graduated with Jackie's teacher, Elroy Kabe." My eyes slide over to Theo. "Did you know that?"

"He never mentioned it." He leans back, frowning. "You sure?"

"I found a website for your father's upcoming reunion and both of their names are listed."

Before he can respond, my phone vibrates with a call from Chief Nielsen. I raise a finger to let Theo know I'll be a minute.

"Did you find her?" I ask the chief.

"Not yet. I wanted to let you know the fire department received a call about a burning vehicle near the industrial parks downtown. It was a 2014 Acura, navy blue. I'm sending you a picture now."

Another vibration of my phone alerts me to a new text. I check the screen, dismissing the low battery warning, and find a picture of a half charred sedan. The earth drops beneath my feet. "That's it," I whisper. "That's the car that was following me."

Theo grips my hand, his expression tight with concern.

"Where's Theo's father?" Chief Nielsen asks.

"I-I don't know. We haven't seen him since we left his hotel a few hours ago."

The chief lets out an exasperated grunt. "Seems awfully convenient he came in here, hellbent on pinning the abductions on the minister because of a car he drove all those years ago, and hours later the car you ID'd was destroyed. I don't remember much about working with Detective Davies back in the day, but something is definitely off now. He seemed to have a hard time reeling in his anger, like you said. I looked into his dismissal with his last precinct and have a bad feeling overall about the guy."

I whimper in agreement as my stomach twists into knots. *Theo may be the son of a serial killer.*

"Is Theo with you?" he asks.

"Yes," I say.

"Is he carrying?" The two men had discussed protection after the break-in, and Theo had assured him that he had a permit to carry along with five years of training with the military.

"Yes," I confirm with fading trepidation.

"Good. Go somewhere safe—somewhere Theo's father wouldn't think to look for you. I'm sending out an APB on him. I'll let you know when we have him in custody."

A rush of anxiety tightens my spine. Will Theo's father come after us because he knows we're too close to the truth? "Okay."

"Sterling," the chief says, his voice edged with a hint of reluctance, "I don't know where you could've possibly been going with that strange conversation we had this morning about the things you witnessed firsthand, but I sense your theories are spot-on. We're going to nail this asshole, and bring little Abigail home. Maybe we'll finally give the others a chance to rest in peace, too."

Once he ends the call, I slowly lower my phone to my lap.

"What'd he say?" Theo demands. "Did they figure out who broke into your house?"

"Someone tried to destroy the car that's been following me." I link my fingers through his as I meet his hopeful expression. "Chief Nielsen is convinced your father is somehow involved."

His Adam's apple rises and falls with a hard swallow. "I feel like a fool." His eyes squeeze shut. "I believed he was only angry with me and didn't have the traits of a killer."

He's not the only one who feels like a fool. "Babe, you can't shoulder the blame for his actions any more than you can accept responsibility for Jackie's abduction." I bring the back of his hand up to my mouth, pressing my lips firmly against it with remorse for once suspecting him spreading through my heart like cancer. If he finds out how much I doubted him, I might lose him forever.

I add, "Besides, we could still be wrong." What else could I possibly say? I'm convinced that Chief Nielsen is right, and we have our man cornered.

Lowering his hand, I unsuccessfully attempt to muster a smile. "The chief wants us to lay low for a while until they bring your father in for questioning. Let's regroup with K.C. and head somewhere to eat."

He responds with a doleful nod. As he steers my car onto the paved road, I call K.C. It rings straight into her voicemail, so I send a text.

CHIEF NIELSEN THINKS *Theo's dad is the killer. They're searching for him. Stay put, we're coming to you.*

. . .

THERE'S a long pause before three dots appear, indicating she's typing. As my phone vibrates with her reply, I become lightheaded.

SHOWS HOW LITTLE YOU KNOW. You should've kept your nose out of this like I told you.

26

STERLING - 2018

lthough Theo exceeds the speed limit by double digits, the drive to the southwest edge of the city where Darrel Heinrich lives feels agonizingly slow. "It can't be K.C.," I tell Theo for what must be the third or fourth time as I check to ensure I haven't received any new messages from her. My phone beeps with an alert, letting me know less than 5% of the battery life remains. "She's been advocating for those girls forever. Someone must've done something to her and taken her phone."

"You don't have to convince me, sweetheart," Theo seethes, cutting off a mini van at our final turn. "But they want us to think it isn't my old man. Who else could it be?"

"It has to be Heinrich. She was sitting outside his house."

Why else would Jackie's memories keep returning to the man from the skating rink? I refuse to believe I was meant to relive her final days on repeat for nothing. She must've known her killer. Whether she's channeling me because I was her in another life, or she's sending me a message some other way, I have to believe it's my purpose in life to solve her murder.

Theo points out the windshield to where K.C.'s empty vehicle is parked in the grass ditch beside a corn field. "There's her Bronco."

My heart sinks when noticing the driver's door was left ajar. Was she ambushed while sitting inside?

We're essentially in the middle of nowhere on a gravel road a few miles off Highway 169, near a yard overtaken by scrub oaks and weeds. In the thick of it, I spot a worn-down farmhouse that I would guess was built in the prior century. One of its widows on the second floor is broken in shards, and the front screen door hangs from one hinge. The house is a mottled gray with spots of chipped white paint clinging with abandon. It emits serious horror movie vibes that I'm unable to shake.

"Is this seriously the address?" I ask Theo, certain K.C. had parked in the wrong place.

He shows me the map on his phone. "I guess so." Then his eyes drift over to the house. "You really think Heinrich lives here?"

"Maybe he got spooked when the police suspected him, and decided to live off the grid." I open the passenger's door of my car. "I'm going to check in K.C.'s Bronco to see if her phone is still in there."

As Theo parks the car behind me, I jog over to the classic SUV, alarmed to discover the keys nestled beneath the driver's door in the ankle-deep grass. I bend to retrieve them and the cup of coffee I had for breakfast nearly comes back up.

Blood covers the sharp tip protruding from a metal ring attached to the keychain—something I'd almost purchased once in a self-defense store in L.A.

What has happened to our friend? My mind races with the possibilities. What if it's *her* blood on the ring?

Sliding my phone from my pocket, I send Chief Nielsen a pin of my location, then a text.

. . .

I KNOW *you told us to lay low, but we had to check on K.C. first. We have valid reasons to believe someone took her.*

THERE'S ONLY a brief pause before he replies.

WHAT IN THE hell was she doing there?

I QUICKLY TYPE out my response while eyeing the red battery on the corner of my screen.

THEO'S FATHER gave us this address, said it's where Heinrich lives. But I'm not so sure. House looks abandoned.

SECONDS after I've hit the sent button, my phone's screen turns black. "Shit," I huff, slipping the dead phone into my pocket. I can only hope the message sent in time.

As Theo heads my way, I hold K.C.'s bloodied

little weapon out for him to see. "I found this discarded in the grass. She must've put up a fight."

"Dammit!" He fists his hair and spins around slowly, eyes sweeping across the landscape. Beyond the vibrant green fields of flourishing crops, there isn't another acreage for miles. "Wait a minute, I know this area. I sometimes go cross-country skiing through this field. We aren't too far from Minneopa park."

Visions of Darrel Heinrich kidnapping those girls at the park and disposing of their bodies somewhere nearby has my bladder threatening to let loose. If this truly is his property, how long has he owned it? Does he still own the house in town? I try to imagine Jackie standing in this same spot, or maybe even being carried inside, and a tear slips down my cheek. If only my dreams had gone beyond her capture...we wouldn't be plagued with so many questions and uncertainties.

Unease creeps down my spine with a new thought, making me shiver. I grip Theo's arm as the earth wobbles beneath my feet. "What if your dad didn't really write down Heinrich's address? What if he tricked us into coming here for a different reason?"

The troubled look Theo gives me when he wordlessly flicks my tear away with his knuckle only increases my growing discontent. "Stash those keys by the gas cap in case someone else comes along. Careful not to touch the blood—could be evidence. I'm gonna take a look inside the house."

"I'm coming with," I say, although I secretly have no desire to enter the decrepit building to find out what diabolical things may be lurking if K.C.'s not inside. "I'm not going to sit here and wait to be taken next."

Theo nods firmly as he takes my hand. "Wouldn't want you anywhere else."

As we approach the old house, my dress pants snag on cockleburs and my short heels dig into the soft earth. The thought of having to run from someone makes it harder to breath in the sweet aroma of weeds and the bitterness of dirt. When we climb the two front steps at the same time, the deck's worn floorboards groan from the pressure, threatening to snap.

Theo removes the handgun from his waistband with one hand and grips the side of my head with the other. His gaze is fiercely protective as it holds mine. "Stay right behind me...hold onto my shirt. If we hear anything unusual, hit the floor as fast as you can. Got it?"

Fear of what we're about to find prevents me from answering, so I simply nod. His lips press against mine, then we're on the move. Despite his subtle efforts, the ancient screen door and the faded green door behind it squeal on their hinges when we enter.

The interior of the house isn't as shabby as I'd been expecting, and has quite obviously been lived in for some time. Beneath a yellowed mirror framed in chipped silver, an oak bench painted a cheery shade of yellow occupies a small parlor with a pair of men's workbooks tucked underneath. I nudge Theo, pointing to the fresh dirt surrounding the boots. His jaw clenches when he nods.

Motioning for me to follow, Theo grips his gun in both hands, aiming it straight ahead. We advance through a door opening on the left, finding a small kitchen where a dirty frying pan, plate, and fork wait to be washed beside a porcelain sink. The faint aroma of fried bacon causes my stomach to growl with envy. A folded newspaper occupies a small round table rimmed in metal with two chairs on either side. Other than the newspaper and dirty dishes, the kitchen is bare. I tug on Theo's shirt, leading him over to the table.

Today's date is printed on *The Free Press*.

Two paneled doors flank either side of the kitchen. Theo crosses over to the first with me hot on his tail and cracks it open enough to reveal a pantry with only a few boxed items and cans of soup. He turns back to face me right as there's a loud thud somewhere behind us. I lean into him, clinging to his arm with all my strength.

"Wait for me in there," he whispers, nudging me toward the pantry door. "Stay low and don't come out until I say it's clear."

My limbs tremor with every rapid beat of my heart as I slip into the dark pantry. The heavy door creaks shut, blocking my view of Theo heading into the next room. Thick dust fills my lungs with every sharp, panic-ridden inhale. I fumble to retrieve my phone from my pocket for the flashlight, belatedly remembering it's dead. My trembling fingers send it clattering down onto the rustic wooden floor. Wincing, I bend to retrieve it and inadvertently push my backside against the wall of shelves behind me.

The wall moves.

A warm golden light fills the pantry, revealing a set of rickety stairs behind me that descend into darkness.

"That's a whole lotta nope," I decide quietly.

There's no way in hell I'm going down there without Theo.

A racket comes from somewhere beyond the kitchen—possibly hurried steps and something or someone falling. I wrap my arms around my trembling body, terrified I'll hear a gunshot next. Attempting to fight against a rush of tears, I hold my breath as I eagerly wait for Theo to return.

The sound of a female whimpering drifts up from the stairway behind me.

K.C.

Adrenaline courses through my blood, sending me tiptoeing down the nefarious stairway without another thought. If my friend is in trouble, I have to act. With every step I take, it becomes a little harder to breathe in the musty air. When my foot comes into contact with a cement floor, I pause to let my eyesight adjust to the dim light.

In the center of a cement room thick with cobwebs and dirt, K.C.'s gaged and bound to an antique chair. Blood smears her face, running down her neck. Her head hangs limp, along with the rest of her body.

Please don't be dead, I think with pain spreading through my chest.

"K.C.," I whisper. "We're here, K.C. Theo's upstairs. Can you hear me?"

I release a slow, quiet breath when her head finally lulls from side to side. Then her chin drags upward and her eyelids lift with great difficulty. A low moan rips from her throat, absorbed by the rag stuffed inside her mouth.

Either she's been drugged or badly injured. Maybe both.

"It's going to be okay," I promise, starting for her.

From somewhere in the shadows behind her, a deep voice sniggers. "That's where you're wrong. Again."

A blow to the back of my head sends me spiraling into darkness.

I COME BACK around with the sound of male voices arguing. Everything's muffled like I'm hearing them through a thick wall, and there's a high-pitched ringing vibrating against my eardrums.

"Who in the hell is that girl? How does she know so much?"

"Far as I can tell she's just some kid who moved here from California to work for Human Services.

She's the daughter of April Marie, the actress. I haven't a clue how she knows things except she's been hanging around this other one, asking questions and digging into the past."

"Great. So if she goes missing, her rich bitch of a mother will come here and raise a fuss, attracting the attention of the entire nation? Why exactly did you bring these two women *here*?"

"They were too close to the truth. I thought it was necessary to shut them up before you ended up serving the rest of your life in prison. She'd spotted you following her around and reported it to that incompetent chief."

"Wouldn't just be me going down, you know. You may not have been equally involved in the beginning, but you were the one who orchestrated things with the Thompson and Tanner girls."

"That's exactly why I came back! Someone had to ensure the past stayed buried!"

"Everything fell apart the moment you nabbed the wrong Tanner sister. The older one would've been much easier to control. Once you got our ol' pal, Dicky, to start selling drugs to their mom, Diane was ripe for the taking. She was too afraid to speak out. We could've kept going if you hadn't taken that mouthy little brat instead. There's no way I was going to take another girl after she nearly exposed us."

"I'm not the one who grew up dissecting family pets as a favorite pastime. I was perfectly content with not doing it again."

"Don't lie to yourself. You got off on getting away with taking those girls just as much as I did. I recall you being the one who volunteered to dig their graves out back."

"That's only because I'd witnessed the piss-poor job you'd done after your first kill in high school. If I hadn't coached you, you would've been locked away before your balls dropped."

Vomit blazes up from my stomach, creating a sour taste in my throat.

The two men are confessing to murdering Jackie and the others—maybe even more.

Every bone in my body aches as I flex my limbs against the concrete floor. At least nothing feels broken.

My head throbs as I attempt to lift it and clear the groggy cloud from my thoughts. From the musty smell that fills my lungs when I attempt a deep breath, I decide I must still be in the farmhouse basement even though I'm unable to see anything.

Goosebumps ripple over my skin as I remember finding K.C. tied to a chair.

Someone struck me.

With a start, I remember Theo was with me upstairs.

Is he the one who knocked me out from behind?

"No," I whimper with tears burning behind my closed eyelids. I refuse to believe the man I love is one of the men speaking in the other room. "No!"

"Did you hear that?" one of the men snaps.

"I didn't hear anything."

"She's already awake! Now we have three bodies to contend with in addition to the girl. What a disaster! What are you planning to do now?"

"Keep a close eye on that door and make sure it stays locked," the other one commands. "I'm going upstairs to make sure my son's still heavily sedated. We'll figure out what to do when I get back."

Theodore, Sr.

This time there's no holding back the hot tears that rush down my cheeks. *Thank God.* Theo's still alive and blissfully unaware of everything I've heard. But he'll be devastated when he learns of his father's involvement.

What are they planning to do to Theo? To all of us?

"Lady, you have to be quiet," a young girl's voice snaps somewhere beside me.

My heart slips into my throat. "Abigail?" I ask, sucking in a gasp.

"Play dead and they'll leave you alone," she tells me in a hushed tone. "At least one of them will. He likes it when you fight back."

"I'm going to get you out of here," I promise, praying that K.C. and Theo are still okay. "I won't let them hurt you."

With the sound of a squeaking door hinge, I remain perfectly still and close my eyes against the pale light.

Feet shuffle over the concrete by my head. I've convinced myself they're going to be satisfied that I'm still out and leave again just moments before a set of fingers press against my neck beside my windpipe.

A heavy sigh rustles my hair before the fingers sweep up my skin, stopping to caress my jaw. Then my lips.

"Beautiful," a deep voice rasps.

With a strong bout of nausea, I strike the palm of my hand toward the voice, satisfied when it lands beneath a jaw as intended. In the faint light I'm able to see a man writhing on the ground in pain.

"Come on, Abigail," I say, scanning my gaze across the dark room. "Let's get the hell out of here."

"Behind you!" she yells.

A terrifyingly familiar face fills my vision just moments before the sharp bite of a needle pierces my neck. This time, instead of drifting off into total darkness, I'm launched back to 1986.

27
JACKIE - 1986

My muscles ache from shivering. At least my breath provides little bursts of heat every time it soaks into the cloth tied around my mouth.

Flashes of J.R.'s dad grabbing me in the park and holding something over my mouth until everything went dark makes my eyes burn, but I've cried so much already that I'm out of tears.

Did his dad take J.R., too? Is he somewhere in the darkness along with me?

What is his dad going to do? Is he punishing me for being friends with his son?

My hands hurt from where they're tied together with rope, but my feet are free to move. The ground is as hard as a rock beneath my butt. I must be in a building. But where? How long have I been here? Why is it so cold if I'm inside?

A faint light shines near my feet with the squeak of a door.

Footsteps pound against wooden steps.

I scramble away from the footsteps until my shoulders hit a wall.

As my eyes take in the tall man with clear-framed glasses heading toward me, my stomach cramps like it does when I have the flu.

He belongs in the classroom with a piece of chalk in his hand, not in this dark, dirty place.

What is Mr. Kabe doing here?

As I stare at my teacher's face, my fears begin to melt away. He has to be here to save me. After all he's *a teacher*.

His eyes pop wide in shock. "Jackie?"

"Help!" I cry as best as I can with the cloth wedged between my lips. "Help me!"

Throwing his fists into the air, Mr. Kabe roars, "No! That imbecile!"

Fear tightens my stomach as he paces back and forth, mumbling to himself. Why is he mad? Why isn't he helping me?

He eventually stops pacing and stares back at me, combing his fingers through his dark hair over and over. "You need to understand this isn't my fault. It was never supposed to be you, Jackie. I've had my eye on your sister for years. I was looking forward to her company."

I shake my head, confused.

"This is a rather sticky conundrum, I'm afraid," he says. "I can't exactly let you go free now that you've seen both me and Teddy, now can I?"

The truth behind his words are like a sword cutting through my middle.

He's not here to save me.

He starts pacing again, talking in a voice so quiet I almost can't hear when he's saying. "I knew I never should've agreed to let him in on this. He was so excited when he realized I'd taken the Myers girl and still taught her classmates every day. I could've told him no, but he would've sent me to prison and continued taking girls without me. I couldn't let him get by with that either."

He stops in front of me and squats down to my level. "Oh, Jackie. We both know you were never one of my favorite students, but it still pains me to have to do this."

When he reaches for me, I draw both of my legs against my chest then shoot them outward like a spring. The heel of my sneaker catches him in the jaw, sending him down on his back with a surprised cry. I jump to my feet and race past him, climbing the stairway with the speed of a rabbit.

I'm in the kitchen of a really old house.

I keep moving until I find a front door. I hear Mr. Kabe yelling my name as I burst out the door and into the cold night.

I run.

I was never a fast runner, but knowing my teacher wants to hurt me provides me with a sudden boost of speed. It's still hard with my hands tied together, but I have a sick feeling I might be running for my life.

A gathering of trees come into view against the dark sky, and I hear the steady pounding of water on rocks. My heart swells with joy.

I'm by Minneopa!

The faraway sound of voices and laughter echoes through the air—probably a group of older kids that snuck into the park to drink beer.

I tug on the cloth around my mouth until it loosens enough to speak. "Help me!" I cry out, my voice sore and scratchy. "He's going to hurt me!"

The sounds of their party continue on. My voice is too weak and I'm too far away for them to hear.

"Over here!" I try a little louder, stumbling

toward the glow of a campfire. "I'm here! Please, help!" The tip of my shoe catches on a tree root and I drop to the ground with a sharp pain shooting through my ankle. My heart beats so hard it hurts.

"If you know what's good for you, you won't yell for help again," Mr. Kabe warns, his voice sharp with danger and way too close by. "Did you really think you could run from me, Jackie?"

I try to stand, but when I put weight on my injured ankle, I'm sent back down to the ground.

As I'm dragged away by the monster who'd been hired to teach children, I close my eyes, remembering the first time I'd laid eyes on J.R. on the river bank nearby.

Thick, sandy brown locks curl around his neck and above his ears, feathering across his forehead. His nose and bottom lip are both a little bigger than the rest of his features, and his cheeks are as round as balloons. Dark eyes beneath thick eyebrows catch the golden hue of the setting sun, making my heart drum a little faster.

I've heard adults talk about love at first sight on TV, and always thought it was something pretend like Santa Claus and the Easter Bunny. My mom taught me that not everyone gets a happy ending. But the first time I laid eyes on Theodore Davies, Jr., I knew true love was real.

I remember the carefree way he laughed as we watched TV together at my house, how he held onto me at the skating rink. He was sweet enough to walk me home from school, and stand up against my bullies.

As a fist is raised into the air above me, I draw strength from the sound of J.R.'s voice, the tilt of his lips that make the dimples pop into his cheeks.

I may not live long enough to marry my crush like I've dreamed so many times, but at least in the short time we were together, we were both really happy. He taught me the meaning of real love. He taught me true friends are something to be cherished. He taught me to be brave in the darkest of times, and embrace the good moments.

He taught me how to live.

28
STERLING - 2018

"**P**olice!" I hear from somewhere in the depths of the darkness. Like before, the voice is muted to my ears as if it's coming from another room. "Drop the weapons and put your hands up where I can see them!"

All at once I remember where I am and bolt upright. "Abigail?" I call out. "Abigail, are you still here?"

A whirlwind of commotion follows.

There's shouting and grunting and sounds of a struggle from the other room.

Then, the blasts of guns. Dozens of them.

I cover my ears and cry.

A few heart-stopping moments pass before an eerie silence follows. Then someone yells, "In here!"

In the course of a handful of shallow breaths, I'm being gathered into a set of arms.

I fight with everything I have, thrashing and screaming with inhuman strength.

I won't let Elroy Kabe hurt me the way he hurt Jackie.

I'll kill him first.

"Get away from me!" I scream. *"Don't touch me!"*

"It's okay, sweetheart! It's me!" Theo yells, gripping my arms and kissing my forehead. "It's over! My father and Elroy Kabe are dead!"

I continue fighting and screaming as Theo guides me to my feet and leads me to where the slain bodies of his father and Elroy Kabe lay in the other room. Their blank eyes stare at the ceiling, unblinking. Theo's father has his hand in a pool of blood, fingers locked around his detective badge. I can smell the bitter scent of grass and feel a roaring in my ears as my hands violently tremble at my sides. My foot rears back and wedges into the corpse's side with a wet, meaty sound. His head rolls, dead eyes staring at me and I can't stop screaming. *"You bastard!"*

Blood sprays across the toe of my white sneaker. I roar with hatred and anger seizing every inch of my bones. I kick him over and over with my stomach sloshing and tightening in unbearable pain. *"You sick, evil, son-of-a-bitch! I hate you!"*

These men destroyed my mom and my sister, broke K.C. and Theo's hearts. If there was a way to bring Mr. Kabe and Theo's father back to life only so I could watch them die with my own eyes, I'd do it—without hesitation.

"Why'd you kill me? Why?" Spittle flies from my lips as I start for Mr. Kabe's body. *"I hate you both!"* Anguished cries rip from my throat, so raw and deep that I'm unable to catch my breath. I can't do anything but fight past the red spots in my vision.

"Get her outta here!" a gruff voice orders.

As I'm launched over Theo's shoulder and carried up the stairway, my screaming rants slow along with my stuttered breaths and become hiccuping sobs. "I hate them," I repeat with far less force. My heartbeat reduces to a painfully slow beat as I'm struck with the truth. "They killed her...they killed her."

Outside, among the confusion of spotlights and a lawn filled with rescue personnel, Theo sets me back down on my feet and takes my face in his hands. "Did they hurt you?"

Gazing into the depths of his whiskey colored eyes—the same beautiful eyes Jackie envisioned as she took her last breath—I choke out, "Where's Abigail...K.C.?"

"They're over there," he tells me, pointing to where K.C. watches with a blanket wrapped around her shoulders as an EMT examines Abigail. "They're both safe."

I fling my arms around his neck, sobbing into his chest. "They killed Jackie, Theo! She's dead!"

"I know," he says, gripping my head with one arm. "But it's over now, sweetheart, and you're safe. They'll never hurt anyone else again."

BIRDS CHIRP their joyous songs and the early fall sunshine beats down onto our shoulders as we stand over the fresh pile of dirt, eyeing the pale pink granite headstone behind Pastor Babel.

Jackie Ann Tanner
Beloved friend
1974-1986

. . .

THE GRAVE-SIDE SERVICE drew in a larger crowd than we'd expected, creating an emotionally charged environment that turned me into a blubbering mess on Theo's shoulder with less fortitude than I'd intended. He's the one who has suffered the most tremendous loss, so I had intended on being his pillar of strength. But seeing those who'd suffered because of Jackie's unexplained disappearance was overwhelming. And I certainly hadn't expected my mom and aunt to be among those in attendance.

Once Jackie's remains were confirmed by the state's forensic lab in St. Paul, Theo and I had gone to the nursing home to break the news to Diane. She didn't remember me, and had asked my name. It was as if the last conversation I'd had with her never happened. I wasn't surprised considering whatever part of Jackie I'd been carrying with me disappeared the moment we left the farmhouse.

The most difficult part of the service occurs when Diane wails in agony as Theo places Jackie's ashes inside the square hole in the ground. I hold her hand and stroke her hair, openly sobbing along. My mom and aunt stand close behind me, each of them grasping one of my shoulders as if transferring some of their strength.

Pastor Babel spreads his arms wide as he gives

his final blessing. Everyone around us responds with a chorus of "*amens*," and his round cheeks rise with a bright smile. Although he retired many years ago, he asked if he could say a few words at the private service when Theo and I stopped by to let him know that Jackie had been found. From the twinkle in his eye, I imagine he wanted to lay her to rest for his own peace of mind.

The minister's gaze holds mine for a moment before skating over the crowd. "On behalf of Jackie's friends and family, I'd like to personally thank every last one of you for attending this very special service today. Our community has suffered in silence for too long. From this day forward, may we all live life a little fuller in honor of her memory and the memories of the other three young ladies who have also been laid to rest."

As those around us begin to break off and start for their vehicles, the orderly from the nursing home tells me it's time to take Diane back for her afternoon nap. I squat down by Diane's wheelchair, holding her hand as our eyes meet. Her face is blotched with red from crying, but her white hair is styled in a fashionable bun and her sapphire dress with a long skirt makes her eyes appear brighter.

"See you later, DeeDee," I say to her.

She tilts her head. "Why did you call me that?"

I glance back at Theo and grin. "A big birdie told me about your childhood nickname. Sorry, I guess it kind of stuck."

Her tired eyes are suddenly as alert as they've ever been. "It's alright. I actually don't mind. It reminds me of happier times."

Theo bends to whisper something into her ear before kissing her cheek. Her eyes fill with tears when he backs away. "I know. She loved you too."

I give her hand a light squeeze before standing. "We'll come by to visit again soon."

Theo loops his fingers around mine as the orderly pushes her wheelchair through the manicured lawn toward the handicap van parked nearby in the gravel road.

Chief Nielsen joins our little circle at K.C.'s side, acknowledging my mom and aunt with a small nod. His wife had stood beside him during the service, wearing a tasteful black cocktail dress with little red flowers that perfectly complimented the red tie her husband wore beneath a black suit. She was a pretty little thing, at least a foot shorter than her husband with large brown eyes and hair the color of sunshine. I'm looking forward to getting to know her after the service when Theo and I have everyone over for smoked brisket and a keg of Theo's favorite craft beer. My supervisor has been ridiculously supportive since I filled her in on an edited version of my reason behind skipping out on work, and also plans to stop by. She even suggested I take a week off to regroup.

"You did a good thing here," Chief Nielsen says, dipping his chin in Theo's direction while shaking his hand. "Gave a lot of folks closure. Just wish it had ended a little differently."

"I don't," Theo replies, his jaw hard. "My old man and Kabe got exactly what they had coming. Prison would've been too easy on them. Only wish someone would've stopped them sooner."

Shortly after our recuse, I learned that immediately after I'd sent my location to Chief Nielsen, he had run a search for the property's owner. Once he discovered it was registered to Elroy Kabe's uncle, he'd rounded up a small army of officers wearing kevlar, weapons drawn.

"I'm just grateful you listened to me and considered my crazy theories," I tell the chief. "If you hadn't come to check on us at the farmhouse that day, who knows what they would've done to Abigail. You probably would've had to bury several more bodies today."

"Ain't that the truth," K.C. huffs. She nudges the chief with her elbow. "Almost makes me feel bad for all the times I harassed you and your department."

"We had it coming," he tells her with a regretful nod. "I'm only sorry I didn't act on it sooner."

"I think it's time we all stop dwelling on the past and move forward like Pastor Babel said," I say to them. "Jackie's finally at peace. We all should be at peace along with her."

Nodding, K.C. squeezes Theo's arm. "I'm gonna head over to your place, see if Beth needs help getting things ready." She leans in beside me and whispers, "I'll give your hot mom and aunt a ride so you two lovebirds can have a minute alone before the party starts. No promises there will be any booze left if you take *too* long."

"I'll see you all there," Chief Nielsen announces, giving a polite nod with his departure.

My mom pulls me in for a bone-crushing hug. She's been giving out a lot of those ever since she learned the details of what went down in the farm-house. She may have her flaws and untraditional priorities, but I'm suddenly able to appreciate the times she's made an effort on my behalf, the times she's shown up. I only wish Jackie would've known a similar mother's love.

"Take your time, baby girl," she whispers in my ear. "Fate delivered you to this man for a reason. Don't let a single minute of his beautiful body go to waste."

"We're in a cemetery, Mom," I remind her dryly.

"Doesn't mean you can't swing home on your way to his place."

With a light-hearted giggle, I squeeze her tight. "I love you, Mom. Thanks for being here today. Your support throughout this ordeal has meant a lot."

"I love you more, Sterling Marie. You're a good person with a good heart. It hurts that you've moved so far away, but I'm glad to see for myself that you're surrounded by so many new friends who clearly seem to appreciate your value."

Once my mom and aunt leave with K.C., Theo and I are the last to remain. I stare at the words engraved on the headstone, wishing I could hear Jackie's giggle one last time.

I haven't dreamt about her again since I was locked in the farmhouse basement. Although I'd told Chief Nielsen everything I'd seen through Jackie's eyes, I decided not to disclose all of the details of her final hours with Theo, and had only confirmed that his father and Elroy Kabe were her captors. Hours following his father's death, we'd made love and he'd cried angry tears after, knowing his father was responsible for Jackie's demise. I held him and let him know that he was the last person she'd thought of in the end.

"I miss her," I tell him. "I miss dreaming about the two of you together...when you were both happy."

"Must be like your aunt said—she was finally able to move on after they found her buried in that yard. She knows my father and Kabe can't ever hurt another girl."

I turn to him, sliding my fingers inside his soft facial hair. "I love you, Theo...so damn much—my heart aches for everything you've been through. Jackie couldn't have asked for a better friend, and I could search the entire world twice over and never find a better man to call mine. I'll alway be remorseful for the suffering she endured, and despise the way they took her life when she was so young, but I'll always be thankful she brought me to you."

"Move in with me," he says, drawing me tight against him. "We can sell your place once I've finished updating it...use the profit to pay for our wedding."

"Our *wedding?*" I choke out, blindsided. "We've

only known each other for a couple of months, Theo. Isn't that moving a bit fast?"

"It's possible we've already been friends for thirty years, right? And I'm obviously not getting any younger." His sinfully wicked lips draw back, popping his dimples into place. "What do you say?"

Tears blur my vision as I snake my arms around his waist. "I can't think of a better way to honor Jackie's memory and make her pleased at the same time. She may no longer be with me, but it's what she would've wanted—for you to be happy."

"What about you?"

I grin. "Do you even have to ask?"

"This isn't all about Jackie, sweetheart. I came out of this nightmare with a strong, confident woman who ripped my heart out of my chest the moment she stood up to my bullshit, gave me hell right back. Never would've guessed a brilliant beauty like you would come to my rescue." His gaze turns determined as he leans in for a kiss. Once he pulls away, I swear I'm floating. "I'll give you my card to pick out a ring you like. A dress too. You should take your mom and aunt along while they're in town...I hear women love that kind of shit."

Laughing brightly, I draw him in for another lingering kiss, then draw back with another bubbling peal of laughter. "Theo, *babe*, my mom and aunt aren't the kind you 'take shopping' anywhere mediocre. Once they know we're getting married, I have a feeling you and I are in for countless trips in private jets to exotic locations. They won't take no for an answer." I finger the curls behind his ears. "Are you going to be okay with them showering us with lavish presents, or do you want to go elope somewhere, just the two of us?"

"I wouldn't care if they insisted we get married atop the Eiffel Tower, so long as I get to spend what's left of my life with you at my side." He grins, his thumbs stroking my jaw in tandem. "You come from a good family, sweetheart. It's important we keep them involved, let them help us celebrate. Expensive presents and fancy trips don't impress me, but if that's how they want to burn their money, that's their choice. Doesn't mean I understand it."

"My dad's gonna love you," I whisper, grinning back.

As we're leaving the cemetery hand-in-hand, my hair lifts into the air behind me and I feel the presence of...*something*. Tingles spread down my spine as I spin back to face the endless rows of headstones and immaculate green lawn. Although I can't see any fresh clippings, the sharp scent of fresh grass overwhelms me as if some has found its way up my nose. I open my mouth to ask Theo if he smells it too, but I'm unable to move. A strong sense of unconditional love and sheer happiness sweeps over me with the strength of an embrace.

I cover my mouth and gasp.

Was Jackie trying to say goodbye?

Theo draws me into his arms, his eyes heavy with concern. "You okay, sweetheart?"

I swallow the ball of emotion rising in my throat. Whatever connection I shared with the blonde little girl who had her life unfairly taken, I sense it's gone. Forever.

I glance up at Theo as a set of tears roll down my cheeks. "I think Jackie just gave us her blessing."

QUINN AVERY is an award-winning and Amazon bestselling author who has written 40 novels, including romantic suspense and mystery/psychological thriller. An avid fan of the beach, a good book, and Dave Grohl, she enjoys spending her free time with her favorite people and biggest fans...her husband and children. Quinn also writes romantic suspense as Jennifer Ann.

www.QuinnAvery.com

f facebook.com/authorquinnavery
instagram.com/authorquinnavery
BB bookbub.com/authors/quinnavery
goodreads.com/quinnavery
pinterest.com/authorquinnavery
a amazon.com/Quinn-Avery/e/B07NLD8Q57

ACKNOWLEDGMENTS

I can't believe I've published my 40th book! I'd be remiss without mentioning the fans who have continued to read my stories over the years and have left glowing reviews. THANK YOU for your loyalty and support! It means everything that readers like you allow me to continue forward in my dream career!

Thanks to each and every blogger and reviewer who agreed to read this book in advance! I know how difficult it can be to squeeze an extra book in on a deadline, so your time is much appreciated!

Thank you to Traci Bentzen for answering my strange questions and Lisa Frommie for lending me your expertise!

Special thanks to Najla Qamber for assisting me with your sharp eye and vast experience on helping me to create a great cover...it's always a pleasure working with you!

To Jodi Henley: I hope you understand how much I appreciate your time and opinion! Your kind words on this project were much needed and valued more than you could know! Here's hoping 2023 is kinder to us both so we can work together again on future projects! 🩶

Massive shout-out to my #1 fan and closest friend, Christy Freeberg, for always having my back and never failing to harass me until I send my latest work. You keep me going on many levels, girl. I treasure our friendship and appreciate all you do for me…especially when keeping me sane with good food, laughter, and Prosecco!

And as always, thank you to my husband and family for your continued support. I wouldn't have made it this far without you!